Magick

Goth Magick

An Enchanted Grimoire

Brenda Knight

CITADEL PRESS
Kensington Publishing Corp.
www.kensingtonbooks.com

CITADEL PRESS BOOKS are published by

Kensington Publishing Corp.
850 Third Avenue
New York, NY 10022

All Kensington titles, imprints, and distributed lines are available at special quantity discounts for bulk purchases for sales promotions, premiums, fund-rasing, educational, or institutional use. Special book excerpts or customized printings can also be created to fit specific needs. For details, write or phone the office of the Kensington special sales manager: Kensington Publishing Corp., 850 Third Avenue, New York, NY 10022, attn: Special Sales Department; phone 1-800-221-2647.

First Printing: October 2006

10 9 8 7 6 5 4 3 2 1

Printed in the United States of America

Library of Congress Control Number: 2006929662

ISBN 0-8065-2736-6

CONTENTS

ACKNOWLEDGMENTS

In deepest appreciation of Amber Gutebier, Goth Girl Gardener extraordinaire and a brightly burning light in the Darkness.

Eternal gratitude to Voltaire in all his myriad brilliance—music, art, and the well-written word.

And to the son of my soul, Duncan McCloud, who back in the Gilded Age of the 80's helped start it all for me—love eternal.

From there come maidens, knowing much,
From the well that waits under the Tree:
Urdh hight one, another Verdhandi—
Score they cut—the third is Skuld.
There they laid down laws, there they chose lives.

—From the "Völuspá"

Goth Magick

INTRODUCTION

The Barbarian Path: The Journey to a Magickal Life

During the Dark Ages, northern Europeans practiced a sort of "primal paganism." The Goths were Germanic tribes, the Visigoths, Ostrogoths, Vandals, Lombards, Burgundians, and Franks, hailing from the area we now know as Scandinavia. Gothic spirituality was informed by a mythology best described by the Roman historian Tacitus, "In their ancient songs they celebrated an earth-god Tuisco, and his son Mannus, as the origin of race, as their founders." Powerful female elders, or "seeresses," passed down this pagan mythology through an oral tradition and the runes were their only writing, a symbolic system used for signs and omens. Goths made quite a name for themselves as they moved across Europe, spreading destruction and even ransacking Rome. Their violent antics earned them the name "barbarian," which was later replaced by the much more colorful term *Goth*, meaning "uncivilized."

Fortunately, modern Goths differ greatly from their ax-toting forebears but both have much in common: a great romanticism, a love of the earth and her magick, as well as a deep tribalism and sense of adventure. For millennia, humankind has been looking to Mother Earth in the search for the answers to life's mysteries, and modern-day Goths are leading the charge. What is Goth magick? It is the modern art of magick deeply rooted in the old ways, a personal path that honors the ancient while harnessing the power of the past to enhance today's daily living. It is a singular craft that heralds and encourages individualism while retaining the all-important connection to a spiritual tribe.

Goth Magick is your all-inclusive guide to the art of magick for this new "dark age" (complete with a Crusade!) in which we live, both the history and the how-to. *Goth Magick* is the next step beyond Wicca for beginners. If you are a spiritual adventurer who likes to look at the other side, the hidden, strange, and mysterious, to discover a marvelous and unexpected world of enchantment, then *Goth Magick* is for you. This volume will help you gain a fuller understanding of what makes Goth magick unique and provides you with a stepping-off point for self-exploration and the creation of your own personalized spells and tribal rituals. Each chapter contains rituals, charms, and spells from simple "quickie" spells to more complex spells that mark very special rites of passage and engender the deepest personal transformation. Reader-friendly and eminently helpful, *Goth Magick* is an instruction book for leading an utterly enchanted and empowered life.

Who are these Goths anyway? To a "mundane" (the uninitiated and non-Goth), today's Goths are weirdos—extremely pale, black-clad creatures who are overly interested in the morose, in other words, in all things gloomy, and don't seem to come out during the day. If you are frequently found in your local record store at midnight, poring over the "Dark Industrial" music section, you are likely to be a Goth. If your idea of a good time is to dress as though you are in mourning, pack a lunch, and head off to the local cemetery for a picnic, you are most definitely a Goth!

Take a closer look, however, and you will find a rich tapestry of ideas and practices in Goth culture; Goths are not only students of history but also cultural anthropologists in a special niche. Goths study Victorian and even medieval style, manners, horticulture, and many other near-forgotten ways of living and reinterpret them for a modern age. For example, Amber Rae, a Goth witch in San Francisco, grows rare flora from the nineteenth century and uses them in her magical tinctures and essences. Similarly, Miss Kat, a ceremonial magician and Thelemite, studies Egyptian mythology and creates ritual music and art. You will also find that Goths are highly literate, spiritual, colorful, and creative people from all walks of life—doctors, attorneys, musicians, teachers, writers, and more. Yes, they all do wear a lot of black, but despite their rather gloomy appearance, the average Goth is probably having an awful lot of fun and is fully pursuing the ancient adages of "know thyself" and "to thy own self be true."

What appears as dark and brooding to some is dark and beautiful to others, and therein lies the essence of "Goth." The Goth way of life is often dismissed as depressing and counterproductive, but Goth in fact reflects a counterculture through music, dress, literature, and belief systems. Goths are those who embrace the dark, the romantic, or the frequently overlooked side of life.

Being Goth is not just about wearing dark clothing and listening to twenty-year-old Smiths B-sides. Goth is a different way of viewing things, combined with a spooky way of doing things. Goth is about an attraction to the unusual, the desire for uniqueness, and the love of the strange. It is a way to dress, yes, but it's also a way to create, learn, and grow as a person, by opening yourself up to the darker side of life and embracing the strange and unusual, rather than ignoring it. The aesthetics of Goth tend to go hand in hand with the love of the offbeat, so much of what this book details will help you become a true Goth magician. Goth will help you to bring out your dark and creative side, your inner poet-artist-musician-freak. Because of its flipside status, Goth welcomes those of all ages, shapes, and sizes to explore their individuality and creativity, along with their macabre side. So, if you're ready to embrace your dark side and all it has to offer, read on!

Chapter One

Under the Darkling Moon: Defining Goth Wicca

Despite their rather scary outward appearance, it is safe to say that modern-day Goths are among the most sensitive souls among us. Aside from their fixation with the Catholic cross, most Goths reject institutionalized religion, as it is not sufficient to nurture the spirit of these very special people. Many Goths report that they turned away from the religious heritage of their families early on in life to explore other options. Many Goths were raised in Evangelical Christian households and are reacting to and breaking away from the strictness of this religion. Above all, Goths seek to explore and express their creativity and chafe at any bonds of confinement or judgment. For those who walk their own path (Goths included) and express their inner nature while honoring nature and living harmoniously with the earth, Wicca is an ever increasing religion of choice. In May 2005, the *New York Times* noted that Wicca is the fastest growing religion in North America. Whether they consider themselves a "white witch" or a "dark Wiccan," something is calling to people on a profound level, something that "feeds" them in a way nothing else does, spiritually and communally. Perhaps it is that Wicca does not preach a prescribed path and rules. Hey—it does not preach at all! There is only a bond of honesty and the golden rule of Wicca that holds true for all Wiccans, and Goth Wiccans as well. In our lives, we have seen suppressed traditions such as Wicca and other traditions of witchcraft enter into the mainstream. Wicca has a wonderfully straightforward approach with a strong ethical code based on moral and personal responsibility.

The Three Principles of Wicca

The Wiccan Rede

"An ye harm none, do as ye will."
Gerald Gardner, *The Meaning of Witchcraft*

This quotation encourages the individual freedom to do as he or she sees fit as *long* as it does not affect anyone negatively. So, while you pursue your own interests, think of how it affects others. This applies to all aspects, especially with ritual and spell work, because you are working with energies that have long-ranging powers to affect everyone and everything. This rede requires a real attention and high degree of consciousness in terms of assessing the consequences of any action in regard to all the possible physical, spiritual, emotional, and psychological consequences that result from all ritual work.

The Threefold Law

"What you do comes back to you threefold" is much like the Buddhist ideology of karma. The Threefold Law is a directive to always think of the consequences of personal actions, including rites, ceremonies, and spells. Negativity comes back to you three times over, so attention to attitudes and thoughts is absolutely essential. The flipside of this law is that the positive comes back to you threefold, as well. Kindness, love, and generosity are all magnified. This is a great guideline for all of life. This is also a reason to do ritual work for long-distance healing and for global issues such as peace, the environment, and world hunger. Send good works and helpful intentions out to others and you yourself will benefit.

The Golden Rule

"Do unto others as you would have them do unto you." Many people might find it amazing that both Goth pagans and Christians share this same basic rule of morality. It places personal responsibility at the highest level. In other words, the "right action" is up to you and is of ultimate importance. These few, simple guidelines are universal in nature and can apply to any walk of life and spiritual practice. It is also vital to respect the diversity of religions. Do not judge in the same way that you do not wish to be judged. In its ability to impact others, creating ritual and working magick is very serious. If you guard your thoughts, intentions, and actions with others, you should be a happy, highly accountable ritualist.

One Web site worth checking out early and often is that created by someone who calls himself "Dark Wyccan" and who has been serving, beginning in 1994, a community of what he calls "Dark Pagans." John Coughlin's Web site, www.waningmoon.com, is a marvelous resource for anyone looking to learn more about this philosophy and wanting to join in with a like-minded community. Waningmoon.com beautifully defines dark Wicca and explains why it is so appealing to those whose spiritual hunger falls outside the margins of our rigid society: "Wicca is a nature-based mystery religion. As a mystery religion, it is not something one can learn in books or even from teachers—its mysteries must be learned through experience. Typically deity is perceived as a male and female (God and Goddess) that are anthropomorphic manifestations of the forces of nature. As with other aspects of the Craft one does not "Believe" in deity, one KNOWS them, from experience." So, Goth Wicca is also this earth-based pagan spirituality but as expressed through the lens of Goth.

Lunaria—That Which Is Under the Power of the Moon

Origins of Goth magick include some ancient and quite historic philosophies. My favorite delineation of "darkling" and night-ruled beings comes from H. C. Agrippa, who wrote the following in the early 1500s:

> Amongst plants and trees, these are Lunary, as the slelenotropian, which turns towards the Moon as doth the heliotropian towards the Sun; and the palm-tree, which sends forth a bough at every rising of the new Moon. Hyssop, also, and rosemary, agnus castus, and the olive-tree, are lunary. Also her herb chinosta, which increaseth and decreaseth with the Moon, viz, in substance and number of leaves, not only in sap but in virtue—which, indeed, is in some sort common to all plants, except onions. Lunary animals are such as delight to be in man's company, and such as do naturally excel in love or hatred, as in all kinds of dogs. The chameleon also is Lunary, which always, assumes a color according to the variety of the color of the objects—as the Moon

changeth his nature according to the variety of the Sign which it is found in.

Cats also are Lunary, whose eye become greater or less according to the course of the Moon, and those things which are like nature, as ceremonial bloods, which are made wonderful and strange things by magicians. The civet cat, also, changes her sex with the Moon, being obnoxious to divers sorceries, and all animals that live in water as well as land, as otters, and such as prey upon fish.

Of the Lineage of Heresy

One usually hears the word *martyr* used in terms of Catholic saints, but many multitudes were martyred among the pagan healers and wise women of old. It is important to remember and honor those who came before and to celebrate the freedom we now have for religious expression. Goth Wicca is definitely one of the latest twists in an ancient wisdom tradition. It is both free-form and prescribes to the ways of Goth—it is sort of a "roll your own" religion. We Goths tend to be keenly aware of history and what we do not romanticize, we abhor. One of the major examples of this is the Spanish Inquisition. Witches and those of the Jewish faith were hunted down and killed in droves after the seemingly insecure Pope Innocent III began a crusade against what he called "heretics" in the twelfth century. These heretics were most often women healers and elders of communities and villages to whom local folks turned to as authorities instead of the Catholic Church. Charges leveled against these so-called witches were that they "consorted with the devil," oftentimes accompanied by descriptions of lewd sexual acts with Satan, conjured up by the twisted imaginations of the clergy of the day. I say let this be a lesson about what happens with the Catholic Church's concept of enforced celibacy for the clergy.

Later, in the thirteenth century, Pope Gregory IX was caught up in a political dispute with the Holy Roman emperor over the Inquisition and issued papal orders that this judicial investigation into heresy would be under the special restricted jurisdiction of the church. Pope Gregory IX was also pursuing so-called freethinkers in Germany and France, but once this pope's lust for blood was raised, his fervor was such that he could not be stopped and the Inquisition spread throughout all of Europe. In 1252, Pope Innocent IV gave his blessing for inquisitors to use torture. The pope and his henchmen certainly were theatrical and knew how to manipulate the public to suit their ends. Sentences were declared in public squares, establishing the circumstances for civic judgment and instantaneous punishment, which could range in severity from a pilgrimage to a holy place, to a high fine of money and goods, to public whipping. The church officers could and did seize properties, but their power ended at life imprisonment—they did *not* have the powers of capital punishment, even though they would come mightily close with their torture. The inquisitors discovered a way around that, however, and began using it immediately. They could hand certain other prisoners and sentenced heretics over to the local civic authorities, and in many thousands of examples the accused were killed.

Inquisitors set up offices anywhere they liked and probed into the lives of locals, making sure the locals knew all the tools for torture the inquisitors had in their arsenal. With the arrogance that can come only from those who believe themselves to be righteous, the inquisitors issued proclamations for any heretics to present themselves. Heretics then had one month's time to confess before such time as a trial. Without a confession, trial proceedings began, which could go quite quickly since the testimony of only two witnesses was considered irrefutable proof. Accused heretics had no chance for asylum or sanctuary. So many times, under threat of torture and extreme pain, villagers agreed to say anything about their friends or neighbors just to end the agony.

"Remember the Spanish Inquisition!" is a line forever inscribed on the popular culture consciousness by the brilliant comic minds of Monty Python. It also refers to the very worst of all the Inquisition. The grand inquisitor of Spain was an ingeniously cruel man named Tomas de Torquemada. He personally undertook and oversaw the torture, persecution, and murder of thousands of accused heretics. His brutality knew no bounds, and he took the art of torment to its apex with instruments such as hot iron chairs, chairs with sharp nails, and the insertion of devices into any and all orifices and then twisting them open while inside the accused. Other special favorite Torquemada torture tools were the Iron Maiden, which was essentially a metal coffin with sharp iron spikes inside, and the rack, a frame on which the prisoner is stretched and tied by the arms, legs, and head until the body is torn apart. Drawing and quartering is a means of death by which each limb is tied to one of four horses and the horses are driven in four different directions, while the body is torn into four pieces.

The inquisitors were phenomenal record keepers, so there are many firsthand accounts and ledgers for modern historians to study. While historians differ over the exact span of time during which these crimes of the church took place, the best estimates show that a million people died over a period of some 500 years. The majority of those who confessed to heresy made their confessions under the duress of extreme torture. It is also important to remember that the majority of those who died were women.

The Inquisition was the Vatican's best effort to wipe out pagans and anyone they viewed to be "heathens" as in not Christian, even Jews and Muslims. In the twentieth and twenty-first centuries, we have "taken back the night" and our rights to religious freedom. To be a Goth Wiccan is not to be a heretic. It is being really and truly yourself, a rather "high-risk" individualist. While Goths have a fascination with the idea of death, life after death, and taking a position of being unafraid of death as a natural part of the life cycle, Goths do not idealize in any way the unmitigated cruelty and waste of human lives, including thousands of witches, that was the Inquisition. Remembering and knowing is an important way of honoring those who died.

We must remember our own who died.

Honoring Our Pagan Past

In 1992, upon the 300th anniversary of the Salem witch trials, the largest number of Goths in history congregated to "reclaim" Salem. Many stayed and have become model citizens and business people with retail outlets, bookstores, workshops, and all manner of successful enterprises. This footnote to our pagan history reflects our high regard for our religious history and how it matters today more than ever.

Another dramatic time in what I call "Witchstory'" or "Witch history" took place in colonial America. When two adolescent girls began having seizures and screaming out, the local doctors immediately declared the ailing girls to be Satan's handmaidens and said that the entire community needed to fast and pray for the two fallen girls. One of the cures for this affliction was "Witch Cake," a hideous concoction of rye meal mixed with the urine of the two girls. This supposedly would cause the girls to reveal the origin of the misfortune. With the entire village of Salem pressuring for a confession, nine-year-old Elisabeth Parris and eleven-year-old Abigail Williams broke down and named three women they knew to be witches who had them under a spell: Sarah Osborne, Sarah Good, and Tituba, the Caribbean Indian slave of the Parris family. While both Sarah Osborne and Sarah Good pleaded their innocence, Tituba was tortured and "confessed" that there was a coven of witches at work in Salem.

A trial took place, lasting weeks, and many of the villagers confessed to having been under the spell of the witches. In 1692, community leaders declared the need for a "witch hunt" and while they were at it, they took the opportunity to clean up the local riff raff. Again, women were under special scrutiny and even those not under any suspicion at all were at the mercy of the judiciary, especially women with property ripe for confiscation by greedy public officials. As always, the desired confession was gained under pain of torture. The first to be found guilty of witchcraft was Bridget Bishop; the sentence was hanging. A sort of "witch fever" spread throughout New England, followed by the Andover witch trials. Fortunately, people began to gather round to protect each other and signed petitions asserting the innocence of the accused. Finally, the newly established superior court, begun one year after the hanging of Bridget Bishop, put a stop to the conviction of witches. Unfortunately, the superior court did not act until twenty people had been executed on trumped-up charges.

Donna Read, in her masterful film *The Burning Times,* explores the history of the Dark Ages when an estimated 3 million women were burned as suspected witches. This repeated torture and murder of millions of women begs the question: Why are women so threatening to men in power? We have seen it time and time again over the millennia, beginning with Eve being blamed for the introduction of evil (read: knowledge) into the world. The sacred feminine is mysterious, with a dark and unknowable aspect that can be threatening to those in power. Women's wisdom, born from women's intuition, springs from the well of the sacred feminine. This frightens people who don't understand or embrace it. Women who spoke their mind, who challenged authority, and who espoused a spirituality other than the codified rule of any church were a risk to strict social order. The unknown and unknowable intimidates and is a menace to the status quo. Thus, it had to be silenced. This silencing cost millions of lives.

While we have progressed in so many ways from 1692, persecution can still happen.

In May 2005, a young woman in England was dunked repeatedly in the river and nearly drowned because her family and neighbors believed she was practicing witchcraft. So, while we believe these dark times are over, we must be ever vigilant. We must never forget.

I meant to find her when I came;
Death had the same design.
One need not be a chamber to be haunted,
One need not be a house;
The brain has corridors surpassing
Material place.

—Emily Dickinson

Goth embraces women's wisdom, and at its essence it is a celebration of the Dark Sacred Feminine. If you look at Goth culture, men also espouse their feminine side and fully flaunt it. Goth remembers the burning times and the times of torture and negation of the female spirit. Goth expresses what was once made silent.

Chapter Two

The Magick Toolbox: Supernatural Supplies and Instruments of Inspiration

As a modern primitive or urban pagan, it is important to establish a sacred space and arm yourself with magickal tools. In so doing, you can create a magickal place where the mundane world is left behind. It can be in your home or your own backyard where, despite the noise of the day-to-day, you can touch the sacred. There is no need to ascend to the top of a mountain or to a silent retreat in search of the sacred, or as a Goth, the deepest darkest dungeon you can find. Nay—anywhere you choose can become the place of magick where you cast the circle.

You can create the magick circle by "casting" or drawing in the air with concentrated energy. Inside the circle you have created, rituals are performed, your spells are worked, and special energy is raised. This sacred space of your very own is where you call on the gods and goddesses and become attuned to your deities. By giving this space real attention and focus, you can make it a truly intense experience. For the first time in your life, all your senses will come alive, and you will feel, see, and hear the energies as you come into the circle because you will have created a tangible sphere of power.

Cast a circle anywhere—out in the woods, on a lakefront, or in the comfort of your own crypt. Wherever the circle is cast becomes your temple. If you are in your bedroom or living room, stack the chairs against the wall to create the limits of your circle. The Goddess tradition specifies that the circle must have a diameter of nine feet, which is the number of the Goddess. That said, a circle can be any size, accommodating a very large group with dozens of people or just yourself. Many witches only cast a circle when they are ready to engage in spell work, and many neopagans cast a circle to celebrate every sabbat celebration. Goth variations on circle casting can include playing hypnotic and rhythmic music, thereby enhancing the creation of sacred space. Covens with which I am acquainted use both live and recorded music to great result and also read from their collective Book of Shadows. One group daringly holds their sabbats in a cemetery because for them the space is double hallowed.

Sacred Tools

Casting a circle is only limited by the imagination or the function you ascribe to it. The magick begins at your altar with your sacred tools—bolline, cord, censor, a cauldron, among other things—for crafting rituals. To fully imbue your tools of magick and ritual with energy, they should reside on your altar. Collecting your ritual tools is a joyful and careful search—don't rush out and get everything at once! As you work to refine your practice, your needs will undoubtedly change, so building a proper tool collection is a process that can take months or even years. Many a Goth magician has acquired a full complement of antique ritual tools; as historians or hobbyists, Goths are keenly interested in tools as *objets*—objects of desire, works of art—as well. Self-proclaimed Goth Marilyn Manson, for example, collects tools from his chosen home in New Orleans used by Voodoo practitioners. Actor Nicholas Cage, who follows the teachings of Aleister Crowley, collects his writings, tarot cards, and tools, because they are imbued with the energy and magick of the founder of the Order Templar Orientalis (OTO). So, again, the use of historic and antique tools of magic can deepen the potential for magick in Goth magick.

You can also find ritual tools in flea markets, metaphysical five and dimes, and craft fairs around the country. Always make sure you cleanse and purify your new tools of magick, whether they are antiques or brand new, to ensure that the energy is yours and yours alone. Think of your ritual tools as energy conductors that absorb the energy of the ritual work that you and your circle perform. If you want to craft tools that are custom made to fit your needs, you can also take the do it yourself approach to making magickal implements. You may well want to laminate the handle of your knife with skulls beads made of bone or take a walk in the woods in search of just the right fallen branch for your wand.

Using Your Tools for Magick

Ritual tools are sacred to an individual who is performing the actual ritual act. Whether you find your tools in a store or they are given to you as a gift, each tool should hold special meaning to you and should feel absolutely perfect to you as you use them. Keep this in mind as you search for just the right tool for your Gothic ritual ceremonies; perhaps your athame will look like a medieval dagger or your Book of Shadows will resemble an ancient tome from the twelfth century. Usually, you are able to "recognize" tools that are meant for you with your inner knowing. I highly recommend using a pendulum while shopping!

Athame—Your Dagger for Designing Magick

Pronounced "a THAW may," this is your magickal knife. Even though it can be used as a ritual dagger or sword for spells, it is mostly symbolic and not necessarily a cutting knife. Your athame represents the yang energy or the male aspect of God. Ritual knives are also associated with the south and the element of fire as such, they should be placed on the right side of your altar. The athame is used to direct the energies that are raised in your ritual. One old witching tradition very much in keeping with the Gothic sensibility specifies that the handle of the athame should be black or very dark in color, since black is the color that absorbs energy.

Bolline

The bolline, usually a white-handled knife, is used for making other tools, such as carving your wand, whittling your own runes, and cutting materials such as cords and herbs. You are creating a magickal tool by using a magickal tool. You should also use your bolline for carving sigils, symbols, names, and deities into your candles and wands as well as your other crafted tools. Usually, a bolline has a curved blade and a white handle to distinguish it from the athame. It is similar to the athame in that it also embodies yang energy. It can be used only within the magickal circle, the boundary you form by marking the four corners and the four directions through a speaking ritual.

Your Book of Shadows

The Book of Shadows is a record of your ritual work and is a very important part of your spiritual journey, as it encompasses the complete body of your magickal thinking and magickal workings. It is, in essence, a history of all your energy work, circles, spells, dreams, and the magick you have manifested over time. It is essentially a diary of all that you have practiced and wrought. In your Book of Shadows, you should keep a journal of your research and the lore you have discovered. For example, is there a particular phase and sign of the moon that works especially well for you? By documenting this type of information, you will be building a practice that you can apply to future spells and circles. Also, many a Book of Shadows has become a published book! This will also be a great aid in recording your ritual work, as you evolve and develop as a ritual designer. For example, I have discovered that the new moon in Virgo (the opposite of my natal new moon in Pisces) is currently the best moon phase for me to work rituals of change. Through trial, experimentation, and much practice, you, too, will discover these secrets of the universe for yourself via your personal records.

Your Book of Shadows will be the most helpful to you if you use it daily or as often as possible. Besides being a record of your magickal work, it should also be a book of inspiration for you, filled with your own thoughts, personal poetry, and observations. Your Book of Shadows should be a tome you wish to turn to again and again. It can be a gorgeous, handcrafted tome of handmade paper and ribbons or a simple three-ring binder. Just make sure it appeals to *you*, so you will use it often and well. I have seen gorgeous decoupaged volumes, some with papier-mâché masks so the book itself becomes a familiar, and also simple ones that reflect the owner (which is the point, after all), with stickers from favorite Goth bands. Try www.insideacauldron.com for some excellent choices you can order.

Black Broom

The broom is a symbol of the practical magick of sweeping the ritual area clean before and after casting a spell. With proper focus and intention, you can rid your sacred space of negative influences and bad spirits from the area, preparing the sacred space for work. In olden days, pagan marriages and Beltane trysts took place with a leap over the broom, an old traditional part of the hand fasting or pagan wedding. The broom, as a significator of womanly domesticity, took hold of the popular imagination as the archetypal symbol of witches. Even Harry Potter has a souped-up broom for sweeping through the skies above Hogwarts!

Your broom is a fundamental tool for energy management, so it is wise to choose your broom very carefully. It's best to obtain a handmade broom from a craft fair as opposed to a factory-made plastic one from Wal-Mart. A broom made of wood and woven from straw will be imbued with the inherent energies of these natural materials. Also, your ritual broom should not be used for housework, which would mix up energies in your home and sacred space. The pagan tradition holds brooms in high regard, and some witches and ceremonial magicians have an impressive collection of brooms, each named to signify their roles as a familiar or kindred spirit. As a Goth, you might be happiest with a black broom and can even buy it at one of my favorite magick stores in Los Angeles called Black Broom! Check it out at www.theblackbroom.com, as it is a purveyor of many marvelous tools, books, and essences, especially the uber Goth black alchemy line of potions, lotions, and perfumes.

Candles and Light

Candles are a simple yet profound tool that can make powerful magick. Today, candle magick is used daily by folks of all walks of life for peace of mind, respite, contemplation, and aromatherapeutic healing. Candlelight transforms a dark room and illuminates the air with energy. Suddenly, the potential for a mystical realm is evident as you will be able to *feel* the latent power. A spell, prayer, or ritual lit by a single candle has the potency of all the stars in the sky. Candles contain the following four elemental energies:

- Air: oxygen feeds and fans the candle flame
- Earth: the solid wax that forms the candle
- Water: the melted wax is the fluid elemental state
- Fire: the spark and blaze of the candle flame

Charging Your Candles

"Charging" a candle means to imbue it with magickal intent. A candle that has been charged carries that intention through all four elements and up to the heavens and fills the very air of your sacred space with your magick. Spell work and ritual candles are chosen for their color correspondences and then they are "dressed" or anointed with the energy of an essential oil. If you are like most of the Goth pagans, you use a rainbow of colors in your magick and have long ago let go of "black only" as your credo. You understand the intrinsic vibratory energy of different colors and their magical properties.

Color Correspondences for Candle Magick

Black: banishing, absorbing, expulsion of the negative, healing serious disease, attracting money
Brown: home, animal wisdom, grounding, healing
Dark blue: change, flexibility, the unconscious, psychic powers, curing
Gray: neutrality, stalemate, cancellation, invisibility
Green: wealth, abundance, growth, luck, employment, gardening, early life, attractiveness, fertility
Light blue: patience, bliss, overcoming depression, tranquility
Orange: attraction, triumph over legal issues, changeability, stimulation, intelligence, clarity, logic, support, encouragement
Pink: love, faithfulness, friendship, goodness, positivity, affection
Purple: healing, aspiration, business success, stress relief, power
Red: vigor, protection, vitality, sexuality, passion, courage, power, love, good health
White: purification, peace, protection, truth, binding, sincerity, serenity, chastity, spirit
Yellow and gold: mental power and vision, study, self-assurance, prosperity, abundance, divination, psychism, powers of persuasion, wisdom, charisma, good sleep

Before you charge your candles, meditate on your intention, then cleanse your candles by passing them through a purifying smoke of sage and incense. You can increase the charge of your candle by carving a symbol or "sigil" into the wax. After you have engraved the appropriate magickal words onto your candle, it's time to "dress" your candle with a specific essential oil. Every essential oil is imbued with a power that comes from the plants and flowers of which it is made. Anoint yourself with the oil of your choice at the crown or third eye to increase mental clarity. By using the inherent powers of the essential oils, you are increasing the effectiveness of your rite and "doubling" the effectiveness by anointing both your tool—in this case, the candle—and yourself. These same oils can also be used in protection spells for your threshold and windowsills, potpourri, anointing yourself, and sacred bathing.

Magickal Correspondences of Essential Oils

Astral projection: benzoin, cinnamon, jasmine, sandalwood
Courage: black pepper, frankincense, geranium
Dispelling negative spirits: basil, clove, copal, frankincense, juniper, myrrh, peppermint, pine, rosemary, sandalwood, Solomon's Seal, vetiver, yarrow
Divination: camphor, clove, orange
Enchantment: ginger, tangerine
Healing: bay, cedar wood, cinnamon, coriander, eucalyptus, juniper, lime, rose, sandalwood, spearmint
Joy: lavender
Love: apricot, basil, chamomile, clove, copal, coriander, geranium, jasmine, lavender, lemon, lime, neroli, peppermint, rose, rosemary, vetiver, ylang-ylang
Luck: nutmeg, orange, rose, vetiver
Peace: lavender
Prosperity: basil, cedar, cinnamon, clove, ginger, jasmine, nutmeg, orange, oak moss, patchouli, peppermint, pine, wood aloe
Protection: anise, basil, bay, black pepper, cedar, cinnamon, clove, copal, cypress, eucalyptus, frankincense, juniper, lavender, lime, myrrh, patchouli, peppermint, pine, rose, rose geranium, sandalwood, vetiver
Sexuality: cardamom, cinnamon, clove, lemongrass, olive, patchouli, peppermint, rosemary

Goth Is in the Details

Carving symbols onto your candles is a simple and profound way to deepen your magick. What symbols are meaningful to you? Certain crosses, vines, flowers, hieroglyphs, and many other images have great associations with Gothdom, so you should feel free to delve in and experiment to find the symbols that work best for you in your spells. The term *sigils* derives from the word for seal. It is a magickal glyph or symbol that is used in ritual to deepen focus or intensify magick powers. Methods for devising sigils can be using the planetary glyphs, runes, Enochian tables, letters, numbers, or even mystical ciphers such as hermetic crosses or kabalistic signs.

Wicked Good Wands

A wand is a symbol of air and is used to project energy in your rituals and magickal workings. It is a very personal tool. While there are many gorgeous, crystal-encrusted wands for sale in metaphysical five and dimes, it is a wonderful thing indeed to *make* your own wand.

Start with a tree branch that has fallen to the ground on its own. Sand the rough edges—it is a wand, not a weapon. Then give it a good saging. Hot glue a large quartz crystal near the handle and any other crystals that feature properties you want in your complement of magick, such as amethyst for balance and intuition, amber for grounding, or moss agate for powers of persuasion and healing. I also suggest chalcedony for power of dark spirits, carnelian for success and fulfillment of all desires, bloodstone for abundance and prosperity, aventurine for creative visualization, calcite for warding off negativity, jasper for stability, hematite for strength and courage, jade for wisdom and for powerful dreams, fluorite for communicating with fairies and other unseen beings, and rose quartz for love. Citrine makes an excellent wand "pointer tip" and aligns the ego with your higher self—after all, isn't that the whole point?

Peerless Pendulums

The pendulum is an indispensable tool for gleaning information from your inner self as it helps you draw on your own inner knowing and psychism. The more you use a pendulum, the more intuitive you will become. Like a muscle, our psychic power thrives by being exercised. Some of the best pendulums are the ones you can make yourself by tying a string or rawhide to a crystal—quartz crystal is a good choice for dependability and clarity. You should tie it so that the crystal points down. Each time you use it, you should ask the pendulum to "Show me yes and show me no," and once the pendulum has confirmed this, you can ask all manner of questions about people in your life, events, decisions big and little, even shopping. The crystal pendulum will swing up and down, giving you answers. Each time you do pendulum work, keep a journal of it in your Book of Shadows, as it will help you to track the pendulum's effectiveness. With time, you will be able to see patterns of information emerging from your unconscious and from the universe. I can't recommend this highly enough. You will learn so much about yourself and your place in the world from this, as your own inherent wisdom is made manifest. Once you start doing pendulum work, you will come to count on it for help with shopping and all manner of decision making.

Creating a Goth Altar

An altar is a place of peace and meditation where your spirit can soar. Adorned with your treasured objects and the tools of your practice, it is a place of extreme focus where you can make magick. Your altar is your most sacred space. It is your power source and the center of all your magickal workings. To unleash your personal pagan power, you must first set the stage—the perfect environment to incubate your dreams and wishes, your hopes and desires. The very first step is to set up an altar, your touchstone for daily conjuring and contemplation. I recommend placing your altar facing north, long held to be the origin of primordial energy. North is also the direction of midnight and an altar oriented in this fashion promises potent magick.

By preparing a place in your home and honoring the sacred on a daily basis, you should adorn your altar lovingly. It should be pleasing to the eye and ultimately reflective of your personal energy. Take a low table or an old chest and paint it a high sheen enamel-red with black details. Get as creative as you wish with the table or chest and carve or inscribe and decorate your altar base with symbols that are significant to you—spiders, bats, skulls, ankhs, crosses, roses, crows, or (my personal favorite) green- and purple-tinged ivylike vines. If you are so inspired, you can go uber Goth by obtaining a sarcophagus-like or coffin-shaped box to use as a chest. One sculptress even hand-crafted gravestones to use for her chest. However, I strongly advise against using a real gravestone, as the energy attached to it would be very difficult to cleanse.

Once you have obtained and decorated your chest, place a favored fabric over your altar table or chest. Optimally, you should have an array of altar cloths, flowers, candles, and stones in different colors depending on the type of spell you intend to cast. The following "color energy" guide will help you to determine the colors of cloth you use for dressing your Goth altar.

Traditional Wiccan Color Correspondences

Red: life, lust
Pink: love, romance
Green: prosperity, friendship, healing
Gray: protection
White: purity, beginnings
Blue: loyalty, creativity, vision
Orange: higher knowledge, enlightenment
Purple: spirituality
Yellow: power, fame

Goth Magickal Color Associations

Black: absorption of negative energy, divination, banishing, protection, binding
Silver: intuition, psychism, balance, spirituality, goddess energy
Red: lust, fire, passion, strength, anger, power, courage

Place the fabric of your choice on your altar. Next, choose two candles and place them on the two farthest corners. If you like, place fresh flowers at the center of the space. Some powerful Goth flower choices are black calla lilies, ivies, or any dark purple flowering vine. You should also place a thurible, or incense burner, in front of the flowers (more on thuribles soon!). If you've not yet found a favorite incense, begin with the ancient essence of frankincense.

Your altar doesn't have to be all about candles, flowers, and incense. To further personalize it, select objects that appeal to you symbolically—a goddess figure such as Isis, a photo you love of your favorite cemetery statue, or an iridescent abalone seashell you found one night on the beach. You can also place your birthstone on the altar or a crystal or stone you treasure. Add anything you feel that adds good energy and represents your singular vibration. Purify the space by "smudging" or burning a bundle of sage over it. Anoint your third eye (the center of your forehead) with a scented essential oil such as the sacred resin amber or one that especially pleases you. Now, anoint the candles with the same essence. Light the candles and meditate in a prayerful way on all the positive and practical magick you will create at your Goth altar.

Goth Is in the Details

Additional Goth altar flowers include:

Solomon's Seal
Moonflowers
Stock, nicotiana
Night-scented roses
Delphinium
Monkshood
Black tulips
Poppies
Belladonna (commonly known as morning glory)

White flowers are always the most highly scented and also glow under moonlight. Moonflowers are a good white flower choice, as they only bloom at night—perfect for Goth nighttime rituals.

Gothic Garden Plant Suggestions

Herein is a list of the most authentically Goth flora for you to grow and procure. These plants emanate a power and magick all their own and make wonderful offerings for your altar, to deities, and for your home lair.

Voodoo lily
Vampire lily
Black calla lily
Andian silver sage
Black mondo grass
Corokia cotoneaster
Black velvet nasturtium
Black violas and pansies
Papaver somniferum var. black cloud
Black hollyhocks
Aristolochia (dutchman's pipe)
Pitcher plants
Flytraps-carnivores
Harry Lauder's walking stick
Dracula vampira var. bela legosi
Ipomoea purpurea (morning glory)
datura discolor var. Kniola's black
Bearded iris var. night queen
Superstition
Cotula "pratt's black"
Baby black eyes (nemophila meziesii "penny black")

After you have been working spells for a bit, an energy field will radiate from your altar! Your altar is the one place you can return to again and again to concentrate your energy and clarify your intentions, so be sure to replenish, clean, and recharge your altar frequently with fresh flowers, candles, and objects. The more you use your altar, the more powerful your spells will be. This consecrated space will center and ground you *and* bring the beauty and bliss of magick into your life.

Cauldron of Life

Cauldrons, which are also called the "Cup of Cerridwen," come down to us from the ancient Gothic and proto-Celtic path where they were used for cooking, scrying, and ritual work. They symbolize abundance and divine inspiration. Your cast iron cauldron represents female energy and the Goddess. The round basin stands for the woman's womb, the giver of life. A true magickal cauldron should be able to withstand fire, which represents rebirth, the phoenix rising from the ashes of the past. Cauldrons are usually used in ritual to hold earth or water as elements for rites of spring. In winter, the cauldron is the sun and should hold fire. In the spring, the cauldron can be a rain jar or a flower-filled fountain. In the summer, the cauldron can be a cup. And in autumn, it can be a pumpkin. Cauldrons are also a very practical tool for mixing your herbs and essential oils. You can scry with a cauldron full of water and foresee the future by reading images on the surface of the water. You can also use this magickal tool to burn papers on which you have written your intentions or a spell parchment. In doing this, you can send your wishes to the Goddess upon the flames and smoke. Cauldrons typically have three legs for ultimate mobility, rather like a tripod altar. You can place a cauldron on your altar or on the floor to the left of the altar. You can and should play with the idea of a cauldron for outdoor ritual and season altars.

Thuribles and Censors

A thurible, or censor, is basically an incense burner. This ritual tool represents the elements of air and fire. Place your incense burner at the very center of your altar or in front of any offering you are wishing to bless such as flowers or fruit, a gift to the gods and goddesses. Your thurible should be used daily to purify your other sacred tools and to cleanse your ritual space. The evocative scent and smoke of the incense can also transport you in a sensory way.

Banishing Incense to Purify Your Sacred Space

This is the optimum mixture of essences to purify your home or sacred working space. Negative energies are vanquished, and the path is cleared for ritual. Open windows and doors when you are burning this clearing incense so "bad energy" can be released.

Supplies:

1 part sandalwood
2 parts cinnamon
3 parts myrrh
3 parts copal
3 parts frankincense

There are many types of thuribles to choose from that will please your inner Goth—gargoyles, dark fairies, dragons, or skulls.

GOTHIC GRAILS

Your chalice is a goblet dedicated specifically for use on your altar. Like the cauldron, it is another vessel symbolizing the feminine, the Goddess, and fertility for women. Holding both fluid and the waters of our emotional body, it is elementally connected to water. Place your special chalice on the left side of your altar with all other representations of the energy of the female and the Goddess. A chalice is also a grail. After all, King Arthur's legend tells that the Holy Grail brought life back to the decaying kingdom of Camelot and restored Arthur and his people, giving rise to the rebirth of England itself. On your altar, your goblet can hold water, mead, wine, juice, or anything you wish to partake of or deem as an offering to share with the deities. A particularly Gothic libation would be Transylvanian Vampire Wine or an absinthe from eastern Europe.

Charging and Consecrating Your Ritual Tools

Once you've accumulated all your preferred ritual tools, you should design a consecration rite for the tools. This consecration will dedicate your utensils for the betterment of all and sets a base of intention for all your good works. Perform this rite every time you acquire a new tool or treasure. If you're a beginner, you can choose a simple "temple template" and build on it as you learn and grow. As your experience in your craft deepens, you can embellish the ritual with your personal preferences. Refer back to your Book of Shadows—is there a certain phase of moon that offers you more clarity? Should you utilize the corresponding colors, crystals, essential oils, incenses, and herbs for your own astrological sun and moon sign? Is there a specific goddess or deity you feel an affinity to? Use these correlations in your rituals and begin designing the ceremonies and rites of your dreams. The more associations you learn and use, the more your effectiveness will grow. Time will tell, so keep good notes of your ritual work in your Book of Shadows. You will soon become a "maestro of magick."

Ritual of Consecration

Now that you have selected your special tools of Goth magic, you need to bless and dedicate them to your magical workings. This is an opportunity to fill your sacred implements with your personal energy; you are encoding them with your unique imprimatur. The more you use your tools, the more charged they will become.

Supplies:

Incense for air
Candle for earth
Cup of water
Bowl of salt

1. Take the new ritual tool and pass it through the smoke of the incense and say:

Now inspired with the breath of air.

Then pass the tool swiftly through the flame of the candle and say:

Burnished by fire!

2. Sprinkle the tool with the water and say:

Purified by water.

3. Dip the tool into the bowl of salt and say:

Empowered by the earth.

4. Hold up the tool before you chant with both hands and imagine an enveloping, warm white light purifying the tool and say:

Steeped in spirit and bright with light.

5. Place the now cleansed tool on your altar and say:

By craft made and by craft charged and changed. This tool [fill in the actual name whether it be the bolline, Book of Shadows, etc.] I will use for the purpose of good in this world and in the realm of the God and Goddess. I hereby consecrate this tool.

Other tools are more intangible—such as breath work, intuition, psychic powers, and the ability to focus your mental power and spiritual intentions—and as they are intangible, only your intention can purify them. You will use other physical tools, such as colors, herbs, oils, crystals, numbers, and all manner of ritual correspondences and associations, which have been passed down through the centuries. Crystals can also be charged, but those tools that come from nature and from the Goddess are not manmade but of divine design, such as flowers, colors, and herbs, so they already contain an intrinsic magick of their own to be used.

Your tools will become inculcated with the magick that lives inside of you, instilled with your energy and stored at an altar or in your sacred space. They will become a power source for you and will magnify the ceremonial strength of your ritual work. Your altar should be a place of peace and meditation where your spirit can soar. Adorned with your treasured objects and the tools of your practice, it is a place of extreme focus where you can enrich your life through ritual. You can create a wellspring of spirit so you can live an enchanted life every single day.

CHAPTER THREE

Elemental Magick: Earth, Air, Fire, and Water

You are now creating a magick to work important changes in your life and to become more connected to the world around you. Goth Wicca is, after all, an earth path, so working in harmony with the elements of which the earth is made is an important step in your personal practice. Just as there are specific influences in the stars and planets astrologically, rhythmic phases of the moon, and a range of crystalline color powers in stones, there are very particular powers in the elements you can call on in your ritual work.

Earth, air, fire, and water are the four elements of the ancients and were developed during the time of the original Goths. The ancient philosopher Empedocles of Sicily refined the theory of earth elements between 420 and 410 B.C., and despite our many modern beliefs, we still hold with the basics of early metaphysics, where science and spirit conjoin.

Earth

Earth is the manifestation of the "solid." It is a real and tangible matter. The earth gives us intransigence, constancy, and durability. All beings on this beautiful planet are made of earth, and we are part of a natural, magickal system. Earth is a stable material and element. In it, you can grow a flowering plant to place on your altar or place some sand in a shell or on your altar to represent this element. And, at the end of our lives, we once again return to the earth. You should call on the element of earth when you want to become more grounded or to build a new aspect into your life.

Earth signs Taurus, Virgo, and Capricorn should perform earth rituals on a regular basis to stay centered. Earth signs are always thought of as the most stable, practical, and organized of all the signs, and the other side of the coin that often manifests in Goths is the sensual, quiet type who works and prefers to entertain at home and has the enviable lair. Tried and true earth rituals are walking meditations, circling in a sacred grove, and a guided visualization into Inanna's cave. Goth magickal earth deities to work with are the Green Man, Venus of Willendorf, Persephone, and elves or trolls.

Earth Element Ritual: Getting Grounded

In Celtic lore, they were called wishing trees. Taoists refer to them as money trees. My group of Goth magicians thinks of them as manifesting trees. Either way, they are trees that give to you and root in the earth, growing, giving stability, and cleaning the air. Plant one in your yard or pot for your home or office. If you have to rely on indoor gardening, the biggest ficus you can find will do nicely in a jade-green ceramic pot. Choose from among the following magickal trees (or trust your intuition in arbored matters).

Willow: healing broken hearts
Apple: divination, spell work
Oak: strength, lust
Peach: love magick
Olive: peace
Aspen: sensitivity
Eucalyptus: purification
Cherry: romance

If prosperity is your real concern, write your wishes on little paper scrolls and bury them in the soil near the tree. Every time you water the tree, you will be bringing your wishes closer to fruition. If you are looking for luck, happiness, or general good, verbalize your wish as you hang charms on the branches of your tree—colored ribbons, crystals, coins, and keys, anything that strikes your fancy. This should also be a custom with friends and guests. Every time you add an ornament, you must take one down. Only when your charm has been removed will your wish come true.

Air

Like water, air is an ever changing element. Air is the unseen form of matter and is formless, but possesses mobility and dynamism. The oxygen in the very air we breathe is essential to the continuation of all life on Earth. Wind creates movement and effects change. Air signs Gemini, Libra, and Aquarius are known for their brilliance and superior communication skills. They can maintain these skills with rituals invoking the element of air. Singing, chanting, and conscious breathing are all invocations of air you can perform every day in your home, at your altar, or outside in the park.

Fire

Fire is heat and is the most visible form of energy. Fire is a powerful element, as it can transform and change the other elements. If you watch the flicker of your candle flame, the embers of your incense, or the blaze of your council fires, you will see a constant transmutation of matter. Fire has the ability to both excite and incite us and is necessary to bring about change. Fire signs Aries, Leo, and Sagittarius are known for their strength and vibrancy. They can maintain this by employing their personal element of fire. Candle magick is a simple, powerful, and direct way you can invoke your native element of fire.

Air Element Ritual—The Energy of Love

While dried, dead roses are very Goth, collecting them and having them around for years actually is dead "chi" and is not only bad feng shui but is also literally dead energy.

To use them positively, bundle all your dried bunches of roses and other flowers together and place them in your fireplace or outside in a fire-safe container (Webers work!). Anoint the dead flowers with rose oil and frankincense or nag champa incense and say aloud, "The fire of love burns in the heart and in my hearth. It burns strong and true. The fire in my heart is a love eternal for [lover's name], for my family, for my friends, and for the world. This fire of my love is eternal." Light the fire with a red candle and repeat once the dried roses are blazing away.

Water

Theorized to be the source of life, water is most certainly the nurturer of all life and is essential for all continued existence. Our human bodies are comprised mostly of water. Water nourishes crops, regulates the weather, and washes away what no longer serves. Where earth is stability, water is the utter lack of all stability. Water is impermanence—in our rivers, lakes, and oceans it is ever changing. Water is a vital cleansing and blessing element, and thus can be used in any kind of cleansing ritual. A fountain in your home or garden or a bowl of water on your altar represents the all-important water of life. Water signs Cancer, Scorpio, and Pisces are highly receptive and creative by nature. They can stay in tune with their gifts with water rituals. Instead of an efficient morning shower, a ritual bath and tea meditation are a wonderful way to connect with your holy personal element.

The human body is like the ocean itself—it is made mostly of water and some salt. Your connection to that sacred element is primal. Thus, we are drawn to the ocean, which is a blend of mineral and water similar to your own chemical mix. Have you ever noticed how blissful you feel at the beach? The negative ions produced by water are soothing to you, creating an overwhelming sense of positivity. In the presence of water, you feel revitalized. The moon's tides are a rhythm of life as well, a regulating force of nature. Water cleanses and restores us, creates our climate, and nurtures our crops and forests. It also reconnects water folk with their native element and keeps them in tune with their true nature.

In India, the sacred Ganges River is the very source of life and cleanses the Hindus' soul from birth to death, where they often float off to eternity in a river burial rite. Christian baptisms are done with the sacrament of water. The Chinese deity Kuan Yin, the goddess of compassion, offers spiritual seekers the comfort and solace of a holy lake. Aphrodite herself rose up from the fecund ocean foam, and the Yoruba divinity Yemaya is believed to rule all the waters of the earth.

I was born with both my natal sun and moon in the astrological sign of Pisces. As a double Pisces, I receive much spiritual substance from water, so I turn to my element for succor.

How the Four Directions Relate to the Four Elements

The four directions we invoke in magickal circles and ceremonies correspond directly to the four elements. Calling out to the four directions creates the sacred space of the circle, the center of ritual work. In so doing, you are calling forth the four elemental entities and energies.

North

The north corresponds to the element of earth and the season of winter.

Colors: brown, green
Totem animal: elk, wolf, bear
Tarot suit: pentacles

South

The south corresponds to the element of fire and the season of summer.

Colors: gold, red
Totem animals: lizard, snake, lion
Tarot suit: wands

East

The east corresponds to the element of air and the season of spring.

Colors: yellow, pink
Animal totems: eagle, hawk, raven
Tarot suit: swords

West

The west corresponds to the element of water and the season of autumn.

> Colors: purple, blue
> Animal totems: swan, whales, dolphins
> Tarot suit: cups

North, South, East, and West—A Ritual for Daily Life

You can purify your home every day and, in so doing, create sacred space for living a life of daily ritual. After cleaning or straightening your home each day, bless the rooms and ensure that you are surrounded with good energy.

Supplies

Cup or bowl of water
Salt

1. Take the cup or bowl of water and add a sprinkle of salt. Then anoint your fingers and forehead.

2. Now turn to the east and say:

Powers of the East,
Source of the sun rising.
Bring me new beginnings.

After speaking, sprinkle some of the water in the east.

3. Face south and say:

Origin of the sun and warmth and light,
Bring me joy and bounty.

Scatter some of the water in the south.

4. Face west and say:

Powers of the West,
Source of oceans, mountains, and deserts all.
Bring me the security of the ground beneath my feet.

Scatter some of the water in the west.

5. Face north and say:

Powers of the North,
Bringer of the winds and the polestar.
Show me vision and insight.

Scatter some of the water in the north.

6. End this simple ritual by sprinkling the water and salt all around your home, especially on or around windows, sills, doorways, and thresholds where energy passes in and out as visitors and delivery people arrive. In this way, you are cleansing and managing the energy of your space. After a distressing occurrence, you can repeat this ritual to clear out the "bad energy."

Chapter Four

The Winter Soul: Spells, Rituals, and Gothic Enchantments

The Winter Soul, Goth and Gloam

What is the Winter Soul? The Winter Soul is mysterious. The Winter Soul is somewhat forbidden and foreboding. The Winter Soul is cold, ominous, and travels alone. The Winter Soul is romantic. Therefore, it comes as no surprise that Goths are drawn to a "winter" sensibility—to the dark, cool, and seemingly gloomy place inside of us—a place most mundanes don't dare venture into. Goths tend to delve fearlessly into their Winter Soul and explore it fully. Still not sure about the Winter Soul? There are plenty of examples in popular literature and culture. Think of Heathcliff tromping across the freezing moors, his heart tormented by a dark, intense passion. Think of the short-lived but never-to-be forgotten Sci-Fi television show *Lexx*, whose star, Kai, was actually *dead* but somehow more beautiful, brilliant, capable, and alive than anyone else on the show. And think of Mary Shelley's Dr. Frankenstein and his monstrous creation trudging over the frozen plain of the Arctic in the dramatic and oh-so-tragic tale of life, death, love, and pain, in the first Gothic novel ever written.

These are all dreams, creations, and expressions of the Winter Soul. From Poe, to Siousie Sioux, to the lone witch on the moonlit hill, these are incredibly imaginative beings who care to go it alone, dare to take risks, and explore a lonesome path to gain the great riches of their own soul at the end of the journey.

If you were drawn to this book, then you, too, are a Winter Soul. You picked up this book to explore a different kind of magick. And as you do so, you will experience a liberation of your spirit unlike any you have ever known before. With the freedom of a Winter Soul, you will come to "know thyself" very well and in this deepened self-knowledge you will gain more personal power and magick. Winter Souls are strong and in that strength comes a calm, potent centeredness and an intuitive brilliance that can lead, help, and command. As you continue along your spiritual path, always pursue the depths of your Winter Soul to the fullest and nurture your spirit to the truest expression of your *self*. When you see a Goth standing out in the crowd, you know this person is unafraid to convey an uncompromising individuality and developed sense of self. Goth magicians are engaged with their inner nature and the outer Nature all around us.

Shadows and Light—Arranging a Winter Altar

There are many ways to nurture your truest nature and Winter Soul; perhaps the most obvious is creating a winter altar. This altar should be unlike any you have ever created before—because you are now recognizing a previously unexplored aspect of yourself and spirituality and focusing them in your altar, your "power center," in the words of Carl Jung, and I concur. Only in accomplishing this can you fully integrate and become whole. Thus, this altar is a tribute to and exploration of your unseen self and should be drawn from your deepest intuition. Select offerings and objects you are drawn to without quite knowing why. The answers will come. Spend as long as possible contemplating the qualities of this side of yourself and collect representations of these qualities carefully. What articulates these unique qualities?

You can go with the obvious symbols of winter—white, icicles, clear crystals, and so on—but do not limit yourself. These types of symbols only skim the surface of possibilities. What of a fossil that is frozen in the amber of time? Perhaps a birch branch with delicate lichen barely clinging to the surface. Think of how a frozen lake glistens with many colors and the mystery that lies beneath the surface, both of which can be represented by an iridescently and glittery chink of labradorite crystal for your altar. As you take a walk in the darkening days in the countdown to the winter solstice, collect a fallen leaf, which is a perfect, dried emblem of the changing of the season. In your own backyard, you see one tiny acorn, tucked in the root of the old oak tree. Place it on your altar as a symbol of all potentiality. As you pass by a yard sale, you spy a bit of beautifully carved ivory, an antique whale-tooth scrimshaw depicting an Inuit ritual, and you instantly know it is perfect for your sacred space. In the back of your closet, you find a snow globe you prized as a child; it has swirling snowy flakes inside a perfect circle. Suddenly, you remember your favorite Hans Christian Anderson fairy tale, *The Snow Queen*. You place the book on your altar and open to its gorgeously pre-Raphaelite depiction of this royal embodiment of the Winter Soul. Encouraged and feeling more open and adventurous, you try your hand at art. You paint on your altar a triptych—the hoary sky, palest sun struggling in its shine, a low-hung harvest moon, all beautiful blues, sapphire night sky, and silver stars. As you think about the heavens above and the firmament in which hang the stars, moon, sun, and all the planets, you are struck by a sense of the sacred. You feel how very special it is to be alive on this planet, maybe an accident and most definitely a miracle. As you think about it, you can almost feel the swing of Earth on its axis as it spins around the sun. Now, more than ever you feel so very alive.

Altar Consecration

Once you have arranged your altar to your liking, it is time to consecrate it. You can use a ritual of your own or follow these simple instructions.

Timing: The best time to perform this ritual is at dusk.

Supplies:

1 violet candle
1 silver candle
Incense
1 goose feather

1. Light the candles and place them on your altar.

2. Light the incense and fan it with the goose feather, as geese are the harbingers of winter. As you breathe in the scented smoke, pray aloud:

I welcome the winter inside of me,
I know my deepest wish is real and right.
I will my spirit to be free
Under this silver moon in this dark night.

Spirits of winter—bless this space with all due grace.
So mote it be!

Rime and Ritual—Spells for the Winter Soul

Have you ever heard the word *rime*? It differs from *rhyme* in that it means "winter frost," which will become integral to your rituals for the Winter Soul. Once you have consecrated your altar, you can begin honoring your Winter Soul with these rituals. The spells and conjurations that follow will enhance your spiritual process as you gradually build on your magickal self.

Guardian's Moon Spell

This little spell will take you deep and far inside yourself. It will greatly empower you and instill you with a much deeper understanding of who you are and what you are here to do. Each of us is as individual as a snowflake and our souls are imprinted with a stamp of specialness. The closer you get to the revelation of your soul's mission, the more you will know why you are here and, more important, what you are here to do. That is real magick.

Timing: The best time to perform this spell is during the new moon, when the night sky is at its darkest.

Supplies:

1 votive candle
Incense
Pine essential oil
Glass jar
Compass

1. Go outside and find a solitary space in which you can cast a circle. Use the compass to find true north. When you feel comfortable and safe to begin, cast an energetic circle.

2. Starting at the north point and moving clockwise, you will now acknowledge each of the Four Directions and call in the winter guardians.

3. Stand in the center of the circle and, with your forefinger, anoint your candle with the essence of pine, a tree that stays strong, green, and alive all through winter.

4. Place the candle in the glass jar and light it, setting both carefully and securely on the ground. Then light the incense with the flame of the candle and stick it into the ground beside the candle votive.

5. Breathe slowly and deeply; make yourself mindful that you are here in the darkest night, celebrating the sacred.

6. As you breathe, look around at the majesty of nature and the world around you. Feel the ground beneath your feet. Listen to the silence around you.

7. Now, open your heart completely to the awesome power of the universe and the magick both inside and outside of you.

8. Using the same forefinger, anoint your third eye, the chakric place above and between your eyes. With your eyes closed, speak aloud this rhyme of rime:

Sitting here beneath the moonless sky,
I open my heart and wonder why
I am here.
Tonight, I will learn
The reason why I yearn
To serve the Goddess and the God.
This night, I'll hear the reason
I serve this darkest winter season.
Guardians, I call on you now!

9. Remain at the center of the circle and keep your eyes closed. You may hear an inner voice or you may hear an outer voice right beside your ear. Listen calmly, staying centered with your two feet on the ground. You will know when it is time for you to close the circle and leave with your new message and mission.

10. Thank the guardians as you seal the sacred space and be sure to leave everything exactly as you found it. Incense, jar, candle, and matches all leave with you.

11. When you return home, write the message on a slip of paper and place it on your altar, where it will be hidden from any eyes but yours.

12. Place the candle, jar, and any remaining incense on your altar and burn it each new moon night.

Final thought: You may also want to begin a special journal of your thoughts, inspirations, and actions regarding the message you received. You have now embarked on an exciting new phase of your life's journey. Your journal will help you as you make discovery after discovery. Your journal may evolve into a Book of Shadows or it may one day become a book like this!

Gothic-Guided Meditation

This "inner work" ceremony will take you into the depths of your very being while you are exploring the depths of Mother Gaia, our earth. It is a way of getting grounded, Goth style, and it also takes you to a very magickal place where you can receive a gift from the Goddess, which will inform you about your truest inner nature.

Crystal Cave Consecration

Blessed beings, you are about to enter the Crystal Cave, our great mother earth Gaia. In your mind, you are standing with bare feet on the ground. You can feel the grass with your toes, the solid earth underneath your feet. Feel the solidity and fastness of the earth fill your body with strength; we are all made of earth, of clay. We come from the earth and we are made of earth. Feel your connection to the Mother. We come from the earth, her womb. We are made of stardust, clay, and the waters of the ocean. Feel the blood in your veins, the water of life. Know that you are alive. Feel her winds, the breath of life. Breathe deeply ten times, completely filling your lungs and completely emptying your lungs. Breathe and feel your chest expand, rising and falling with each breath.

Now feel your backbone connecting to the earth; you feel a silver cord connecting you and your life to the earth. Concentrate on the cord until you can feel it running all the way through you and deep into the earth. Tug on the cord; feel it give. Now, take the cord in your hands and follow it down, down, deep into the earth. It is dark as you go down and down, but you are not at all frightened, as you are a denizen of the dark. Trust in the universe and keep descending into the bosom of the mother. Down we go, not falling, but moving purposefully, gracefully, following the cord of the earth. Now you see light. Keep moving toward the light and keep holding the cord as it leads you to the shining distance.

The light grows nearer and you see that it is an opening, a cave, a safe place for shelter. Enter the cave. It is filled with firelight reflecting off a thousand crystal points. A lovely and mysterious older woman sits near the fire, warming her bones in her comfortable and dry cave. She is bestrewn with jewels and is dressed in a velvet and gossamer robe that is iridescent and shines in the firelight. Her visage is that of an incredibly wise woman and you can simply tell she has all the knowledge of time and the history of the world.

The cave is beautiful, more beautiful than the palace of any king or queen. It is the crystal cave of the Goddess and you are with her. Show your respect to the Goddess and light the incense at her altar at the side of the cave, which has piles of many shimmering stones and priceless gems, the bounty and beauty of our generous benefactor. Sit at her feet and take in her love, power, and grace. Sit quietly and hear the special message she has for you. You are her child and she has dreamed a dream for you. When you have received your goddess-gifted message, let the cord guide you back to the surface. Release the chord and bow in gratitude to the Great Goddess.

Winter Solstice Grave Mound—A Goth Gathering Place

You have gone to the Cystal Cave in the center of the earth for a centering ceremony. An actual site for a Gothic pilgrimage would be what is believed by locals to have been the location for winter solstice rituals. Goths gather on special occasions at cemeteries and burial sites. The Stone Age–era Newgrange Mound in Ireland is the ultimate site for a Gothic ritual gathering. For 5,200 years, ritualists and tourists alike have gathered at this mound to wait for the renewing of the sun's light and the promise that life will continue for another sacred year.

In a masterwork of sacred architecture, the artisans who erected the mound designed it so that only during the winter solstice can sunlight pass through an aperture in the roof of the mound. Magickally, the the sunlight illuminates the entire passageway floor, almost as if it is pouring on to the floor of the mound like liquid gold.

While any day is appropriate to visit this deeply special and spiritual site for spell work and magickal workings, there is one optimum day of the year when your spirit can be renewed and reminded of the most simple and powerful sources of life and that death is a part of life. At sunrise on the winter solstice, the great Irish Neolithic mound of Newgrange captures the rays of the rising sun in a vigorous celebration of light as life. Each ritual celebrant enters the site under the enormous lintel stone of the gateway in the mound and proceeds though a sixty-foot-long darkened passage, which is believed to be representative of death. At the end of this darkened hall, the celebrant comes across a highly significant spiritual carving, known though legend as the Spiral of Life. At this point, the mound opens into a circular chamber, which is believed to resemble a woman's womb. In the case of the Newgrange Mound, several burials have been found inside, but in many sacred mounds only one special holy and royal personage has been found.

The sunlight continues to flow inside the space until it rises up the Spiral of Life. At the moment the sun reaches the spiral, the sun glints and sparkles off the bas-relief of the spiral shape and the symbol itself flashes fiery colors of yellow, gold, orange, and red. It is a magickal experience—as if the Spiral of Life comes alive this one moment of the year in a marvelous light play and resurgence of the sun as the giver of life. After a moment or two, the entire chamber room, or cairn, is awash with yellow-gold light.

The Spiral of Life is one single line with no beginning or end. People the world over believe it is a symbol of rebirth. Irish scholar and goddess historian Sonja Geoghegan purports the theory that the central chamber in the Newgrange Mound site was a birthing chamber as well as a burial chamber to encompass the entire circle of life and to "encourage transmigration from one generation to the next." Fascinatingly, the single steady line of the spiral itself has also traditionally been linked to a ninety-day period, showing that the creators of this uniquely beautiful triple-looped spiral symbol may have had in mind the three trimesters of the human pregnancy cycle. Geoghegan's work on the Newgrange Mound is very compelling, especially in conjunction with the fact that the design and layout of the mound itself is very much like a woman's uterus and birth canal. The simple wisdom of these Stone Age builders has lasted many lifetimes and provides connection to the eternal cycles of life and death, light and dark, sun and moon.

Goth Is in the Details

James Churchward calls the triple spiral the "Roadway of the Soul" in his seminal source work on spiral symbology: "It will be seen that the spiral has no end, but when the center is reached, the line returns on itself. There is no starting point either of the spiral and no end given, consequently, these spirals are also the equivalent of a circle. . . . We are told man's soul lives on until finally it reaches the source of its origin. Ana, 1320 B.C., Egyptian Papyrus, 'if we live on we must continue for ever, and if we continue for ever, life, the circle and eternity, man had no beginning.'"

—James Churchward, *The Sacred Symbol of Mu*, 1933

Our Lady of Silver Magick: A Full Moon Invocation

While the winter solstice occurs but once a year, the full moon is an opportunity for thirteen holy celebrations a year. The full moon is also the most powerful time of the month and the perfect time to celebrate with special people in your life. The following ritual will heighten your spirituality, your friendships, and your connection to the universal powers.

As I write this, it is a full moon in Libra and I look forward to getting together with some of the sisterhood, some fellow Wiccan Goths, kicking up our heels in celebration of life and asking for what we need from the universe. We will wait until midnight, the traditional witching hour. We will gather in one of our favorite spots near water under the bright moonlight. You can perform this ritual in your home, garden, or sacred place of your choosing.

Midnight Goth Goddess Incantation

At "the witching hour of midnight," the power of magick is strongest. This is also the optimal time to call down the Goddess of the moon for a power boost of blessings and strength. By honoring her and inviting her into your circle, you will receive untold gifts of wisdom, joy, and beauty into your life. This mystery rite could be incorporated into your coven's monthy moon sacraments.

Timing: The best time to perform this ritual is midnight.

Supplies:

1 large crystal (a geode, amethyst, or quartz or rock crystal would be a good choice)
Goblet of wine
An image of the Goddess
Candles in sturdy glass votives
Each participant's personal touchstone
Rattles, drums, or other instruments of your choice

1. Place the large crystal in the middle of the altar, along with the goblet of wine and image of the Goddess.

2. Designate a leader who performs all the incantations as the group forms a circle. Begin with the appointee saying:

Oh, lady of silver magic,
We honor you here.
In this place, sacred and safe.
This circle is in your honor.

3. The person in the north point of the circle places his or her candle and crystal on the ground as the leader says:

Blessed one, all earth is yours.
May we all heal.
May we all draw strength.

4. The person in the east places his or her candle and crystal on the ground as the leader says:

Oh, lady of laughter and joy,
So is the sky yours, too.
May the air be clear and pure.
And the clouds sweet with wind and rain.

5. The person at the south point lays down his or her crystal and candle while the leader says,

Oh, lady of summer,
Each season is yours.
May each spring bring
Flowers and crops for all.

6. The person in the west lays down his or her candle and crystal while the leader says:

Goddess of the waters,
The rivers and the ocean are yours.
May they once more flow crystal clear.
Lady, we have built this circle in your honor.

7. Now the whole circle goes to the altar and kneels, with each member placing his or her candle and crystal on the altar. Each member takes a sip from the goblet of wine and says:

I toast thee bright lady
In your honor,
Blessed be.

8. Then pick up the rattles and drums and sing and dance under the sparkling sky.

New Moon, New You

The new moon is the optimum time for new beginnings, and it happens a lucky thirteen times each year. With each passage of this dark moon, you can ask for and sow the seeds for the life and love you want. Goths are known for their lust for life; performing this simple spell will bring your desires to you.

Timing: This ritual is performed on the new moon night.

Supplies:

2 pieces of rose quartz
2 red candles

1. Take the two pieces of rose quartz and place them on the floor in the center of your bedroom.

2. Light the two red candles and say aloud:

Beautiful crystal I hold this night
Flame with love for my delight.
Goddess of love I ask of you.
Guide me in the path that is true.
Harm to none as love comes to me.
This I ask and so it shall be!

Invoking Angels

A brooding, pale, and soulful Goth resembles a dark angel. The concept of the watcher angels and "Nephilim" are favorites among Goth lore and fantasy. Dark metal and Goth bands such as Morbid Angel and Fields of Nephilim attest to the fascination with this mythology or hidden history of the relationships between angels and humans.

Angels are messengers; in fact, that is the exact meaning of the Greek word *angelos*. Angels appear in many of the world's wisdom traditions: Mormonism, Zoroastrianism, Judaism, Islam, Hinduism, Tibetan Buddhism, and Christianity. In every case, angels are messengers who carry the message of God's will to his people. They are spiritual beings on the chain of being between God and humans. Views of angelic beings vary in how they conduct their "personal" lives when they are not serving God. Jews view angels as male and the Christian tradition sees them as without gender. Certainly, the angel of God who helped Peter escape from his imprisonment and enchained bonds seemed very masculine. In the apocryphal Book of Enoch, however, angels referred to as "the Watchers" were sensual beings who "lay with human women" and fathered a race of half-human, half-angel beings with supernatural powers called "Nephilim." Enoch is described as being brought to heaven by the angel Michael and is transformed into an angel known as "Metraron." Perhaps the great English poet John Milton was influenced by Enoch, since he wrote of angels as supremely sensual beings who enjoyed sex often and well.

Theories about angels vary nearly as much as the theorizer. Emanuel Swedenborg believed that angels are not physical or material in any way and can only be seen when we humans open our inner or "spiritual" eye. St. Thomas Aquinus was called the "Angelic Doctor" for his miraculous ministerings, but he, too, believed angels came from our own intellect and were creations of our own thoughts. The great medieval mystic Hildegard of Bingen saw angels as great beings who shined as stars in the firmament or like red flames.

Calling All Angels

In your travels along the sacred path, you should have by now gathered up seashells, driftwood, crystals, and small pebbles. You can create a simple "Angel Accessing Tool" from your collection of nature's blessings. Make a wind chime any time you want to gather up the good energy of those unseen who can help and protect you (and drive away the *not* so helpful energy). Here's how to make a wind chime.

Supplies:

A stick (a small piece of sea-smoothed driftwood is perfect)
String
Chunks of crystals (celestite, aquamarine, muscovite, morganite, and selenite can all help you make contact with your guardian angels)

1. Tie string around the pieces of crystal.

2. Attach each string to your stick of wood.

3. Hang your chime in your home or wherever you want to "make contact."

Once you have crafted your magickal tool, you should store it in a safe place and bring it out when you really need angelic intervention. You can welcome unseen and benevolent spirits into your home and life with this conjuring charm.

Spell for Welcoming Benevolent Spirits

We can all use more angels in our lives. Some angels take human form such as a helpful friend who is always there in a crisis. Still others are above in the ether and can be invoked with a few words and focused intention. Use this spell when you need a guiding hand and angelic assistance.

Supplies:

Sage
Your wind chime

1. Bless the new wind chime by smudging with sage smoke.

2. Jingle the chimes energetically and say aloud:

I call on my angels to guide joy to my door.
Such gladness as I receive, so I shall give.
By the moon and the stars
I call on my guardians
To show me the best way to live.
For this, I am grateful.
Blessed be.

The Ranks of Angels

The Book of Revelations (8:2) reads, "And I saw seven angels which stand before God." These are the archangels. Jewish tradition holds that the highest rank of angels consists of the angels "of presence" of God and these are the seven archangels. The First Book of Enoch lists these archangels as: Uriel, Michael, Gabriel, Saraqael, Remiel, Reqiel, and Raphael. In the Third Book of Enoch, they are presented as Gabriel, Michael, Sahaqiel, Satqiel, Baradiel, Baraqiel, and Sidriel. In Islam, there are only Michael, Israfel, Azrael, and Gabriel. Current Christianity has reduced the list of archangels down to Raphael, Gabriel, and Michael.

The duties of the archangels are to serve the presence of God, assist humanity, and watch and care for the lower ranks of angels. Concerning each angel's special tasks, Raphael is the angel of healing, Gabriel can be called on for personal guidance and prophecy, and Michael is the angel of courage and personal protection. A study of angelic lore across the traditions indicates that the archangel Michael is the oldest and most powerful of all angels, and as a personal protector he can be called on or "invoked" when you need him for courage, insight, and spiritual growth.

The seven archangels are:

Raphael: healing
Gabriel: strength
Michael: protection
Uriel: light
Ariel: wisdom
Cammuel: divine love
Cassiel: understanding

Who Is Archangel Michael?

Michael is the only angel to cross all the major wisdom traditions because he appeared to Old Testament prophets including Enoch, to Mary, among others, in the text of Christianity, the New Testament, and to Mohammed, the founder of Islam. His very name places him close to God, as it translates to "who is like unto the Lord." Gnostics believed that Michael was present at the creation of the universe. It was Michael who God charged with casting Lucifer out of heaven. Michael has been the subject of devotion of several religions including a powerful "cult of Michael" during the Crusades that rampaged through Nordic tribes, converting with the aid of a sword. It was shortly after this Nordic and Germanic conversion crusade that the cult of Mary took precedence, replacing the goddess. Joan of Arc began receiving visitations from Michael at the age of thirteen, guiding her, quite successfully, in battle.

Angelology—long a secret aspect of pagans practicing ceremonial magick, such as the OTO, founded by Aleister Crowley—has "crossed over" and has been embraced by Wiccans, most especially dark Wiccans. There are many ways to call on the guidance of the angels, and you can invoke Michael anytime you need guidance or as a spiritual touchstone. You can do this with a pendulum or meditation ritual; ask him to join you in a walk or in your dreams. In fact, in your dream, you will be much more open to receiving his messages. Before inviting Michael into your dream world, breathe deeply and achieve a state of total calm. Then, think about why you feel the need for his guidance. Write down in your dream journal or Book of Shadows a specific invitation to him, "Michael, please come to me and help me to know if this job opportunity is right for me." Yes, you can be that specific! As you fall asleep, think about the situation and ease into your sleep and your dreams. The answer will be in your mind when you wake up. Write it down in the same journal and thank your angelic guest with a prayer.

Ritual of Angel Evocation

We all have matters that weigh us down. Whether you have an abusive boss or relationship or you find yourself lost in a dangerous block in a strange town, every now and then you will need the tools to call up guardian energy. Here is how to get an urgent message out to an angel if you are in need of protection.

Timing: Perform this ritual whenever you feel in need of some angelic protection.

1. Face the east with your arms by your side and your head bowed down. Now, shut your eyes and with creative visualization envision yourself surrounded by the four archangels.

2. Visualize a pure, white light descending from above that expands and surrounds both you and the angels.

3. Breathe deeply three times and then turn to your right.

4. You are now standing before the archangel Michael. Open your eyes and say aloud, "Michael, I need your help," and describe to him what you need. He is a true helpmate in a time of need!

Vampire Protection

Part of the lore of angels includes the fascinating theory that "fallen angels" who battled with God and were kicked out of heaven became vampires here on the earthly plane. The apocryphal chapter of the Holy Bible, the Book of Enoch, states that when the children of angels and men had exhausted the supply of good, they then began drinking the blood of humans, even resorting to eating their flesh. The modern notion of the vampire has been so influenced by cinema, Bram Stoker, and the very prolific Anne Rice that hardly anyone has a real idea of its early origins. Goths, of course, know quite a bit about this! The idea that the dead require blood to restore them to a semblance of life predates even Homer and his poetic posse in ancient Greece. Prehistoric peoples believed that women's lunar flow of blood was the mysterious source of all life and that this blood was the vehicle of reincarnation for all souls waiting to come back after death. The Greeks did think that "shades," or ghostly spirits in the underworld, thirsted for blood and sought it from living people. If you recall, Odysseus acted as a necromancer and was able to call forth the spirits of his dead solders and comrades by pouring out offerings of blood for them. And come forth they did—in droves. It is almost entirely forgotten, except by modern heathens, that the gods likewise lived on blood and could be invoked with a blood offering.

This lore in and of itself does not account for all the fascination and centuries-old stories of vampires. Medieval folks thought vampires were a sort of cannibal and that they were mostly women. There is even a historical account in the pre-Roman Germanic law records called the Salic Code of a "she vampire," who was charged with and found guilty of devouring a man. As Christianity evolved, clerics came to believe in vampires and demons and were on the lookout for them, especially during witch hunts, as it was believed they were in league with each other. In northern Europe, especially the Balkans, Hungary, and Bohemia, vampire legends are legion. In these regions, the locals take a more proactive approach to vampires with many techniques for capturing them, such as trapping them in bottles or killing them with the classic stake through the heart, which is still practiced in the Balkans today.

Psychic Vampires—Chi Suckers

So, you've been going through your day your own way and it is just fine. Then, you run into someone you know and after you've talked with her for a bit, you feel the positive energy draining out of your body. While you try to keep the conversation positive, she is doling out the woe in bucket loads—icky boyfriends, creepy bosses, heinous landlords, on and on. You listen, make helpful suggestions, make a date to get together, and boom—she walks away happier and smiling. What just happened?

You just encountered a psychic vampire (PV)! If you don't guard properly against PVs, you will find yourself in this situation time and time again. Certainly, it is fine to be a sympathetic friend and to be helpful and kind, but it is most unhelpful and unkind to *yourself* to allow anyone to suck you completely dry of your life force, your chi. Most often, PVs are not aware on a conscious level of their incessant chi sucking, but they are on an unconscious level. And when you are victim to this, you are giving away your power, which is energetically and utterly negative.

Who are PVs? Big time narcissists! It is all about them—notice how they rarely ask how *you* are. They have been running a victim script for a very long time and being a victim is a chosen and much prized role. If you are kindly and generous of spirit—good for you—but watch out, because you are a favorite target for PVs. But with the right tools, you can protect yourself from PVs. The psychic shield is an effective magickal way of shielding yourself from the neighborhood PV.

Psychic Shield

You would not leave your house on a cold windy day without a coat, right? Please don't leave your house without a psychic shield—you'll thank yourself later.

Visualize whatever feels like a secret defense against unwarranted psychic intruders. Some folks see garage doors, others utilize an enclosing egg, and I have even heard of a big wet blanket as a shield, but I prefer science fictiony silver shields that I put up or down and a hooded robe that I wear. Anytime I go out into groups where I feel unsure about the people, I cloak myself in my silver robe and do a brief silent meditation. Also, the best defense is a strong, positive attitude and sense of self. The more you practice your meditation and creative visualization, the greater your skill will grow.

Goth Ritual of Protection

Goths are, as a rule, incredibly sensitive folks even if they have twenty rivets decorating their neoprimitive heads. With sensitivity comes the reality of being greatly affected by energy—both bad and good. It is important to constantly perform energy-cleansing rituals for this very reason, such as saging yourself and space, taking purifying baths, and doing some mental clearing.

You are about to learn a wonderful basic energy cleanser known as the Lesser Banishing Ritual of the Pentagram (LBRP), sometimes simply referred to as the Pentagram Ritual. It is a marvelous template that you can add to and personalize after you are truly familiar with it. This ritual will become an extremely important tool in your magickal arsenal for keeping at bay any unwanted forces, both worldly and otherworldly. Some even believe that the LBRP casts out not just negative forces, but all forces. At the end of the LBRP, you have an utterly neutral environment in which you can perform your spells and magick. As you perform this ritual and advance in your magickal practice, bear in mind that positive and negative forces do not automatically mean good and bad. The Goth way is a mixture of positive and negative—a mixture of romanticism and fascination with all things dark. It is a balance of energy, and to use it properly, you must stay aware.

Lesser Banishing Ritual of the Pentagram

The Hermetic Order of the Golden Dawn is a pagan pathworking dedicated to preserving western esoteric traditions. As such, it is an important source for pagan rituals of all kinds, as well as for many important practices for psychic and self-protection. The following is a variation on a Golden Dawn ritual, the Nuosphere Rite:

1. Stand facing the east to create the Cross of Light; visualize a brightly glowing sphere of white light above your head, reach inside this ball, and pull a beam of light toward you until it touches your eyes.

2. Now speak aloud:

My god and my goddess is above me.

3. With concentration, pull the light down through your body, forming a vertical pillar. Touch your second, or sacral chakra area and say:

My god and my goddess is below me.

4. Touching your right shoulder say:

My god and my goddess is to the right of me.

5. Drawing the light across your body to form a horizontal bar, touch your left shoulder and say:

My god and my goddess is within me.

6. Throw your hands and arms upward and outward above your head to form a V and say:

There is no god and no goddess where I am.
This forms the Cross of Light.

7. Move to the eastern quarter and draw a large pentagram facing upright in the air before you. Then stand in the sign of the Enterer, arms outstretched in front of you, left foot slightly forward. Again, creatively visualize energy streaming out of your hair and into the pentagram and visualize the word:

Therion.

8. Pull your arms back in the sign of Silencia, your left thumb pressed to your lips; your feet together.

9. Turn to your left, moving widdershins, or clockwise. Repeat this procedure of drawing the pentagram in each of the quarters—North, West, and South. When you create the pentagram in the North, vibrate the word:

Nuit.

In the west, say the word:

Babalon.

In the south, say the word:

Hadit.

10. Return to the center of the circle and, facing east once more; stretch out your arms to each side and say:

Before me the power of the earth.
Behind me, the power of water.
On my right hand, the power of fire.
On my left hand, the power of air.

11. Visualize the body of the Goddess Nuit arched above your feet in the north, hands in the south, filling the circle with starlight. Invoke with the words:

Around me burn all the stars of Nuit.
And within me burns the star of Hadit.

Now repeat the Cross of Light and close the ritual.

Chapter Five

Goth Rocks and Heavy Metal: Magickal Jewelry

You can recognize Goths by the striking array of jewelry and gemstones they are wearing. Goths have been real pioneers in the art of bejeweling as they were some of the first to wear multiple earrings in eyebrows, ear lobes, tongues, and noses. Goths are wonderfully experimental in their use of metals and gems in personal adornment from rings that stretch from knuckle to knuckle to chains that run from nipple to navel and beyond! That jewelry is spiritual is doubtless in the world of Goth magick. A marvelous way to take greater advantage of Goth magickal powers of your gems and crystals is to wear them on your sleeve—literally! Not only will you be adorning yourself but also these rocks will interact with your energy systems while you are wearing them. As you choose your jewelry, give a lot of thought about what constructive changes you wish to see in your life or what good qualities you want to develop further in yourself.

For example, if you want to get more organized, you should get some lazulite and incorporate it into your jewelry or clothing. Another example of a powerful stone is jade. Jade is a grounding and stabilizing stone, so you may want to incorporate it into your wardrobe when you are going through a period of change or transition. Also, I have never really had any jade, but recently I feel like I need the grounding and stabilizing of this stone. Also, I need to get more prosperity minded. I need to be better about saving money and thinking in terms of my future security so I'm not reading tarot out on the sidewalk when I'm ninety! So, I have been walking through San Francisco's Chinatown and feeling very attracted to different jades. I'm sure you feel such urges and attractions, too. Often, this might be your subconscious giving you a gentle nudge about some growing you need to do. If you listen to those inner voices, you will reap the benefits again and again.

Understanding the Language of Jewelry

A little thoughtfulness about how and where to wear your crystal and gem jewelry can go a long way toward your health and happiness. The left side of your body is the most sensitive side. Information and energy flows into your left side much more quickly, so you can protect yourself by wearing crystals that act as "energy guards." Jewelry worn on the right side of your body helps with work, productivity, and success. Your left side is the "feeling" side and your right side is your "action" side.

Necklaces, Pendants, and Chokers, Oh My!

Chokers are a popular Goth accessory, a variation on the popular dog collar of Goth's punk rock roots. Perhaps you want to be a better communicator or to sing, chant, or simply express yourself more freely. To do any of these things, you will need a clear throat chakra. A blocked throat chakra can result in your feelings and ideas being blocked, so a necklace or choker can open this center and bring more possibility into your life. A strand of pearls for your throat is not only timelessly elegant but also boosts your self-esteem and sociability. If you're more into precious metals, try silver, copper, and gold. You will want to avoid aluminum entirely, as it has been linked to some health issues including Alzheimer's disease. The best throat chakra stones are amethyst, azurite, blue obsidian, lepidolite, aquamarine, blue topaz, amber, kunzite, blue tourmaline, and turquoise, as they harmonize with the blue color of this chakra.

The Old Rugged Ankh and Other Crosses to Bear

The brilliant psychologist Carl Jung put forth his belief that crosses are a key symbol for the creative process, which usually leads to a crossroads and a choice and artistic direction the creator must take. Goths are nothing if not creative. Even if you are not an artist by trade, by cultivating your unique look, you become an artist. Another important aspect to consider is that crosses represent crucifixes and the passage from life to death. To me, this explains why so many Goths, including myself, have an inordinately high number of crosses among their jewelry and accoutrements.

Even though the cross is most often associated with Christianity, pagans and most especially Goth pagans are well aware of the fact that crosses are an ancient symbol that predates Christianity by a long shot. There are dozens of different kinds of crosses, including the Egyptian ankh, which is a revered symbol of everlasting life.

A Compleat List of Crosses

Anchor Cross: a cross that's made to look like an anchor
Ankh: an elongated oval at the top of a long bottom bar and shortened cross bar
Button Cross: a perfectly squared cross with four small bulbous ends
Church Cross: small centered cross bars with a quarter length at all four ends
Coptic or Egyptian Cross: a perfect circle at the top of a Latin-like cross
Cross Dissimulata: very like an ankh with an anchor-like semicircle line at the bottom
Crossed Cross: like the Church cross with a small extension beyond the bases at each end
Cross of Archangels (Golgotha Cross): same as the Patriarch cross with a base
Cross of Christ: like the symbol for number one crossing at the center at a 45-degree angle
Cross of Endlessness: an upended rectangle with four triangles connecting on four sides
Cross of Peter: cross bar is three-quarters down from the top
Cross of Phillip: a Latin cross on its side with the cross bar on the right side
Cross of St. John's: like a four-leaf clover with a tiny circle connecting the four leaves
Cross of the Patriarch: a short cross bar just below the top and a longer cross bar one-quarter down from the top
Cross of the Pope: same as the Patriarch cross with the addition of a long bar halfway down

Death Cross: a miniature Peter cross meeting close to the bottom at a 45-degree angle
Evangelists Cross: cross bar at the center with a gradated base of four bars, large to small
Gamma Cross: a cross formed in an outline of four L-shapes facing different directions
Greek or St. George's Cross: perfectly square outline filled in all black, with indented ends looking like a ribbon
Heraldic Dagger or Pointed Cross: a cross that looks like a short sword
Inaugural Circle: a small circle inside and connected by cross bars to an outer circle
Invocation Cross: a doubled and shorter version of the Cross of Peter
Iron Cross: a larger version of the Maltese cross with an outline and the center blacked in
Latin Cross: cross bar is one-quarter down from the top
Lily Cross: an open circle at the center with Y's at all four ends
Lutheran Cross: Latin cross with a small circle at the cross bar and cross bars at each end
Maltese Cross: a short and centered outlined cross with concaved ends at each cross bar
Pentagram or Solomon's Seal: one line forming a five-pointed star
Portuguese Cross: like a Latin cross but with flanged-out ends on all four bar ends
Restoration Cross: perfectly square outline of a cross with a circle at the center
Ring or Celtic Cross: a Latin cross with a circle connecting all three ends of the cross bar
Roman Holy Cross: a twelve-ended maze of crossed bars with four dots at four ends
Russian Orthodox Cross: like the Patriarch cross with a diagonal bar halfway down
Shield, or Star, of David: two overlapping triangles, one up, one down, forming a six-pointed star

Square Cross: an upended, blacked-in rectangle with a small cross on every side
St. Andrew's Cross: two lines meeting at the middle at 45-degree angles
Sun Cross: a perfectly centered and square cross in the middle of an outer circle
Tali Cross or St. Anthony's Cross: like an ankh with no oval and no bar at the top
Threefoil or Lazarus Cross: the Crossed cross with rounded ends and heavier lines

Many of these crosses come in and out of vogue; the Iron cross fell out of favor after it was adopted by the Nazis as a symbol of the pure race and the totem of their genocide, a meaning those Germans attached to it. The Latin cross and its many variations represent two disparate elements intersecting: life and death. When Christians adopted the cross as their symbol, to be a reminder of the crucifixion of Christ, it gained popularity that has never ceased. Interestingly, the pentagram has gained new popularity, even outside of Wiccan circles, since 2004 as a result of the astounding popularity of author Dan Brown's *The Da Vinci Code*, which spends a good deal of time explaining the history, origin, and meaning of this symbol. The hieroglyphic ankh meant both "life" and also "the mirror." Designed to represent the Goddess, it was also a representation of the sexual union and eternal life. Most depictions of gods and goddesses in the Egyptian pantheon are holding the ankh.

Goth Is in the Details

Traditionally, vampires and those who died by suicide should be buried at a crossroads.

Chains of Being

Chains of all kinds are Goth favorites as they represent the sadomasochistic (S&M) ethos inherent in punk from which Goth sprang.

Chains represent links between people, the ties that bind you to another. Other mystical meanings for chains are happiness and justice, prayer, reason and the soul, communication, and command. Plato referred to a "chain of being," a golden chain linking earth to the heavens above, a bond between humans and the immortals. Socrates tied our human happiness to the concept of justice with a concept of a chain of steel and diamonds. Pseudo Dionysius the Areopagite compared the practice of prayer to an infinitely luminous chain going from earth to heaven. An astral cord, akin to a golden chain, binds the spirit to the psyche or reason to the soul.

Waist jewelry has recently made a big comeback. People are going beyond belts and wearing belly chains and lariats. Gemstone belts and buckles can really enhance your joie de vivre and give you greater physical strength and health. Turquoise grounds and agate raises the energy level. For healing power, try bloodstone. For constancy and achieving life on an even keel, the organic gem family of shells, corals, and abalone are optimal. For impetus and motivation, wear carnelian. Health and well-being boosting stones include red coral for the lungs, bloodstone for the heart, and moonstone for pregnancy.

Kiss My Ring

Rings mean eternity, unity, reincarnation, safety, union, power, and energy. Rings symbolize the eternity of the circle shape—the universe. Wearing rings was believed to help ward off any kind of malevolence through continuity—nothing could "get in." A ring "binds" you with the energy of the stone. In dream psychology, a ring represents the desire for reconciliation of the different parts of your being and personality—it shows you want to be an integrated whole, which is the first step in making it happen.

When wearing rings, be sure the bottom side of the stone is open, in other words, not set in metal, to give greater connection to the stone and your skin. As a general rule, you should wear gems that awaken and release emotions on your left hand and that power career and personal goals on your right hand.

Though thumb rings have become a big trend, they are not recommended, as they tend to block the energy of the thumb or, even worse, awaken egotism and selfishness. If you need an esteem boost, do wear a ring on your thumb, but if you have any tendency toward egotism, resist the temptation for a thumb ring.

The index fingers are the achievement fingers and adorning them with the right gem can really aid you in striving for your dreams. For wisdom, wear lapis lazuli. For greater love of yourself and others, try pearl, moonstone, or garnet. For success, wear carnelian. For a quiet mind and greater calm, wear sodalite, chrysocolla, or turquoise.

Your middle fingers are all about ideas and insight as well as intuition. Your left hand receives and can even channel intuitive information. In palmistry, your left hand shows the future or potential in your life, so your left is the antenna, if you will, for the future. Therefore, only wear stones on the middle finger of your left hand when you want to get a lot of psychic input from the world around you. For greater sensitivity and creativity, wear amethyst. To awaken your inner and outer beauty, wear rubies. To access your higher good and know your life purpose, wear sapphire or quartz crystal.

The ring finger represents creativity and, of course, the ring finger on the left hand is a direct connection to your heart and love center. For deep and loyal ties of love, wear a diamond. For inspired creativity, wear emerald. To express the love inside you toward the world, wear moonstone. For practicality in your work and art, wear turquoise. For service to your community and the world, wear opal. For serenity both within and without, wear ruby. To meet creativity goals, wear tiger's eye.

Your pinkies represent change. The right gem on your little finger can help you find and pursue new opportunities and change the direction of your whole life. This is a lot of power in one little ring! For better organizational habits, wear a pearl. For unwinding and simplifying, wear turquoise. To bring new energy and new prospects, wear aventurine.

Vestal Victoriana—Brooches

Brooches symbolize virginity, faithfulness, and protection. Brooches were once the costume jewelry of the medieval Irish, as decorating themselves with gems and valuable stones showed they were part of the aspiring warrior caste. Brooches were one of the most useful ornaments to the Goths of old as they were used to clasp their robes and cloaks together for protection against the harsh Dark Age winters. Brooches have recently come back into great favor due to the popularity of J.R.R. Tolkien's *The Lord of the Rings* and the magickal Elven brooches used by the hobbits, dwarves, elves, wizards, and men in the *Fellowship of the Ring*.

Victorians, who are a constant inspiration for Goth style, loved cameo brooches of ivory and colored corals, as well as obsidian. These gems were beloved for their relative softness and ease in carving silhouette portraiture and miniatures in the popular jewelry of this Gilded Age. A common belief stemming from that era was that coral warded off evil. A diamond-studded brooch is a double symbol of love and safeguard.

Crowning Glories—Head Dressing

It is no accident that kings, queens, and emperors wore crowns. The ancients expected their leaders to be wise, and a bejeweled crown bestowed the brilliance and power of the gems to the royal personage. The word *crown*, literally means a circlet and signifies the special status of the person wearing the crown. Crowns could also be a circlet of flowers such as those worn by the king and queen of May Day for the sabbat of Beltane, for a hand fasting, and for candled crowns for Brigid's Day and Yule. While you may not want to wear a tiara to the office or a crown to the grocery store, you can wear hair clips and barrettes with crystals and stones attached for some of the same reasons. Why not be smarter and smartly accessorized? Bejeweled barrettes worn at the temple confer wit and wisdom, a kind of brain-boosting power energy.

Cuff Me—Bracelets

We can thank the Romans and Egyptians for bringing jewelry for the arm to the fore—cuffs, bracelets, and arm bands. By the Roman era, many gem stones that we use today had already been discovered. Myth and magick was the rule of the day and gemstones were treated with respect. Arm bands are symbols of power and strength. Cuffs bespeak your relationship to the world and, quite often, to one other special person. Cuffs are embraced by Goths in the spirit of the punk, S&M style. Bracelets are worn on the wrists and upper arms. The arms connect the body to the hands and, as such, connect the energy brought in through the touch of our hands. Bracelets on the wrist are important protection and energy blockers. The wrists are perfect protection pulse points. The organic gems such as coral and abalone are very helpful for energy flow and release. Turquoise is great for stabilizing and calming you physically. Ancient cultures loved to wear arm bands and cuffs, which have gone out of style except for the most dramatic of fashionistas. Perhaps we should try to bring this style back because gems and crystal armbands are a very good thing for the body and soul, conferring physical strength, vitality, and positive energy.

I'm Your Slave—Ankle Bracelets and Toe Rings

Bejeweled feet and ankles are very sexy. Jewelry in this area of the body is also grounding and stabilizing. If you are dealing with anxiety or substance abuse issues, wear amethyst around your ankle. If you are feeling drained of energy, jasper or rock crystal will come in handy. Rhodonite will do the trick if you are feeling disconnected or restless. You can cleanse all your jewelry by placing it in a bowl of sea salt for seven days to make sure nobody else's energy is retained in the pieces of jewelry. This is especially important if it is antique or estate jewelry.

Magick Heavy Metal

Just as the first ancients sensed that stones contained energy and special properties, they also discovered that metals hold energies with tremendous influence and power. Metals used to be very commonplace in magick but their popularity waned during the late medieval era when alchemists began to become scientists. Magick metallurgy has rebounded and plays a definite role in the magick of jewelry. Goths connect most directly with the magick of metal with studs and sacred piercings.

Gold

In Mexico, gold is linked to religion and faith. Gold crucifixes and crosses are worn for protection and as a link to God, Christ, and Mary.

Parents in India give their young children tiny gold amulets to guard against harm and illness.

Gold nugget jewelry brings in a continuous flow of wealth!

Gold is beloved for its sheen and purity. Gold is a fantastic energy conductor in either white gold or yellow gold. Gold enhances any gem or stone and encourages the action of said stone with a dose of quickening energy. Gold is a symbol of wealth and personal power and "honors" any gem or crystal. Gold also honors *you*. Gold is both the softest and strongest metal—it is mutable for shaping and design and resilient no matter how many times it is melted and reshaped. Gold never tarnishes and seems to stay beautiful and perfect through anything—it is impermeable to any weather, damage, or aging. Gold is used for jewelry, in industry, and in medicine. Gold is a viable energy conductor and has wonderful healing properties. It has been used for arthritis and, since it is impervious to harm, it is a tremendous element of renewal and regeneration. Gold has been said to help with blood and circulation, chemical and hormone imbalances, stress illnesses, pulmonary problems, the brain, and also the emotional realm.

Gold can enhance the power of any gem or crystal, with a dose of "quickening" energy, a magickal boost. Gold can give you courage and self-esteem. Gold, associated with the zodiacal sign of the royal Leo, confers the confidence of this sign and spirit. It accentuates the positive in yourself and in your regard of others. This metal of kings and queens will cast a golden glow over your life!

SILVER

> In China, parents gift their children with silver locket necklaces.
>
> One French tradition is to wear silver chains when getting engaged.
>
> Lapis, jade, emeralds, and pearls set in silver attract love.

Silver is aligned with the moon and the planet Mercury, named for the quicksilver messenger god Mercury, and contains the properties associated with excellent communication. Silver has been associated with the moon for thousands of years. As such, it enhances the power of any crystal or gem. These are traditional associations that come from mythology and astrology. It secures the energy of the stone and doesn't add to the energy. Silver is a healing metal that should *not* be worn all the time; let your body tell you when it feels right. With this simple safeguard, you will not exhaust the power silver has to heal *you*. Silver offers a reflection of your self-esteem and this should be paid very special attention. Silver is a detoxifying agent and communicates with the body to alert about raised levels of hormones and other chemical imbalances. Silver is good to wear as a necklace as it is very beneficial to the throat and lungs. Your synapses even fire more efficiently because silver acts as a transmitter. Consequently, silver is good for people encountering memory reduction, psychological issues, and brain disease.

In olden days, women wore silver around their waists for fertility. Men can do the same, a silver belt buckle, perhaps, for impotence or any other sexual dysfunction. Moonstones are wonderful in combination with their sacred moon metal—silver. Amethyst is also great in a silver setting. Jasper and agate are very suitable along with fire agate and opal. While diamonds are more often set in gold, silver is a terrific combination with the pure-carbon gem, as is the case with sapphires. Zircon, tourmaline, and amber should not be set in silver. I see amber set in silver all the time, which is unfortunate because amber is a *hot* stone and works better with any other metal.

Copper

> Copper is ruled by Venus and attracts love, especially if set with emerald.
>
> Copper is a lucky metal, twice as lucky if containing crystals of tiger's eye, coral, opals, and Apache tear.
>
> Copper jewelry has immense healing properties and, if worn on the left side of the body, can actually prevent sickness.

Copper is the metal most consciously worn by healers. Because of copper's power as a conductor, healers place their faith in copper's power to heal the body and mind. Copper helps the mineral content of gems and crystals interact with your body. One school of thought propounds the belief that a crystal wand wound with copper is supercharged. You will notice that some of the healing rocks discussed in this book mention copper as a trace element, amping up the power of these kinds of crystals greatly. Some of these copper ore gemstones are azurite, chrysocolla, malachite, and turquoise. Copper reacts best with stones containing a lot of metal and reacts very little with stones that lack metal ore in their makeup. Tiger's eye, aventurine, rhodonite, and mica are metal-rich stones that combine energies beautifully with copper. Do not place most crystalline stones in copper; the same holds true with pearls and coral. Amethyst is one of the only crystalline stones that combines well with copper. Copper combined with gold and silver and a multimetal bracelet with the right stone is a powerful piece of healing!

Copper is found around the world and has been used since ancient times for decoration and jewelry. Copper plays a significant role in the cultures of prehistory, Greece, Rome, Native America, India, and Egypt, along with China and Japan. Copper was believed to be able to protect against evil and attract love. The Egyptians relied on copper for the ritual of the dead. Copper is deeply ingrained in our history in use as sacred knives, candleholders in early churches, Asian copper prayer diagrams, purification vessels, and countless other holy instruments.

Copper stimulates the flow of energy throughout the body and mind. Copper can raise personal energy. People who suffer from lethargy should wear copper to get out of their rut. (That reminds me, where is my copper bracelet and wand?) Copper is believed to be a helpmate to the blood, soft tissue, immune system, metabolism, and mucous membranes. Copper has been associated with positive effects on self-esteem, giving its wearer a feeling of freedom and possibility and acting as a purifier. Copper gives confidence and, quite frankly, who could ask for anything more?

BRASS

> Brass is a wealth attractor.
>
> Brass offers healing and protection, especially if shaped into a dog-, falcon-, or snake-shaped brooch.

Brass is the result of combining copper and zinc. Brass has been successfully used to treat hair loss! Healers favor it as a detoxifier, a blood cleanser, and for people who actually have too much metal in their bloodstream. Brass has often been used as a shiny substitute for the much more costly gold. Brass is also a strengthening ally for the body and supports gems and crystals in their energies and abilities to interact in a positive way with your body. The iron content in brass makes this possible; it makes brass a real stabilizer. The ancients loved placing their gems in brass for the way it made the beautiful colors really stand out.

Bronze

Bronze is also an alloy of copper and zinc, having much the same healing power as brass but with one exception: bronze is said to give greater strength of character. My favorite aspect of bronze is that it helps people conceive of and achieve their goals. Bronze is Gothic in the original sense in that it was favored by Vikings almost above all other metals. The Romans also embraced bronze in their adornments as well as in coinage, statuary, and decor. Bronze mirrors were used for scrying in ancient times.

Platinum

Platinum is an extremely precious metal and makes for a very special setting for gems and jewels. Careful consideration must be given to determine which gems can be placed into a platinum setting, because they need to have an energy that can withstand the high energy of this metal. Diamonds have a strong enough brilliance and are enhanced in their power in this way as are the ruby, tourmaline, sapphire, and emerald. History takes us back to circa 1000 B.C., where the remarkable metalsmiths of Egypt became extremely skilled in the art of working with platinum. A 2,500-year-old coffin of an Egyptian priestess was discovered, beautifully decorated with platinum hieroglyphs. Their polish and luster were still perfect, giving dramatic proof of platinum's incomparable strength and resilience. Another ancient people who created beautiful objects from platinum were the Incas. But the invading Spanish conquistadores, seeing little use for this metal, deemed it "silver of lesser value," *platina*. They even went so far as to throw great amounts of the metal into the sea, thinking that it might become a cheap imitation for silver. Little did they know that it is even more valuable than gold! Finally, during the eighteenth century, platinum's value as a metal supremely suited for jewelry started to take hold. Then in the nineteenth century, platinum became the de facto standard for setting the finest of the newly discovered gemstone, the diamond. In fact, the most famous of these gems, the Hope diamond, was set in platinum.

Gemstone Don'ts

The following are some tips about stones not to mix together in jewelry as their energies cancel each other out:

Carnelian cancels out amethyst, as it connects more strongly with the body.

Lapis lazuli stimulates the mind and blue lace agate relaxes the mind.

Lapis lazuli and turquoise also cancel each other out, although I can't help but notice it didn't stop the Egyptians!

Turquoise dampens the energy of malachite.

Diamonds and turquoise are so energetically different that they conflict.

Gems of Protection—Amulets and Talismans

Rarely will you see an unjeweled Goth, even if it is just a series of silver studs along the ears or eyebrows. Goths know well that jewelry can be used as defense. Modern Goth, as inspired by punk, recognizes that a fierce skull ring with ruby eyes sends out a message. Goth magicians take it one step further by knowing the meaning, power, and property of each stone and metal and wielding that energy for the good of others and themselves.

The term *amulet* comes from the Latin word meaning "defense." Indeed, amulets are a way to protect yourself that dates back from earliest human beliefs. Pliny himself subscribed to the use of amulets and wrote about three common kinds used by the Romans of the classical age. A typical amulet of that era was a bit of parchment inscribed with protective words rolled up in a metal cylinder and worn around the neck. Evil eyes might be the most global of all amulets, as they are believed to ward off a hex by simply reflecting it back to its origins. Phallic symbols, such as horns, hands, and the phallus itself are also popular amulets. Some amulets were devoted to a specific god or goddess, offering that deity's shelter of protection.

Organized religions appropriated the idea of amulets from pagan peoples; in medieval times, it was very popular to wear a tiny verse from the Torah, Bible, or Koran. Many a Catholic wears a saint medal such as

St. Christopher, the patron saint for travelers. Wiccans and modern pagans are great proponents of protective amulets, thereby causing a resurgence in Celtic symbols and imagery.

The Assyrians and Babylonians favored cylindrical amulets encrusted with precious stones. The ancient Egyptians absolutely depended on their amulets, and we have many preserved in burial displays in museums. The Egyptians employed a type of blue-green copper-glazed baked clay called "faience." Wealthier denizens of the Nile, royalty, and the priestly class wore precious and semiprecious gems and crystals as amulets. Lapis lazuli was perhaps the most revered of these, a lapis lazuli Eye of Horus being the most significant of all, followed by scarabs, symbolizing rebirth, frogs for fertility, and the ankh for eternal life.

Enchanted Amulets

This following is a detailed list of stones from which to choose for the specific kind of safeguard you feel in need of. Amulets are very easy to make and make nice gifts, as long as you feel your friend will truly benefit and is aware of the special qualities and power of this gift. Select a stone that is endowed with the desired energy. Hold it in the palm of your hand until it is warm from your touch. Then do a visualization about the gift the stone is offering. Wear your amulet as a pendant or tuck it in your pocket or purse for "a guardian to go."

Amber is one of the oldest of talismans and has great power for general safety.

Amethyst can help with sobriety by preventing inebriation.

Aquamarine is good to wear if you want to attract wisdom or have fear of water and drowning. It is a guard against malevolent spirits.

Bloodstone is also lucky and is good to wear when traveling.

Carnelian is to the devil what garlic is to a vampire—it keeps 'em away

Chrysolite can drive away evil spirits and aid in peaceful sleep, especially if set in gold.

Diamonds in the form of a necklace are good fortune and should always touch the skin. This dazzling stone works best when it is received as a gift and lends force and valor.

Emeralds can cancel out the power of any magician!

Jade offers protection for children and guards their health. Jade also creates prosperity power.

Jasper was reputed to be a defense against the venom of poisonous insects and snakes.

Jet set in silver will help expel negativity.

Moonstone is also a boon to travelers and brings fortune and fame.

Turqouise is believed to be great for a horse's gait if affixed to its bridle.

Talismans

A talisman is an object or "objet" that also provides protection and has magickal properties. Ancient peoples, including the Mesopotamians, Assyrians, Babylonians, and Egyptians, loved animal talismans for the qualities associated with different animals for courage—bulls for virility, cats for stealth, and so on. A talisman can be *any* article or symbol that you believe has magickal properties. As we know, many gems and crystals naturally have very special innate powers. With talismanic magick, the special powers have to be present by nature or in the contest of a ritual in which the magick is instilled. Even though people often confuse amulets with talismans, they differ in this significant way: amulets *passively protect* the wearer from harm and evil or negativity, while talismans are *active* in their transformative powers. For example, the supernatural sword Excalibur, a tailisman, imbued with supremacy by the Lady of the Lake, gave King Arthur magickal powers. Another way to look at it is that talismans are created for a specific task and amulets can have broader uses. So, an amulet can be worn all the time for general protection whereas a talisman is for a specific use and a narrower aim.

The varieties of talismans are many: for love, wealth, gambling, the gift of a silver tongue, a good memory, or the prevention of death. Whatever you can think of, there is probably a talisman for that exact purpose!

Sorcerer Stones and Alchemical Crystals

Goths usually have a fascination with medieval history, commonly called the Dark Ages. Late medieval and early Renaissance literature is very worth study by Goth magicians—John Dee and Michael Maier in particular. They were alchemists and often called "wizards" for their immense wisdom, knowledge, and magickal powers. The Dark Ages are a treasure trove that informs Dark Wicca in regard to alchemy, herbology, astrology, and the marvelous world of gems and crystals. The following is a guide to the medieval mythology that you can use in Gothic gem magick.

Amethyst—Stone of Sobriety

The Chinese have been wearing amethyst for over 8,000 years. Tibetans consider this stone to be sacred to Buddha and make prayer beads from amethyst. One lovely legend associated with the purple crystal is that it comes from Bacchus, the god of wine. Mere mortals had angered this divinity, so he vowed a violent death by tiger to the very next mortal he encountered. A pretty girl by the name of Amethyst was enroute to worship at the temple of Diana. The goddess Diana protected Amethyst by turning her into a clear crystal quartz so she could not be torn apart by the ravaging tiger. Bacchus regretted his actions and anointed Amethyst with his sacred wine. However, he didn't pour enough to cover her entirely, leaving her legs without color. Thus, amethyst is usually uneven in its purple color. This also relates to the healing power of this stone to help with sobriety because it already has the wine within. The Greek word *amethystos* means "without wine." In the Victorian era, the paler amethysts were called "Rose de France" and were a favorite stone in jewelry. They sometimes left amethysts out in the sun to fade them. Nowadays, the darker purple stones are considered much more valuable.

If you are seeking stability and sobriety, this is your stone. It also opens intuition, a great asset for Goth witches. Amethyst is a stone of compassion, which is why bishops wear amethyst rings to signify their station in the church.

Aquamarine—The Stone of the Sea

A favorite of sailors and mariners, this stone is said to keep them safe. This stone is the signifier of the oceanic divinities and sirens. Egyptians loved this gem and gifted it to the dead as part of their treasure hoard to grant safety in the next life. Egyptian high priests wore two aquamarines, or "shoham" as they called them, on their shoulders engraved with the names of the six tribes of Egypt. Giving aquamarine to the gods of the nether world was a guarantee of safe passage. This sacred stone was also one of the twelve sanctified gems used in the breastplate of the biblical King Solomon. This gem is also a boon to a couple as it helps maintain a long and happy marriage. It is also a defense against the devil! The sun is the nemesis of the blue gem as it fades the color if exposed too long to sunlight, making it a favorite of night-dwelling Goths.

Beryl—The Stone of Power

The medieval historian Arnoldus Saxo, a seminal source for the Gothic history of his contemporaries, said that warriors used beryl to help in battle and also reported that it was good for court cases. Saxo was perhaps a bit hyperbolic in his declaration that the wearer was made "unconquerable" and smarter and cured of any laziness! Thomas de Cantimpre's German classic *De Proprietatibus Rerum* spoke about the power of beryl to reawaken the love of married couples. Early crystal balls were frequently made of beryl polished into spheres, rather like J.R.R. Tolkien's "palantirs" used by wizards. Druids and Celts used beryl to divine the future and legend has it that Merlin, King Arthur's magician, carried a beryl ball around him for exactly that purpose. Beryl is clearly a stone that assists in divining the future, but it also is a wonderful talisman that protects pregnant women. It is a calming agent and soothes the nervous system. A Goth pagan should have a crystal ball in his or her bag of magick tricks.

Bloodstone—The Martyr's Stone

In medieval times, Christians used bloodstone for sculptured bas reliefs depicting the martyred saints and Christ's crucifixion, thus the name "martyr" stone for bloodstone. The myth behind bloodstone is that some of Christ's blood dripped down and stained jasper, which lay at the foot of the cross. The Louvre in Paris has in its collections the German emperor Rudolf II's seal, which was carved into bloodstone. The ancient Egyptians loved bloodstone and gifted it to pharaohs, great warriors, and kings, believing it had the power to calm their tempers and prevent wrath and bloodshed.

An ancient book of Egyptian magick, known as the Leyden Papyrus, recorded the high regard for bloodstone, "The world has no greater thing; if any one have this with him, he will be given whatever he asks for; it also assuages the wrath of kings and despots, and whatever the wearer says will be believed.

"Whoever bears this stone, which is a gem, and pronounces the name engraved upon it will find all doors open while bonds and stone walls will be rent asunder."

Damigeron, a classical historian, wrote that bloodstone could disclose the future through what he called "audible oracles" and could also change the weather. He further claimed that this favored stone kept the mind sharp and the body healthy and protected the reputation of the person who wore it.

Bloodstone is an aid to divination and a stone of strength and healing for the blood and body. Most important, it is a remover of obstacles. Wear it during a job interview, important meetings, your art show, or any time you don't want anything to get in the way of your success and happiness.

Calcite—The Bones of the Earth

The ancients believed that calcite placed at the base of a pyramid could amplify the pyramid's power. Bosporus, one of the first sites for mining and gathering calcite, was also raided early on by the Gothic tribes and later by the Huns, who were led by the legendary chief Attila. After discovering its healing power, the Celts collected it on the cliffs of their island homes. It strengthens the bones and functions as an aid to psychics. For today's Gothic tribes, calcite is a powerful boost to psychism and can be worn during tarot readings for greater intuition.

Carnelian

"He who wears carnelian will have whatever he desires."
—Jafar

Wearing carnelian dates back from at least biblical times; there are several mentions of soldiers and priests wearing it. Carnelian was a favorite in ancient and medieval times, when people believed that wearing the stone would protect them against injury from falling stones with the saying, "No man who wore a carnelian was ever found in a collapsed house or beneath a fallen wall." Other lore associated with this jewel includes the Armenian belief that an elixir of powdered carnelian would lift any cloud or darkness from your life and fill the heart with happiness. In olden days, carnelian was credited with being able to defy no less than the devil! So, people wore this lovely red-orange stone with the intention of protecting themselves from evil, oftentimes repeating the prayer, "In the make of God the just, the very just, I implore you, oh God, king of the world, deliver us from the devil, who tries to do harm and evil to us through bad people, and from the evil of the envious."

If you have lost your lust for life and fallen into a pattern of old habits and uncreative day-to-day drudgery, this is the stone for you. Carnelian, also referred to in bygone days as carbuncle, is a type of quartz from the chalcedony gem family. It is an "earth" stone and acts as an anchor to the earth. Carnelian is thought to eliminate fear of death and grounds and clarifies. In olden days, carnelian was used to recall historical events in a sort of backward mirror.

Celestite—Angel Stone

The lore about this sky-blue stone is that it is "star seed" from the Pleiades. It is a truth-telling crystal, rendering anyone holding a celestite crystal unable to tell lies. Angelite is a condensed form of celestite with a highly unusual pattern of striping that looks like angel wings. Both forms of the magickal stone will get you in touch with spirit and helpful energies from the angelic realm. You can use this stone to get in contact with your guardian angel. A geode of celestite crystal is believed to be filled with angel energy and brings one to the highest consciousness. It is a great balancing stone, in that it creates attunement with high intellect and evens male and female energies within any person, making it an essential stone for Goth pagans.

Celestite is the stone to keep with you before any speaking engagements or writing that needs to be done and done well. It aids the flow of thoughts and words. Most interesting of all, it is a "listening stone." Hold a piece of celestite and listen carefully to the voice within; the wisdom from this stone will reveal your deepest intuition and lead you to right action. Meditation is greatly assisted by this crystal as it is believed to hold the wisdom of the archangels. In meditation, you can ask celestite for any knowledge you need and it will be made known to you, whether it is memories of a past life, a vision, or an out-of-body experience. Celestite is also a dream guide to keep by your bed for dream guidance.

Chalcedony—The Stone of Protection

Chalcedony, made of earth's ancient living things, has incredible powers of protection. It was even used to chase off "boogey men" or anything that went bump in the night in the eighteenth century. Associated with the Holy Grail, chalcedony was a favorite material for chalices and was believed to even be able to protect against poison.

As chalcedony is actually stone from primeval organisms, it is a powerful vessel for ancient energies. This stone has been with us since the earliest days of humans and has been used as a tool and gem. Chalcedony, the "stone of brotherhood," was sacred to Native Americans and was a powerful stone used to unite tribes in holy ceremonies. It is a stone of stability, kindness, endurance, and balance and is said to create peace. Chalcedony creates a desire for introspection and can help overcome low self-esteem and bring about a new lease on life, new enthusiasm. This star-powered crystal can also prevent loss of mental faculties with age. You can use it to great effect to bring your coven or Gothic tribe together for the betterment of all and for ceremonies and group rituals of the highest order.

The Most Goth Rock of All—The Crusader's Stone

Chiastolite is an exceptional variety of andalusite mined in China, Sri Lanka, and Brazil. What sets chiastolite apart is the dark-colored clay and carbonaceous inclusions in the stone, usually black or brown. These inclusions line up in symmetry and often take the form of a cross, garnering the name "Crusader's Stone." The black specimens are called "Iron Crosses." Chiastolite is a mineral that assists the mental faculties in critical and analytic thinking. Chiastolite is greatly valued as a creativity stone and is held dear for the remarkable ability to combine originality with practical thinking. This crystal will take a notion and give you the impetus to make the dream real. As is fitting for a Crusader's Stone (think Knight's Templar!), chiastolite will bring answers to mysteries. It is used by metaphysicians to support astral travel. It is also a symbol for transmutation, death, and rebirth; this is very much a stone of change. Healers believe it can reduce fever and even repair any material! This significant stone is held in immense regard, perhaps due to its cross marking, making it like no other rock in the world.

Chrysophrase—The Love of Truth

The seventeenth-century Swedish theologian, scientist, philosopher, and metaphysician Emanuel Swedenborg credited this apple-green chalcedony with giving people a "love of the truth." Other lore regarding chyrsophrase is a most rare capability to give a man set to be hanged sure escape from his executioner. Supposedly, all he has to do is place this crystal in his mouth.

Chrysophrase is important for one major quality: it is the stone of the scholar. This brilliance booster is an agent of calm while stimulating intellectual curiosity, two seemingly incompatible situations that chrysophrase brings together.

Diamonds—Fragments of the Stars

There is a charming legend that Europeans first discovered diamonds from Africa in a shaman's pouch, who used them for healing magick. Prehistoric peoples believed they were fragments of the stars and teardrops of the gods. In the most ancient times, diamonds were worn simply as an adornment in their unpolished and rough state. While diamonds are more commonly thought to bring luck, there is another school of thought among diamondphobes who believe that diamonds bring sure misfortune. The legend of the Hope diamond is a fascinating history wherein every owner of the royal rock was bankrupted until it was nestled safely in the Smithsonian Institution in Washington, D.C.

Diamonds have an association with lightning and give sure victory to warriors wearing them. Diamonds are thought to be powerful enough to fend off madness and even to stave off the devil himself! Rabbi Benoni, a medieval mystic, believed that diamonds were conducive to true spiritual joy and had power over the very stars and planets in the heavens.

A curiosity regarding most of this lore is that diamonds are supposed to be effective only if received as gifts; the outright purchase of a diamond is ruinous to the magick.

Renaissance astrologer and scholar Gerardus Cardano was wary of the crown jewel of crown jewels. He proclaimed this about the diamonds, "It is believed to make the wearer unhappy; its effects therefore are the same upon the mind as that of the sun upon the eye, for the latter rather dims than strengthens the sight. It indeed engenders fearlessness, but there is nothing that contributes more to our safety than prudence and fear; therefore it is better to fear." Alchemist Pierre de Boniface was far more confident about this queen of crystals, claiming it could render anyone wearing diamonds invisible! Still other medieval healers and humbugs claimed diamonds could cure poisoning and were themselves a powerful poison if ground up. Perhaps the most obvious unfounded claim regarding diamonds is that they could overcome and cure the plague.

EMERALDS

"Every emerald of significant size was smuggled at some point in its history."
—National Geographic

Emeralds were believed by the Romans during the early part of the empire to have been brought to the earth from the planet Venus. This precious stone is one of the only ones that retains its value among gemologists and jewelers even if it is deeply flawed. Emeralds have a richly varied mythology attached to their glowing green history. For thousands of years, Hindu physicians in India regarded this stone as an aid to many stomach-related illnesses—an appetite stimulant, a cure for dysentery, a laxative, and a way to control the overproduction of stomach-irritating bile. In India of old, Hindu physicians also believed emerald could drive away demons or rid a body of ill spirits.

Another antiquated belief about emeralds is that they portended events from the future, rather like scrying or seeing things in mirrors, in this case, the glassy surface of the gem. Emeralds were believed to be a foe to any and all sorcerers, a belief stemming from a legend that emeralds vanquished all wizardry in their wake. The ancients loved emeralds and connected them with the eyes. Theophrastus, a student of Plato, taught that emeralds protected the eyesight. He was taken so seriously that engravers kept emeralds on their tables to refresh their eyes.

Egyptians valued emeralds almost beyond any other stone and claimed their goddess, Isis, wore a great emerald. Anyone who looked at Isis's green jewel was ensured a safe trip to the underworld, the land of the dead. Egypt had been the main source for emeralds until the sixteenth century. The Cleopatra Mines south of Cairo were the mother lode, and emerald traders from as far away as India sought the stones, which had been obtained at great human cost under wretched conditions of extreme heat and dangerous underground shafts. Hopefully, the other common belief that these stones also protected people from any poison and all venomous serpents was true here. Emeralds were anathema to snakes as they were also supposed to be struck blind by merely looking at the stone.

In ancient Rome, emeralds were also sought after by the wealthy class. Nero watched the games in the coliseum through a set of priceless spectacles made from emeralds. However, with the capture of South America by Francisco Pizarro and Hernando Cortés, the Spanish in the 1500s fed the insatiable European appetite for jewels with a bounty of New World emeralds. The discovery of the Muzo Mine in Colombia, in 1558, uncovered emeralds of incredible beauty and size, prompting the Spanish conquistadores to take over the mine and declare the natives slaves. Perhaps part of Montezuma's Revenge involved the seizure of the emerald mines. Emeralds were a popular cure for dysentery in the sixteenth century, if worn touching the torso or held in the mouth. As with all valuable gems, the people who actually mine them have no access to them unless they are smuggled out of the mines. According to a recent article in *National Geographic*, however, this is done more frequently than one might think, especially with larger stones.

Garnet—Noah's Lantern

Garnets, with their beautiful deep red colors, are surrounded by much lore. The ancients ascribed to them protective powers that prevented travelers from accidents and mishaps and also guarded the sleeping from nightmares and bad dreams. It is said that the fiery glow of a garnet kept Noah and his ark afloat. Garnet was also a popular biblical gem—King Solomon used it as one of the stones on his breastplate. In Asia, garnets were used as bullets, most notably in the 1892 rebellion in India. Garnet's name comes from the Greek word for pomegranate and is associated with the Greek myth of Persephone. This daughter of Demeter tasted three seeds from the pomegranate fruit, dooming herself to spend half the year in the underworld, married to Hades, god of the underworld.

Iron Pyrite—Fool's Gold

Iron pyrite was supreme in early Mexico, where it was polished into mirrors for shamanic scrying, looking into the future and the past. These people also carved sacred symbols into these vessels of interdimensional viewing. Iron pyrite helps your skin by enabling it to ward of contaminants. This mineral is also a plus for circulatory and respiratory systems and has a strong connect to the iron levels in the blood and oxygen flow. Many people get relief from digestive ailments, too, and those who overeat can seek help.

Iron pyrite is highly regarded for its nearly unmatched support for mental workings, boosting creativity, intelligence, ability to communicate, and logic, and for providing invaluable soothing relief from mental fretfulness and angst. These crystal clusters radiate stability. Native Americans revered iron pyrite as a protective amulet

Jade—The Concentrated Essence of Love

Jade has been called "the concentrated essence of love." The word *jade* comes from the Spanish word *piedra de hijada*, which was prompted by the Indian use of jade as a cure for kidney disease. It literally translates as "the stone of the flank." Jade has been used as a birthing aid by midwives and birth mothers; on the opposite end of the spectrum of life, Egyptians, Chinese, and Mayans placed a small piece of jade in the mouths of the dead. The French literary legend Voltaire, author of *Candide*, was involved in a "kidney stone scandal" caused by the innocent generosity of a Mademoiselle Paulet, who gave Voltaire a lovely jade bracelet. She wanted him to be cured in the same way she had, but French society thought it was a token of love and his reputation as a serious artist and intellectual was irrevocably damaged. French society at the time judged what they deemed as impropriety most severely and this included their beloved intelligents as well.

Sir Walter Raleigh, the erudite world-exploring nobleman, wrote this about jade, "These Amazones have likewise great store of these plates of gold, which they recover by exchange, chiefly for a kind of greene stone, which the Spaniards call Piedras Hijada, and we use for spleene stones and for the disease of the stone we also esteeme them. Of these I saw divers in Guiana, and commonly every Kind or Casique had one, which theire wife for the most part weare, and they esteeme them as great jewels."

Shades of jade include yellow, orange, blue, red, purple, white, brown, black, and the classic jade green. Jade brings with it the power of love and protection. Jade is a dream stone, bringing prophetic and deeply meaningful dreams. Purple jade heals the broken heart, allowing understanding and acceptance in, and pain and anger out. Green jade is the "counselor stone" and can help dysfunctional relationships become functional; this shade is also a boon for the brain. Red jade promotes the proper release of anger; it also generates great sexual passion! Blue jade helps bring about patience and composure and for conveying a sense of control. Yellow jade is for energy, simple joy, and the sense that we are all part of a greater whole. Black jade, which is favored by Goths, offers protection from negativity and confers a wise use of personal power.

Jasper—The Building Block of Heaven

The authors of the Bible mentioned jasper quite frequently; their great city of heaven is reputed to have jasper walls. This opaque kind of chalcedony is found on every continent on this planet often with striated bands in exquisite shades of brown, yellow, green, and red. Ground up into powder and added to potions, jasper has been an ingredient in healing elixirs for thousands of years. It has gradual, encouraging effects that can happen over a long period of time. Jasper is a patient rock but it does good work. It is an energy crystal, as well as a stone of sensuality that engenders immense ardor.

Jasper was also favored by the ancients as a cure for snakebite and for controlling the weather as a bringer of rain. In *Lithica*, a fourth-century epic poem, this stone is praised, "The gods propitious hearde to his prayers, who'ever the polished glad-green Jasper wears: His parsed glebe they'll saturate with rain, and send for shower to soak the thirsty plain." Jasper was also believed to be able to repel evil spirits.

Lapis Lazuli—Babylonian Blue

Ancient Babylonians and their south-of-the-Mediterranean neighbors, the Egyptians, could not get enough of this bright blue jewel. The Egyptians named it "chesbet" and usually listed it to be paid to subordinate nations and to the great kingdoms of the Nile. The Babylonians piled it high in their tributes to Egypt and had it in plentitude as they were the earliest people to mine lapis lazuli; they were mining it from mines that date back to 4000 B.C.!

Lapis lazuli was so holy to the Egyptians that the high priest himself wore a pendant of the blue stone in the shape of Mat, the goddess of truth. The Egyptians seemingly wished to swim in seas of lapis as they used it in daily adornment, for funeral masks and tools, and as an ingredient in their art, a methodology that continued for many generations into the future. Because lapis has the unusual ability to hold its pigment even when it is ground up, it was used in makeup for Egyptian priests and notables, including the unforgettable queen Cleopatra.

Lapis lazuli is a stone on the path to enlightenment and is altogether powerful. As with any other crystal, it must be used with thoughtfulness and caution, but do double your vigilance with this one! It is one of the major mental stones; lapis lazuli is a thought amplifier very nearly second to none. Lapis also enhances psychism and can open the third eye by being laid very briefly over that center on your forehead.

MAGNETITE—THE HERACLEAN STONE

This gray or dark brown stone is also known as "lodestone," a poetic name much preferred. in Gothdom. It has a major quantity of iron and is, as the name implies, very magnetic. The ancients called it lodestone, while Plato wrote that it was "the Heraclean stone." All iron-based crystals are considered to be very helpful to the blood and circulatory systems and it is true in this case as well. Magnet therapy has come into vogue in the last twenty years and is becoming commonplace nowadays. Even athletes and physicians are trying magnetic therapy and any controversy about this one-time "New Age healing" method is fading thanks to many positive endorsements.

The ancients were fascinated with magnetite and its mysterious workings. The great Pliny wrote that the first instance of the discovery of magnetite happened when a shepherd was walking Mount Ida with his flock and the nails of his shoes clung to a rock in the field. The shepherd's name was Magnes. Pliny also recorded a tale of Ptolemy who wished to make an iron statue of a woman for a temple dedicated to his wife and his sister. The great trick was that he wanted to have the statue suspended in air without any visible means of support by using the new art of magnetism! Unfortunately for us, Ptolemy and his architect, the Alexandrian Chirocrate, died before its completion. Otherwise, there might have been an eighth wonder of the world.

Lodestone was held to be a protection against spells and other magick mischief. The ancients also believed that a small piece of lodestone beneath the pillow would be a testimony to virtue. Alexander the Great gave his soldiers a piece of lodestone to defend against unseen evil spirits.

MOLDAVITE

Here is a rock so rare because it is extraterrestrial! Moldavite is the only known gem-quality crystal that comes from outer space. About 20 million years ago, a meteorite fell into the modern-day Czech Republic's Moldau Valley. An unusual crystal of greenish-blue translucence, moldavite can only be found in this one valley. Some folks claim it is the result of the burning meteorite crashing into terrestrial rock, but in either case, it is still utterly unique. Perhaps the most fascinating thing about moldavite is its association with the Holy Grail. Excalibur, the sacred sword of King Arthur, was supposedly forged from the iron of a meteorite, for one. In Wolfram von Eschenbach's *Parzival*, the grail is a "lapsit exillis," a stone out of the heavens. Many other moldavite theories equate it with the "Philosopher's Stone," the long-sought source of wisdom for all alchemists, and it is even thought to perhaps be the sacred stone of Islam in Mecca, the center of the Muslim faith.

OPAL—CUPID'S STONE

Early humans believed that opals were pieces of rainbows that had fallen to the ground. These exquisite iridescent gems were also dubbed "Cupid's Stone," because the ancient Greeks compared it to the incomparably beautiful skin of the love god Cupid. Opals had many superstitions attached to them. There was the belief that an opal wrapped in a bay laurel leaf could cure any eye disease and combat weak hearts and infection.

St. Albert "the Great" was one of the most learned men of the thirteenth century, studying natural science as well as theology, literature, and languages. He fancied mineralogy and waxed quite openly about the opal, "The porphanus is a stone which is in the crown of the Roman Emperor, and none like it has ever been seen; for this very reason it is called porphanus. It is of a subtle vinous tinge, and its hue is as though pure white snow flashed and sparkled with the color of bright, ruddy wine and was overcome by this radiance. It is a translucent stone and there is a tradition that formerly it shone in the nighttime, but now, in our age, it does not sparkle in the dark, it is said to guard the regal honor."

In the Middle Ages, opals were called "opthalmios," the eye stone. The great Scandinavian epic, the *Eddas*, contained verses about a stone forged by the smithy of the gods that formed the eyes of children, doubtless a reference to opal. In olden days, it was thought that an opal would change color according to the mood and health of the owner, going dull and colorless when the owner died. Blond women favored opals because they believed they could keep their hair light in color! (I trust they were not using black or dark blue opals!)

It was even believed that opals could render the wearer invisible, making this the patron stone of thieves. Black opals have always had top ranking among global gemological societies, being the rarest and the most dramatic. One legend told that if a love relationship was consummated with one party wearing a black opal, the gem would soak up the passion and store it in its glow. Opals can help you if you want to get the special attention of a certain someone or if you have to give a speech or presentation. Opal is one of the really rare stones that has both male and female energies within; it contains the energy of the sun *and* the moon. It can generate flashes of intuition and inspiration. Opals can be stones of wonderful dreams and can facilitate positive change. Opals can bring submerged feelings and trapped emotions to the surface. Opals can help "uptight" people get in touch with their emotions and loosen up.

Opals are best worn as pinkie rings on the little finger. They are also a popular engagement ring as a symbol of faithfulness and as a stone that is effective in bringing stability and longevity to relationships. Fire opals are good for business by promoting positive action and prosperity.

Pearls—The Tears of the Gods

Pearls have a romantic past. The Chinese regarded them as the physical manifestation of the souls of the oysters. One of the prettier names of the pearl is the Persian "Margarithe," meaning "child of light." The Arabs called them "tears of the gods" and said they were formed when rain drops fell into oyster shells. In India, it was the perfect wedding gift, promising devotion and fertility. A Hindu wedding ritual involved the piercing of the "perfect pearl," a virginity ceremony.

Throughout human history, pearls have fascinated and have been used as a favored adornment. Pearls are an energy amplifier and are especially good in combination with emeralds and diamonds. People so lusted after pearls that they began introducing sand into oysters for forced pearl production, resulting in the cultured pearls we see on the marketplace today.

Pearls have affinities to the moon, femininity, and fertility and are a sacred symbol for pregnant women. The great tradition of pearls, especially in Asia, was of modesty and wholesomeness. Pearls are truly soothing. That is why they exist in the first place—for soothing the irritated shellfish. They are an excellent helpmate in any stress-related illness and are good for stomachaches, ulcers, hypertension, headaches, and fatigue.

Pearls are environmentally sensitive and pick up vibrations from the person wearing them. What is more, they *remember* feelings and hold them inside. If you are in a sad or bad mood, remove your pearls so you don't unknowingly keep that negativity hanging around you. By the same token, do not ever loan your pearls. Cleanse your pearls regularly by laying them in a bowl of sea salt and make sure you do this before wearing if you buy antique or vintage pearls.

Malachite—The Stone of Juno

This stripy green stone belongs to Venus! The Greeks believed it had major magickal powers when set in copper jewelry. The Romans associated malachite with the goddess Juno and cut it into triangle shapes to indicate her sacred peacock symbol. Another popular bit of early medieval malachite lore is that drinking from a goblet cut from malachite supposedly gave understanding of the language of animals!

Moonstone—Stone of Prophecy and Passion

It is a milky bluish-white feldspar gemstone cut from albite and is beloved the world over for its pleasant and somewhat mysterious smooth surface. Moonstone is quite obviously connected to the moon and is as soothing to the psyche as it is pleasing to the eye. The properties associated with moonstone are sensitivity, psychism, loyalty, sleep and dreams, and emotional balance. It is also associated with female sexual organs and cleansing organs, especially the skin. Moonstones have a very rare ability to help with eating disorders, particularly overeating. They can calm the stomach and adjust the vibrations so you are directed to eat the proper amount in the future. Moonstones open the heart chakra and, very importantly, help overcome any anger or hard emotions toward the self. Pagans have seen it as a Goddess crystal for a millennia and as a source for nurturing, wisdom, and intuition. Moonstone is a powerful protective and loving talisman for pregnant women. In India, moonstone is sacred and is very lucky but it's even more valued on the subcontinent because it helps make you more spiritual. Moonstone is at its very best on your behalf if worn in a ring with a silver setting. In olden times, it was believed that wearing a moonstone during the waning moon would give prophetic abilities. India has held moonstone as holy for thousands of years and had a superstition against displaying the sacred stone except on a yellow cloth, since yellow is the most spiritual color in this culture. Indians also believed it was very potent in the bedroom and not only aroused enormous passion but also gave lovers the ability to read their future together. They had to hold the moonstone in their mouth during the full moon to enjoy these magickal properties.

Peridot—Pele's Tears

Peridot is one of the most misidentified gems on the planet—it is really a combination of two other stones, fayalite and forsterite, with a bit of iron, a dash of nickel, and a pinch of chromium. The world's oldest source for the green charmer was the mist-shrouded desert island of Zeberget, also called St. John's Island off Egypt's coast. Unfortunately for the peridot miners, this island was full of deadly, venomous snakes! The pharaohs so treasured their peridot that any uninvited visitors to the island were put to death. Perhaps the stones from the breastplate of King Solomon and his high priest Aaron came from this odd little island. Peridot was one of the twelve stones believed to have the power to create miracles for the rituals of these priests and to help protect them in battle. Furthermore, Solomon drank "soma" from cups carved from peridot, thus gaining his wealth of wisdom.

Peridot can also be found in some meteorites. In the 1920s, a farmer in Kansas awoke one morning to find lumps of a peridot-studded meteorite in his fields. It is believed that Cleopatra had really adorned herself with high-quality peridot instead of emeralds. The Romans called peridot the "evening emerald." Brought back as booty by the Knights Templar and by crusaders, peridot was used to adorn cathedrals in medieval times. On the Shrine of the Three Magi in the Cologne Cathedral, there is a huge 200-carat peridot.

The powers of peridot are believed to be twice as intense if it is set in gold. The Romans believed peridot had the power to drive away evil and if those who were so lucky as to have a goblet carved out of peridot, any medicine they drank out of it had magickal healing powers. In Hawaii, the lore of this gem is that Pele cried tears that turned into peridot. Now that the mines on the island of Zeberget are no more, most of the world's supply of peridot is mined by Native Americans in Arizona and in the exotic locales of Myanmar, Sri Lanka, and the Kashmir Himalayas.

This is a creativity crystal. It frees the imagination and counteracts negativity. For people who feel hampered by the rules of society and unable to truly express themselves and their inner being, peridot is a great boost to personal freedom. Depressives can also find solace here. This uplifting stone also increases psychic insight and receptivity, and is a great aid to meditation. Peridot is fantastic for dark wiccans as it can keep them from becoming "too dark."

Ruby—The Mother of the Earth's Blood

In the tenth century, Chinese gem carvers engraved depictions of dragons and snakes on the surfaces of rubies to gain money and power. In India, worshippers give rubies as an offering to their god Krishna, and in China it is an homage to Buddha.

In Phillippe de Valois's famed *Lapidary*, he lavished praise on the royal red rock, writing that "the books tell us the beautiful clear and fine Ruby is the lord of stones; it is the gem of gems and surpasses all other precious stones in virtue." Sir John Mandeville similarly enthused with his opinion that ownership of a ruby would accord safety from all peril and bring about wonderful relations with friends and neighbors; he further recommended that rubies be worn on the left side of the body.

In Myanmar, the ruby was viewed as a stone of invincibility; a radical approach to this protection was inserting the ruby into the skin of the wearer! Soldiers had the gem imbeded in them before marching into battle. They also believed the color "ripened" inside the earth. Prehistoric people believed that rubies were crystallized drops of the "Mother of the Earth's Blood."

Rubies come in a range of colors from a really vivid red to a deep purplish crimson. Rubies will magnify whatever is present, whether it is positive or negative. Ruby's red color can quickly give rise to passions of romance and to anger and rage. You must bear this in mind with rubies and remain conscious of your feelings. The most valuable color of this stone is the delicate rose color. The energy of ruby is extremely intense. People who do energy work and healing also say that rubies can fill in and repair holes in the aura. The ruby affects the base chakra and is therefore connected to our most primal drives as humans: sex and survival.

Rubies are stones of loyalty, confidence, and courage. Rubies protect you. If you are exhausted, this wonder worker will replenish your drained chi and restore you to peak levels of vitality, strength, and stamina. Rubies eliminate blockage of the reproductive system and keep healthy energy flowing. Rubies are even good for hypoglycemia.

Rubies help overcome and eradicate negative thought patterns and habits. Rubies hold the singular power of love for the self and for others. If set in white or yellow gold, ruby's regenerative love power is greatly enhanced. A blood-red ruby is a jewel par excellence for any Goth pagan.

Sapphire—The Eye of Horus

The ancient Persians believed that the earth rested on a giant sapphire and the blue of the sky reflected its color. The Greeks identified white sapphires with the god Apollo; they deemed this stone very important indeed—the oracles at Delphi used it to make their prophecies. The Egyptians designated the sapphire as the eye of Horus. Star sapphires are especially prized, as the lines crossing the blue of the stone were believed to represent faith, hope, and charity. Sapphire had been used for an eye cure for centuries until modern medicine came about. Medieval scientist Albertus Magnus the Great recorded incidents in which he had seen sapphire used with success as a healer, stating that it was necessary for the stone to be dipped in cold water before and after surgery. A contemporary of Magnus by the name of Van Helmont advocated the use of sapphire as a remedy for plague boils by rubbing the gem on the afflicted spot. Van Helmont did offer the disclaimer that the condition could not be too advanced and explained the science behind his cure with the early theory of magnetics in which a force in the sapphire pulls "the pestilential virulence and contagious poison from the infected part."

Part of the myth and magick of sapphires is myth and magick itself. Magicians and seers love this stone as it adds to their sensitivities and enables them to perceive their augurs better. Historically, it is regarded as a gem of nobility and any regal personage wearing this noble gem would be protected from harm, particularly the threat of poison. Another dubious legend is that Moses wrote the Ten Commandments on tablets of sapphire, but it is more likely that they would have been carved into the softer and more readily available stone lapis lazuli. One notable instance was the twelfth-century bishop of Rennes, who commended this gem as an ecclesiastical ring, especially due to its obvious connection to the heavens above. The religious and legal-minded also favored this stone as it was believed to help counteract fraud and deception. Once, sapphires were believed to have gender. Dark sapphires were "male" and light stones were "female."

Sir Richard Burton always carried a star sapphire with him while he traveled through Asia and the Middle East as his talisman. According to Burton, the stone brought him excellent horses and ensured he received attention right when he needed it. It does seem to have worked as he is still receiving accolades and consideration long after his passing. A generous soul, he showed his star sapphire to the friendly folk as this gem is a giver of great luck.

Blue sapphire carries the blue ray of harmony, nourishing the mind, giving perspective, and putting the mind and thoughts in order. Blue sapphire also increases mental flexibility. Sapphire helps achieve mastery of the self—mind, body, and spirit. Sapphire is simply a light on this most complicated thing, the human mind, with its myriad levels and endless new thoughts. On a soul level, sapphire is about discrimination, clearing, and focusing the mind. Discernment is the key to soul growth, deciding what to process and what to let go.

Topaz—St. Hildegard's Cure

Sailors once used this golden gem to shed light on the water during moonless nights. Topaz was also used by Egyptians both as an aphrodisiac and to prevent the excesses of love—a rather large contradiction! Ground into a dust and mixed with rosewater, topaz was used to treat excessive bleeding. Similarly, wine mixed with powdered topaz was a treatment for insanity. The ancients used topaz to guard against magicians by setting it in gold and wearing the bracelet on the left arm. St. Hildegard of Bingen suggested topaz as an aid to poor vision; placed in wine for three straight days, it was then gently rubbed into the eyes. The wine could then be drunk, after removing the stone, of course. This is one of the first written records of a gem elixir. Medieval physicians also used topaz to treat the plague and its accompanying sores, with several miracles attributed to a particular stone that had been in the possession of Popes Clement VI and Gregory II.

Turquoise—Turkish Stone

One pretty legend relating to turquoise is that it is generated by rainbows touching the earth. Turquoise seems to have always had a mythic link to horses, beginning with the medieval belief that anyone wearing this stone would be protected from falling off a horse. Phillippe De Valois's *Lapidary* further claimed that this blue-green stone prevented horses from the harm of drinking cold water when they were sweaty and hot. Turkish equestrians went so far as to attach this crystal to the bridles of their horses as a talisman for the animal.

An unusual story about turquoise comes from the court of Emperor Rudolph II, whose court physician was given a specimen that had faded completely. The doctor's father gave it to him with these words of wisdom, "Son, as the virtues of the turquoise are said to exist only when the stone has been given, I will try its efficacy by bestowing it upon thee." The young man set it in a ring and in one month's time the splendid color was completely restored. The story involved several mishaps with horses in which the physician came away unharmed but with the stone cracked, which was perceived as a "warning."

Zircon—The Legacy of Hyacinth

A charming tale is the medieval use of zircon in exorcism. The methodology was simple: A cross was cut into a loaf of freshly baked wheat bread, then a zircon was used to trace along the cross shape and the bread was eaten.

Chapter Six

The Gothic Conjuring Calendar

Goth Sabbats

Sabbats are the "holy days" that were created around the season of the year, the phases of the moon, the setting of the sun, and the wheel of constellations as the stars circle our sky. Some of these holy days celebrate spring and the start of new growth, while others celebrate harvest in preparation for the dark and chilly days of winter. Nearly all of our modern festivals and holy days have ancient roots in the farming customs and fertility rites relating to this all-important aspect of life. Goth sabbats stem from this same source and add a new layer of the modern mixed with reverence for the past. As Goth paganism is a path of intense self-expression, the Goth sabbats are reinterpreted through the dark lens of Goth. So, perhaps you have a ritual with an amplified band instead of just drums or perhaps your coven always performs at group rituals during the "witching hour" of midnight. Perhaps you hold a hand fasting at a graveyard or maybe for you everyday is Halloween!

The Year of Two Seasons—The Ancient Norse Calendar

The Germanic and Nordic Goths saw the year as only two seasons—winter and summer—and split the year into two twenty-six-week halves, which they kept track of by the moon. The Old Norse words for both *harvest* and *year* are one and the same because the years were counted as harvests. The Old Norse word for the sun year was "Silarbangr," and the year began around June 21, midsummer, the longest day of the year when the sun prevailed over all. These northern European tribes began the new year at the setting of the sun, a ritual they shared with two other tribal peoples: the Celts and the Hebrews.

Due to their proximity to the north pole, wintertime came just four months later and was celebrated with a winter night festival with offerings to please the gods. This was followed by the summer feast day in June called "Sumarmail." The Norse folk who migrated to Iceland had to adapt this schedule slightly to accommodate the even more extreme winter times. Iceland was on its own specialized climatic schedule and for Icelanders summer began in mid-April, so they celebrated Sumarmail then. Some scholars theorize this was the true origin of Ostara, which was Christianized as Easter. The inventive Icelanders further compensated for their slightly out-of-sync seasons and calendar by adding four more days during summertime and adding in an entire week every seven years.

Yule was a big festival for these tribes and was timed with the winter solstice. For the peoples living in Scandinavia and the extreme far north, Yule came when the sun returned to the sky after a long period of darkness. In olden Scandinavia, the majority of the holidays and festivals took place in summertime when people could be outside together for more than a few minutes. The "Varthang," or Spring Thing, named for the goddess Var, who hears oaths and promises, was the big spring celebration when important business matters were taken care of. Legal cases were heard and preparations were made for the meeting of the assembly. The seventh week of summer, known as the "Fardagar," was a time for moving into new homes and new tenancies and properties were transferred from one owner to another. The Althan, or midsummer festival, usually occurred when ten weeks of summer had passed Traditions celebrated in other European areas such as the Maypole dance were performed with feasting and sacred rituals. Two months before the end of summertime came the "Leith," or Autumn Thing. This was the time of the "Althing," the political assembly of the people. Month names varied from tribe to tribe and according to location. Some of the names are lost to us and some historians theorize that the months were not named but counted instead. The winter moons were often named for the festivals.

Today's Goth, imbued with the soul of winter, will draw much spiritual sustenance from the ritual of "Needfire," which acknowledges the element of water as ice and the opposite with the life-giving heat of the element of fire. Goths study history and pull from the past to inform the present. The ritual heritage of the "original Goths" links us to and authenticates the magickal lineage that is ours to carry on. This practice can be done in the month of January, typically the coldest month of the year.

Ritual of Needfire

Without fire, there would be no life.

Supplies:

Altar space
Wood, matches, kindling, and a safe place for a fire
Candles
Cauldron or large pot
Ice cubes, water
Drums
Fire tool or poker
Apples, apple cider, or apple ice cream
White ice cream
Spoons and bowls
Bowl of tarot cards

1. Place the bowl of tarot cards on the space designated as the altar.

2. Ask for a volunteer to be in charge of the fire and to be the leader of the ritual. The fire maker should then select three women to represent the Norms or the Three Fates. One of the fates will be in charge of "giving fire." With a candle in the cauldron, she keeps fire safe and gives it to the fire maker. Another fate hands out the future to ritual participants with a one-card tarot reading. The last fate gives life in the form of the foods—the apples, hot cider, ice cream, and so on.

3. The participants should get as cold as possible before beginning the ritual—take off your coats and sweaters and open all the windows and doors if you are inside. You need to feel the winter deep in your soul. The leader should pass around the ice cubes so the participants can engage sensorily with freezing cold and the need for fire.

4. While the participants get good and chilly, the leader should start the fire. People who really want the totally authentic experience of fire-making can try to create fire from sparking with a "drill," but the ritual could take hours unless the fire maker is well practiced in the art of making fire.

5. The following is the chant to be spoken while the fire is being made. The ritual leader should pass out the drums and begin the rhythmic sounds to underscore the chanting.

Winter winds howl and wail.
We feel the cold in our bones.
This is an old familiar tale.

The ice binds and surrounds us all.
Fates above, please hear our call.

Fire thaws the ice.
Fire creates the water.
The heat warms our bones.
Fire and ice bind our lives.

Now feel the fire!

6. Holding hands, everyone should dance slowly around the fire, feeling the life-giving warmth. Next, repeat the chant.

7. The fate of the future goes around the circle with the bowl of tarot cards and performs one-card readings for each individual. If time allows, she should also do a reading with the full set of tarot cards for the group about the future of the community.

8. Last, the fate who gives life serves the group celebratory food—the ice cream and other cold foods are a remembrance of the cold of the ice times and the hot cider and other hot foods represent the life-giving heat of fire. The head of the ritual should lead everyone in a discussion of the importance of the ritual of the Needfire and any other topic important to every participant and the community.

The Old Norse Calendar

Thorri: name of a frost giant or popular deity (mid-January to mid-February)

Gói (originally indeclinable feminine, but later became Góa)—another giant; the daughter of Thorri

Einmánudr: Solitary month

Gaukmánudr, Sádtíd, Harpa: Cuckoo month, Seed tide month

Eggtíd, Skerpla: Egg tide Month

Sólmánudr, Selmánudr, Stekktíd: Sun month, Shieling month, Lamb-fold time

*Auknætr (four days): Addition nights

Midsumar, Heyannir, Ormamánudr: Midsummer, Hey time, Snake month

Tvímánudr, Heyaanir: Double month, Hey reaping

Haustmánudr, Kornskurdarmánudr: Harvest month, Corn cutting month

Gormánudr: Slaughter month

Frermánudr: Frost month, Yule (mid-November to mid-December)

Hrútmánudr, Jólmánudr, Mörsugr: Ram month, Yule

The coming of the sun marks the summer holy day, while the departure of the sun marks Yule, but all other sabbats are under the domain of the moon.

Dark Sides of the Moon—Lunar Phases

Performing a spell at the optimal time of the lunar cycle will maximize your power. As you read the spells in this book, keep this elemental magick in mind.

Each lunar cycle begins with a "new" phase when the moon lies between the sun and the earth so the illuminated side cannot be seen from the earth. The moon gradually "waxes" until it has moved to the opposite side of the earth. When the moon has reached the far side of the earth, its lit side faces us in the "full" moon phase. It then begins to "wane" until it reaches the new moon phase again. The entire cycle takes a month.

To determine the sun sign governing the moon, you will need a celestial guide or almanac. My favorite is Llewellyn's *Daily Planetary Guide*. The moon moves from sign to sign every two to three days.

Before we had handy guidebooks such as the *Daily Planetary Guide*, the Norse used a wooden stick called "Primestave." It provided the means for relating the lunar calendar to the solar calendar. Up until about 1700, the Primestave was the primary means of keeping track of time in Scandinavia. The name originates from the old Norse word *prim*, meaning "new moon." Normally, it was carved out of wood, with lines for each day of the year and special symbols marking important dates. Often, it was shaped like a long stick, with one side for winter (October 14–April 14) and one for summer (April 14–October 14). Since it was based on the Julian calendar, it could be used year after year without modification. But in 1700 the more precise Gregorian calendar replaced the old system, and the Primestave became obsolete. Nevertheless, it was still made for another two centuries because of the strong tradition it represented.

Major Sabbats

Candlemas, Beltane, Lammas, and All Hallow's Eve comprise the most important feast and ritual days of the year. These are great occasions for gathering and marking time and for attending to the passages of our lives and our spiritual development both as a group and individually. By honoring these sacred days, you imbue your life with meaning, and life becomes a purposeful journey that is filled with wisdom and joy.

CANDLEMAS—FEBRUARY 2

Candlemas is the highest point between the winter solstice and the spring equinox. This is the time to honor new Goth witches in your circle and acknowledge their progress on the path.

This is the celebration of the waxing light that I learned from my mentor Z. Budapest, a Hungarian priestess to the goddess in the Dianic tradition. She shared her generous knowledge with me, and I am very pleased and grateful to share it here. (Candlemas, also called Imbolc, is the highest point between the winter solstice of December 21st and the vernal equinox of March 21st and the summer solstice of June 21. Z has utilized this sabbat as the special day to initiate new witches, which has been practiced for generations in the Hungarian tradition and handed down to her. She calls them "genetic witches," she says with a Transylvanian twinkle in her eye.

Transylvanian Candlemas Ritual

This ritual has been handed down to us through Z's Hungarian lineage and bears the "Transylvanian touch," which really means "across the woods." It must, if at all possible, be done outdoors in the forest.

Supplies:

Cauldron
White candles
Cedar
Pine
Juniper
Holly
Incense
Stone such as quartz crystal for an altar

1. Cast the circle in the customary manner, as discussed in the beginning of this book. The leader of the circle should purify the circle with the fire of the incense while invoking the four directions to raise power. Place your altar stone in the north part of the circle and place white candles on and around the altar.

2. Face toward the east and say:

Welcome guardians of the east, bringing your fresh winds, the breath of life. Come to the circle of Imbolc!

I explained earlier that it goes by both names, so I'd like to keep it this way.

3. Face toward the south and say:

Welcome guardians of the south, you bring us heat and health. Come to the circle on Brigid's Day!

4. Face toward the west and say:

Welcome guardians of the west, place of the setting sun and light rains. Come to us!

5. Face toward the north and say:

Welcome guardians of the north, land of the life-bringing rains and snow. Come to our circle on this sacred day!

6. The high priestess or priest should then serve the sacred food and drink, then let the merriment begin!

Beltane—May 1

Beltane is the sexiest high holiday for witches, and it is anticipated all year. Look forward to having a joyful spree every May. Witchy ones celebrate Beltane on the very last eve of April, and it is traditional for the festivities to go on all night. This is a holiday for feasting, dancing, laughter, and lots of lovemaking. May Day, when the sun returns, is when revelers erect a beribboned maypole and dance around in gay garb followed by pagan picnicking and sexy siestas. Another bonus of Beltane is that this is the one day in the year when it is "officially okay" to enjoy sex outside your existing relationship. This is the day we look the other way.

First, serve a sensual feast of foods, along with beer, wine, ciders, and honeyed mead you can make or obtain from a microbrewery. Gather together some of spring's bounty of flowers—narcissus, daffodils, tulips, and my favorite, freesias—in your favorite colors. Also set out candles in spring colors—yellow, pink, red, green, white, and purple. With arms extended, point to each of the four directions and say, "To the east, to the north," and so on. Then recite the old-world rhyme, created especially for Beltane:

Hoof and horn, hoof and horn,
Tonight our spirits are reborn.
Welcome joy to my home.
Fill my friends with love and laughter.
So mote it be.

Now is the time for you and your partner to retire to a comfortable place, be it a bed or a blanket in an outdoor hideaway, and explore the magick of each other with a Beltane Body Blessing. Explore and map out your partner's body, inch by inch, very slowly from head to toe, awakening every erogenous zone and raising sexual energy. As you both become intensely aroused, continue touching, tasting, and smelling your lover's body, taking deep pleasure and sharing sensations. Decide who will give and who will receive, taking turns. Practice tantalizing touch with hands kneading, stroking, and teasing. Apply feather-light kisses and caresses, especially around the breasts and buttocks. Every part of the body is suitable for kissing—feet, toes, fingers—let your imagination run wild. During this intimate experience, you will gain a sacred connection in what is a form of mutual worship.

Beltane Brew

Honeyed mead is revered as the drink of choice for this sexy pagan holy day. It is an aphrodisiac most definitely, and with its sticky sweetness, is perfect for dribbling on your lover's body and licking off—yum! This is my special recipe for honeyed mead, handed down through generations of Celtic witches.

Ingredients:

1 quart honey
3 quarts distilled water
1 tsp cinammon
1 tsp clove
1 tsp nutmeg
1 tsp allspice
pinch cardamom
yeast packets

1. Mix the honey and water and boil for five minutes. You can vary the herbs to your liking, but I prefer a teaspoon each of clove, nutmeg, cinnamon, and allspice. (One of my friends adds cardamom for a chai taste.)

2. Add a packet of yeast and mix. Put in a large container.

3. Cover with plastic wrap and allow it to rise and expand. Store the mixture in a dark place and let it sit for seven days. Then refrigerate for three days while the sediment settles at the bottom.

4. Strain and store in a colored glass bottle, preferably green, in a cool, dark place. During this fermentation process, your brew has magickally transformed into an alcoholic "spirit." You can now drink it, but it is even tastier after it has aged for a period of at least seven months. This Beltane Brew packs a punch—it is 60 proof!

Non-alcoholic Mead

This recipe has all the taste of Beltane Brew—with none of the sin!

Ingredients:

1 quart honey
3 quarts distilled water
½ cup lemon juice
Lemon, sliced
½ teaspoon nutmeg
Pinch of salt

1. Add the honey, lemon, and nutmeg to the pot of water and place on the stove, stirring gently to a slow boil.

2. Boil five minutes and then cool and bottle immediately.

3. Keep in the fridge to avoid fermentation and enjoy.

LAMMAS—AUGUST 1

The Celts called this time of the year "Lughnassadh" or "Lunasa" for their god of wisdom. The tradition of Lammas comes to us from the Celts and is still celebrated to this day far and wide. The custom is that when the first corn is cut, it must be baked into a loaf and offered to Lugh in a sort of thanksgiving devotion. Native Americans called August "Corn moon," and even the Franks referred to this time of the year as "Aranmanoth," or "Corn Ears month." Lammas used to be known as "Lammastide," meaning "loaf day," as it is a true celebration of the harvesting of grain that can now be baked into nourishing loaves of bread. It is a time of abundance and the sheer joy of life. Gather your friends together and be grateful for life's blessings.

Lammas August Eve Ritual

There are many ways you can create your own variations on Lammas Day with your own unique views on the summer season and how you show appreciation to nature and spirit. One lovely way to celebrate Lammas Day is to have a feast that begins and ends with gratitude and blessings for the food and wine, which is also shared with a place setting for the great godly guest of Lugh.

Supplies:

Acorns
Sheaves of grain
Cauldron
Water
1 floating candle and 13 pillar candles (one for each person)
Essential oils

1. To create the sacred space of the ritual, arrange the acorns and sheaves to represent the four directions around a cauldron. Fill the cauldron with water three quarters of the way and add essential oils of the flowers of summer.

2. At this point, the leader of the ritual should light each of the thirteen candles and then hand them to each person and guide the participant to form a circle around the cauldron. If there a less than a full coven of thirteen, each person can hold more than one candle.

3. Next, the floating candle should be lit and placed in the cauldron by the leader who says:

Oh, ancient Lugh of day-long past,
Be here with us now.
In this place between worlds,
On this Lammas Day.

4. Rap three times on the cauldron and after a few moments say:

Harvest is here and the seasons do change.
This is the height of the year.
The bounty of summer sustains us,
In spirit, in soul, and in body.

5. Now, the group should perform a processional spiral dance five times around the cauldron. All present should speak about their gratitude for the gifts of the season and the riches of the summer bounty. Storytelling, singing, and dancing should all be a part of this rite.

6. The leader determines when the rite is done by putting out the candles and proclaiming:

This rite is done.

Ritual Recipe—Lammas Bread

Makes 1 large or 2 regular loaves.
Ingredients:

2 cups whole-wheat flour
2 cups bread flour, plus more if needed
¼ cup toasted sesame seeds
2 tablespoons active dry yeast
2½ teaspoons salt
2 cups milk, scalded
2 tablespoons smooth peanut butter
2 tablespoons honey

1. Mix dry ingredients in a large bowl.

2. Add peanut butter and honey to hot milk and stir to combine. Cool milk mixture to very warm, approximately 115º. Stir milk mixture into flour mixture.

3. Knead for 15 minutes, adding enough additional flour to make smooth, elastic dough.

4. Oil the surface of the dough, cover with plastic wrap or a damp tea towel, and let rise in a warm place until double in bulk, approximately 90 minutes.

5. After the dough has risen, punch it down and shape it into two rectangular loaves.

6. When risen a second time, bake in a preheated 375° oven for 30 minutes until golden brown and hollow-sounding when you tap the bottom.

ALL HALLOW'S EVE—OCTOBER 31

Solo Samhain—All Hallowed New Year's Eve

Samhain, also known as the Celtic New Year is the most profound, important, and best-known of all pagan sabbats. Samhain is perhaps the Goth pagan's favorite high holiday of all. After all, it is the witch's New Year celebration and the time to honor and commune with your elders, your family members who have passed on to the other side, and to celebrate the passing year and set intentions for new blessings in the coming new pagan year. Plus, it is the time to get your Gothiest in a glamourous costume or your skyclad best!

Supplies:

Altar space
3 candles
Powdered incense
Bread
Salt
Wine

1. Prepare for this most holy night and rite by setting up an altar. Place the three candles on a stone altar to represent the Triple Goddess and five to represent each point of the pentagram. The star of the pentagram should be drawn with powdered incense to be lit later. Gather together bread, salt, and wine for the sacrament.

2. After you have made your preparations for the altar, ready yourself by bathing and meditating. Anoint your body before dressing in a robe or gown befitting this night when the veil between the worlds is the thinnest. As you ready your body, mind, and spirit, consider what has taken place in the preceding year. Cleanse your mind and heart of old sorrows and most especially of angers and petty resentments. Bring only your best into this night. After all, this is New Year's Eve and you want to truly connect with those who have gone on to the other side.

3. Walk alone to the place of the ceremony and kneel before the altar. Before lighting the candles on the altar, say aloud:

This candle I light for the Maiden's brightest glory.

Light the candle and bow to the Maiden.

This candle I light for the power and passion of the Lady, the Queen.

Light the candle and bow to the Queen.

This candle I light for the unsurpassable wisdom of the Crone.

Light the candle and bow to the Crone.

4. Light the incense and then place the candles on the altar saying:

These do I light in honor of the Triple Goddess on this sacred night of Samhain
I create this holy temple in honor of the Goddess and the God
And all the ancient ones.
From time before time,
I pay my tribute and my devotion
In love and greeting to those behind the veil.

5. Now, light the candles that represent the power of the five-pointed pentagram. Rap three times on the altar with your hands or with your wand. Then say:

This is a time outside of time
In a place outside of any place.
On a day that is not a day
Between the worlds and afar.

6. Pause and listen to your heart for thirteen beats, then hold your hands in benediction over the bread, salt, and wine. Now say:

For this bread, salt, and wine,
I do ask the blessings
Of our Maiden, our Queen, and our Crone
And of the God who guards the Gates of the World.

7. Take the bread and sprinkle a bit of salt over it saying:

I ask that I and all whom I love
Have health and abundance and blessings.

Eat the bread and hold up the goblet of wine saying:

To a spirit that remains strong and true!

Drink the wine and declare:

By the Triple Goddess and her godly consort, so mote it be!

8. At this point, a dance macabre to any Gothic music of your choosing can end the ritual—I suggest any music by the band Dead Can Dance. You should also spend time meditating or allowing yourself to ease into a trance state to communicate with your beloved dead. Hear the messages they have for you and let them know you.

9. When you feel the ritual has ended, quaff the candles, and say:

Though these flames
Of the material world
Be darkened,
They shall ever burn
In the world beyond.
This rite is ended.

The Four Lesser Sabbats

The four lesser sabbats contain the solstices and equinoxes, the astronomical beginnings of the seasons. Their dates may vary by a day or two each year, depending on the sun's entry into the zodiacal signs of Aries (Spring), Cancer (Summer), Libra (Autumn), and Capricorn (Winter). The lesser sabbats are:

Ostara: March 21, also known as the Spring Equinox
Lithe: June 21, also known as the Summer Solstice
Macon: September 21, also known as the Autumn Equinox
Yule: December 21, also known as the Winter Solstice

Yule rules, but Christmas itself is very un-Goth, with the exception of Tim Burton's visionary film *The Nightmare Before Christmas*. All those bright twinkling lights, garishly colored packages, and dreadful thematic sweaters are the antithesis of Gothic sensibility. How can buying gifts for people you don't even talk to most of the year (your family, maybe?) be spiritual? In early tribal times, Goths stoically went through the winter seasons making sure there was enough food for everyone and hunkering down against the bitter frozen cold. How can a goddess-fearing Goth get through "the dark time of the year" while maintaining dignity? The following are some suggestions from the world's wisdom traditions.

December is named for the Roman goddess Decima, one of the three fates. There is much more going on in December aside from the Christmas festivities. Nearly every solar god is celebrated during this month—Ball for Syrians, Apollo for Greeks, Freya in Nordic mythology, Osiris in Egypt, to name but a few. Scots celebrate Hogmany, in honor of their solar god Hogmagog. Yule is one of the sabbats, or the eight solar holidays, and is celebrated on December 21, the shortest day of the year. The word *Yule* comes from the Germanic *jol*, meaning "midwinter." The old tradition was to have a vigil and a bonfire from dusk to dawn to make sure the sun does indeed rise again on this longest night of the entire year.

At the Gate of the New Year—December 31 Celebration

Instead of hosting a large energy-draining New Year's Eve party that competes with a half-dozen other large energy-draining New Year's Eve parties thrown by your friends, why not host a different kind of event? Open your home to your tribe of Goths and partygoing friends who are traveling to or from bigger and wilder celebrations and give them a chance to pause and refresh themselves before going on to the great celebrations or returning home to their cozy beds.

Besides the ritual recipes offered herein, offer your guests the opportunity during their visit to divine their fortunes for the coming year. Tarot readings, scrying, the I Ching, and all manner of divination systems should be available, and if you are not a tarotist, engage the services of a friend who is skilled in the arts of divination for your guests' pleasure. This quiet oasis in an otherwise loud and raucous day and night provides your fellow revelers a rare chance to truly reflect on their lives in the year that is passing away and the possibilities for the year to come—to both look forward and backward like the two-faced Roman god Janus, the god of gates and doors, beginnings and endings—and the month of January.

Your wayfarers' magickal experience begins at the threshold of your front door. It's a simple ritual that was inspired by the great temples of Japan. Before entering the temple, the pilgrims pause at an outdoor shrine and ceremonially wash their hands with pure water that is poured from a bamboo ladle. Then, with clean hands they take a stick of incense, light it from a perpetual flame, and place the burning incense in a container of sand. Sometimes they clap their hands as if to call the gods' attention to this offering, or they pause for meditation and prayer. Finally, they leave a few coins in another nearby vessel and continue their pilgrimage.

You can create your own shrine with a beautiful array of ritual objects: on a table near the entrance to your home, place three large china bowls, one filled with pure water, one with sand, and one for coins. In the back of the bowl of sand, place a lit votive candle. In front of the bowl with sand, stack a large amount of Japanese stick incense.

Post a beautifully drawn and decorated sign at your simple shrine that simply reads:

At the Gate of the New Year
Purify your hands with water so you may receive peace.
Light a stick of incense so you may receive freedom.
Offer a coin so you may receive stability.

Can you think of better gifts for the New Year?

A similarly simple ritual for this time of year is the Shinto custom of clearing away any accumulated debt at the new year. While that would be impossible for me and many people I know, you *can* accomplish this in small and doable ways. Why not pay back the twenty dollars you borrowed from your friends that night at the night club or return all the books, CDs, and clothing you borrowed from your friends? We all borrow things from our friends and family and this is a "karma cleansing" rite that will leave you feeling psychically clean and also reconnect you to members of your tribe and remind you of the simple joy of being honorable.

CHAPTER SEVEN

Goth Mythology: Flying the Fields of the Dead

Nifheim—The Ancient Gothic World of Ice

The northern European tribes that made up the Goths had a rich and varied mythology. Long, dark, and icy winters dominated the world their gods and goddesses inhabited. Winter, the longest season for these folks, was the time for the rebirthing of the world. For example, in the hardy Vikings' mythos, they believed in a "quintessence." Besides the revered four elements so essential to pagan belief—earth, air, fire, and water—they believed that winter itself had a unique energy that made it the fifth element. In ancient and medieval philosophy, the fifth and highest essence after the four elements was thought to be the substance of the heavenly bodies and latent in all things. At this time, the Goth's entire tradition held that all life on the world came from Nifheim, a world made entirely of ice. It was a cold white world of snow and sleet. The counterpart world to the south was Muspeliheim and was hot and fiery, teeming with volcanoes. The first being to ever set foot in the world was a frost giant, Ymir, who materialized from an enormous block of ice.

Unfortunately for us, unlike the Greeks, Romans, and peoples of the Middle East, India, and Asia, Vikings were too busy surviving to write down their tales and mythologies. We do have the vast epic poems that were sung, passed down, and recorded to consult, the *Eddas* being among them, which are a rich resource for understanding the Nordic mind. Vikings were great storytellers and had an incredible capacity to recite hours of story and song from memory. The storytellers themselves were held in high regard and were called "skaids." A visiting skaid was an occasion for a great feast attended by both king and commoners in a great hall with a roaring fire, roasting meats, and many a jug of mead. Iceland was the last stronghold of the old Viking religion and tales as it was too remote for many invasions and Christian military missionaries to visit. Keenly aware of their role as preservationists, they began recording the Old Norse sagas and songs and thus we have the *Eddas*, which were written down in the late thirteenth century. The *Eddas* is the single most important original text for understanding the true nature of the Norse mind-set, the original Gothic pagans. As modern dark wiccans, we are continuing the legacy and the mythology of Old Norse's oral tradition with our stories, ceremonies, and writings.

Valkyries—In the Domain of the Dead

Valkyries, the dark goddesses of Norse mythology, made many appearances in the *Eddas*. In Old Norse, Valkyries were called "choosers of the dead." The great Viking skaids referred to them as "battle maids" and they were like angels of death. They were the nine daughters of Odin and flew over battlefields and actually chose who were to die. Later, they took on the form of black ravens and flew back to the field of the dead and determined who was to rise to the status of hero. In old Saxon, they were called "man-eating women"; they sometimes appeared as corpse-eating carrion crows. The dead Viking warrior's blood was described by skaids as "the raven's drink." The Valkyries then carried the fallen heroes to Valhalla, the great hall of the gods. Those not selected as heroes were left to Freya, who visited the battlefield in her cat chariot.

Valkyries were believed by the Vikings to be beautiful, young women who were also fierce and warrior-like, dressed in full battle armor. Valkyries were also capable of shape shifting, disguising themselves as mares or swans and exploring earth on bird's wings. A mare-woman in Swedish was called a "volva," which was related to very old Nordic words for priestesses who conducted ceremonies for the dead—vila, vala, wili, among them. Once in Odin's halls, however, they garbed themselves in lovely white robes and gowns. They treated the dead heroes with the respect that was their due: a horn brimming with honeyed mead and a feast. The heroes then became members of Odin's army and spent their next incarnations in even more exciting adventures. One ancient saga, the Grimnismal, said that the Valkyries' number was thirteen, the number of moons in a year and the number of a coven. The greatest heroes such as Siegfried took Valkyries as lovers. Today, Goths can invoke a valkyrie lover in the more gentle form of a swan maiden. Swan maidens were also known as "wish maidens," and you can obtain your truest wish with obeisance to a swan maiden.

The Norns

The Norns of Scandinavia are some of the older representations of the Triple Goddess, similar to the Moraie of Greek mythology and Saxony's weird sisters. Each norn was charged with an aspect of fate: past, present, and future, and their salvo was "Become, Becoming, and Shall Be." They resided in a cave at the root of the Tree of the World. Minding the fate of every living thing on Earth, their rule was ultimate, even over the great god Odin. Also part of their domain was the Well of Urd. Urd, related to the Saxon word *wyrrd* or *weird*, is also the name of the first of the Norns, a manifestation of Mother Earth. Verthandi is the second and Skuld is the last of the Norns, the goddess of death.

Mother Holda

Mother Holda was a maternal cave-dwelling crone who had power over weather. One of the more charming tales from this time is that snow came from Mother Holda shaking out her fluffy feather mattress. This wise woman had the additional duty, aside from her climatic work, of nurturing children in her snug cavern home before they were born and tending to them after their untimely deaths.

Odin

Odin is a god of war and death, but also the god of poetry and wisdom. He hung for nine days, pierced by his own spear, on the Tree of the World. Here he learned nine powerful songs and eighteen runes. Odin can ask questions to the wisest of the dead and have those questions answered. Equivalent to the Persian Mithras, he is the lord of the underworld and master of wisdom, language, and poetry. You should successfully appeal to him by carving your invocations into runes on candles or through the medium of oral poetry. Odin can help you with any kind of writing, giving you the energy to forge ahead with purpose and passion. He can even help you write your own rituals and poetic magickal chants.

LUGH

Lugh's name comes from the Celtic word for "Shining One," and he is indeed a warrior sun god and also guardian of the crops. Lugh has his own pagan festival, which takes place every year on August 1 to celebrate the harvest time. To honor Lugh, you should perform a ritual of gratitude for life, luck, and prosperity, which will help to keep the bounty flowing in your life. If you need a guardian or help with interpersonal problems at work, turn to Lugh as your defense divinity with invocation and ceremonies of your own inventions.

TALIESIN

He lives in the land of "summer stars" and is invoked in higher degrees of initiation in some esoteric orders. Taliesin, which means "Shining Brow," is the harper poet god and comes from the Welsh tradition, which is steeped in magick and mystery. He is the wizard's god and embodies wisdom and clairvoyance. Taliesin is a helpmate to musicians and any creative folks. If you are a solo practitioner and want to create a ceremony of self-initiation, Taliesin is a potent power to engage.

THOR

He is the Norse sky god of justice and battle who uses a thunderbolt to exact his will. Scandinavians of yore believed the crackle of lightning and thunder was Thor's chariot rolling through the heavens. The Norse believed that during a thunderstorm Thor rode through the heavens on his chariot pulled by the goats Tanngrisni ("gap-tooth") and Tanngnost ("tooth grinder"). Lightning flashed whenever he threw his hammer Mjollnir. Thor wears the belt Megingjard, which doubles his already considerable strength. His hall is Bilskirnir, which is located in the region Thrudheim ("place of might"). His greatest enemy is Jormungand, the Midgard serpent. At the day of Ragnarok, Thor will kill this serpent but will die himself from its poison. His sons will inherit his hammer after his death. Donar is his Teutonic equivalent, while the Romans see in him their god Jupiter. Thursday is named after him.

Turn to Thor when you need to use spirituality as an approach to solve a legal matter requiring a spiritual approach. He is also a powerful protection deity to use in ritual. You can and should do prosperity rituals every

Thursday through prayer and obescience to this old Goth god of abundance.

TYR

He is the northern European god who lends his name to the second day of the week,"Tyr's Day." Variations of his name include "Tiw" in Saxony and "Ziu" in Germany. Tyr is related to Odin and is known as the "sly god." Tyr is the original Germanic god of war and the patron god of justice, the precursor of Odin. At the time of the Vikings, Tyr had to make way for Odin, who became the god of war himself. Tyr was by then regarded as Odin's son (or possibly of the giant Hymir). He is the boldest of the gods, who inspires courage and heroism in battle. Tyr is represented as a man with one hand, because his right hand was bitten off by the gigantic wolf Fenrir (in old Norse, the wrist was called "wolf-joint"). His attribute is a spear, which is a symbol of justice and a weapon. Invoke him in rituals you perform on Tuesdays or for help any time you need to be more aggressive in your job or life, if you are asking for a raise or promotion, or debuting your Goth band's CD at a party; a show of respect to Tyr will abet your bold moves and set you in motion for success.

SUNNA

She is the ancient Germanic goddess of the sun, indicating that the big star in the sky is not always deified as male. The Teutons also referred to this very important divine entity as "Glory of Elves." In the great poetic epic the *Eddas*, it was said she bore a new daughter Suhn, who sheds light to a brand new world. Other sun goddesses include the Arabic Atthar and the Japanese Ameatuse and Sulis. As you rise each morning, speak your greeting to Sunna. Morning rituals set a positive tone for the day, ensuring that you are indeed living a magickal life.

CERNUNNOS

He is the Horned God of the Celts and is sometimes also called Herne the Hunter. He is a virile, very male figure of the hunt, symbolic of man's sensual power, the land, and animals. Cernunnos is the one to call on for animal magick, for fertility, and for any earth or environmental ceremonies you want to create. He is the wild man spirit of the woods. This deity is depicted with the antlers of a stag and sometimes carries a purse filled with coins. The Horned God is born at the winter solstice, marries the Goddess at Beltane, and dies at the summer solstice. He alternates with the goddess of the moon in ruling over life and death, continuing the cycle of death, rebirth, and reincarnation. Paleolithic cave paintings found in France depict a stag standing upright or a man dressed in stag costume, which seem to indicate that Cernunnos's origins date to those times. Romans sometimes portrayed him with three cranes flying above his head. He was known to the Druids as Hu Gadarn. He is also god of the underworld and astral planes. Creating an antler headpiece to wear during ritual work connects you to the power of Cernunnos and takes you outside the world of the mundane and into the magickal plane.

Fairy Myth and Magick—Goth on Gossamer Wings

Fairies have long been described in the legends and lore of nearly every culture. Today, Goths have claimed the fairy world for their very own. While the appearance of the fairies varies greatly from culture to culture, these gossamer and gothic beings are generally genial, gentle, and magickal in and of themselves. Fairies can appear as golden-haired maidens, hideous hags, black maws of bad and malevolent energy, a fleeting shadow, a golden glinting in the distance, or some natural phenomena such as twinkling lights in the sky, a rustle, conspicuous and surprising in the leaves, or a rippling of the water when there is no wind. They seem to be members of the same family, scattered over the earth and throughout history, but somehow all in league with each other. Whether harpy hags or beautiful blondes wafting through the woods, *Lord of the Rings*–style, fairies have long been believed in, sight unseen—they are invisible entities, unseen yet altogether powerful.

For centuries, country folk placated the fairy world with offerings of cookies, flowers, and a special cup of sparkling ale. While blessings and good fortune were the hoped-for outcome, when something in the home went awry, it was generally believed that the fairies were at fault. The mischievous and malevolent were to blame for missing babies, sudden illness, disappearing horses and sheep, and all manner of mishaps and mayhem. Even though modern minds believe that that the crops are not the result of meddling spirits, it might still be a really good idea to create insurance with charms and incantations.

While belief in fairies has declined greatly in many parts of the Western world, due to the Age of Reason, Darwinism, scientific exploration, industrialization, and urbanization, the fairies still rule some of the deepest corners of the forest in the densest backwoods, where the thicket grows the thickest and the green is greenest.

The magickal realm is teeming with spirits, mostly unseen with the exception of a few who like to startle mere mortals. Knowledge is power and knowing spirit names is greatly powerful. We know from the story of Rumpelstiltskin that saying the name of a fairy or magickal being can render it powerless long enough to escape! The following is a field guide to the Goth world of the unseen beings who can make mischief and ensure that life is never boring!

Affric—Water Nymph of Ancient Britain

Affric is probably derived from the ancient name Glen Affric, a very special place in Scotland. It contains one of the largest ancient Caledonian pinewoods in Scotland as well as lochs, moorland, and mountains. This wide range of habitats make Glen Affric a haven for wildlife. There are many rare and special birds, animals, and plants found here. Glen Affric has been described as the most beautiful glen in Scotland and has some of the most natural phenomena and long traditions associated with it. When Christianity came to Scotland, Affric lost her status as a local goddess and became known as a nymph who protected her river homes.

Aganippe—Muse of the Spring

Aganippe's abode was on Mount Helicon in ancient Greece in a wellspring that was sacred to the muses. Living in these sacred waters gave Aganippe the ability to confer inspiration to poets and water to anyone who drank from the rivers and brooks flowing from her spring. She is the daughter of the river deity Ternessus. An especially charming part of this myth is that the wellspring was caused by the hooves of Pegasus.

Agere—The Wild Woman

Agere is the "wild woman" spirit of Melanesia and is a dark spirit, considered by some to be a female demon. Agere has a rich legend in the folk tales of this area of islands north of Australia. The Melanesian people are literally the oldest peoples of the Pacific, having a culture thousands of years older than anywhere else and a rich mythology of the spirit world. Agere is believed to be a young woman who seduces men from her home in the waters of a lake. Part of her magick is that she has the power to cause rushes, plants, and reeds to grow around and hide her so she can lure unsuspecting men into the weedy waters and have her way with them. Many are never seen again!

Aiwel—Sudanese River Spirit

The Dinka people have a rich river mythology. Their world is inclusive of many unseen nature spirits all tied up in the delicate ecosystem that depends on the river for sustenance for crops as well as for spiritual well-being. Aiwel is the son of an elder river being and is utterly benign. A helper spirit with great magickal powers, this Dinka deity aids with livestock and herds and can also be counted on to help people in need.

Ashai—The Shropshire Water Fairy

Make no mistake, just because you see a very small and perfectly human-looking creature in the lakes of rural England, it is probably *not* a little person; it is very likely an Ashai. If you happen across one, just leave it alone. Otherwise, you will cause both the Ashai and yourself much misery. You may even cause the Ashai to disappear entirely! Stories abound of fisher folk catching these water fairies instead of fish. One of the more cautionary tales from Cheshire tells of a fisherman who reeled one in, despite the Ashai's despairing cries, and tied it up. The fisherman noted it had cold, clammy, damp skin like that of a fish. As they neared shore, the fairy faded away from sight as it writhed in the ropes, leaving no trace except a scar where the fisherman's hands had touched the fairy. Sometimes, one must simply leave well enough alone—look but don't touch is my advice.

As-Iga—Siberian Protector Spirit

While most of us think of the northernmost part of Russia as a frozen plain, it also has rivers and mountains and an exceedingly rich religious history and complex belief system dating back thousands of years. Siberian shamans have only now begun revealing their healing systems and mysteries to the world. One of the more benign beings in the fertile lore of these Finno-Ugric folk is As-iga, which means Old Man of the Ob. He guards the Ob River and protects the lives of all who depend on the Ob for their lives—every fish, reed, minnow, and all the Ostyak people, whose livelihood comes from the waters of this Siberian river.

Ben Varrey—Mermaid of Mann

The Isle of Mann is a most mysterious place. My family, the Stuart branch, that is, moved there for a time before sailing to Virginia in the 1800s. It seems they needed to escape Scotland for reasons I would be keenly interested in knowing. The Manx word for mermaid is *Ben Varrey*, and she is also depicted as a most beautiful golden-haired creature with great glamour for unsuspecting fisher folks, who are always smitten shortly before meeting their ensured doom. Thankfully, Ben Varrey is occasionally benign. The most famous example of this is a tale in which a mermaid showed her gratitude toward a man who rescued her by giving the man information regarding a secret buried treasure lost by the Spanish during the time of the great Armada. Sadly, the mortal man was unable to recognize the worth of this fortune and thoughtlessly threw it back into the water where it lies even now in wait of a wiser person.

The Blue Men—Mermen of the Minch

The Outer Hebrides off the coast of Scotland have less kindly water spirits. In fact, the island denizens believe them to be fallen angels. They are believed to float in the area called the Minch, between the island of Lewis and the Shinat Isles off the mainland of Scotland. They are reported to be cave-dwelling blue men with long, gray beards who navigate this especially treacherous sea with ease, having the power to control both the weather and the water. When they emerge from their underwater cave, beware for they summon up powerful winds and storms and even swim up to any ship out in the storm and chide those onboard. The only way to deal with the blue men is to challenge them to a rhyming contest and win, and thus, to stay alive.

Boann—Queen of the Well

Boann was a queen of old Irish folklore, the wife to Dagda, and the mother to Angus Og. Boann's singular sway was over a well of Nectan, and anyone who looked down this well would go blind, in fact, their eyes would pop out of their sockets. Boasting that this curse would not touch her, Boann was herself bested by the well. The harsh justice of this curse was such that the water splashed up out of the well and began tearing her apart. Her only escape was into the Boyne River, where she remains as only a faint memory and a name.

Bonito Maidens—Sea Spirits of Solomon

The Sa'a folk of the Solomon Islands believed deeply in these spirit maidens of the sea. They are somewhat similar to European mermaids of legend but are the guardians of the Bonito fish and live in deep pools in the ocean bed where they are seldom seen. Exceedingly beautiful, they bedeck themselves with jewelry made of shells and ivory. If you lose anything in this region of the sea, only they can return it to you. The Sa'a folk pay homage to these maidens by building shrines and sacrificing fish to them in respect.

Brounger—"A Flint the Son of a Flint"

This Scottish coastal sea spirit is a malevolent meanie who hailed from the Firth of Forth. The old-fashioned expression for the Brounger, "a flint the son of a flint," points to a link to St. Elmo's fire and also to thunder storms and the unearthly fiery sparks associated with lightning. According to legend, the Brounger is said to have bribed all fishermen he encountered with a price called a "teind" or tythe of oysters and a portion of their catch of the day. If not appeased by his fee of fish, the frightening water spirit might appear at any time on the riggings of a boat and make his demands. The cure for this evil appearance was to turn the boat, no matter the size, a full 360 degrees three times.

Bucca—Sprite of Cornwall

Sometimes called Bucca Boo, Bucca Dhu, or Bucca Gwidden, this invisible sprite visited fishermen in Wales and Cornwall, England, who tried to keep the Bucca at bay with offerings of beer and fish. If not sated, this water spirit could turn suddenly stormy and cause terrible weather that beached and sank boats. Wily fishermen would give succor to the Bucca and beseech him to divine a future of favorable weather for fishing by leaving part of their catch on the beach for him. The Bucca was also believed to be the spirit who disturbed tin mines, called the Knocker when he was deep in the mines and out of the water.

But Ia—Russian Water Devil

But Ia are freshwater spirits who safeguard lakes and other bodies of water. Sometimes called a "water devil" or the "water master," But Ia most often manifests as an ox or a horse but can also take on the appearance of a giant fish or a very scary old man or woman with horns and long gray hair. Folkloric convention has it that the garments of the water spirit, if any, reflect the grandeur of the water he protects. If it is a great lake or sea, the garments are grand, silvery robes, and if it is a mere pond or creek, the spirit wears humble rags. The But Ia are believed to live in an underwater town with families, friends, and belongings commensurate with their status.

The best way to handle a But Ia is to ply him or her with money and vodka to ensure good fishing and safe waters. To ignore these water spirits is to court danger, however, and if you chance to encounter one with long gray hair sitting by the shore, it is a certain omen of death.

Song of the Siren Spell

Mermaids and sirens are extremely erotic symbols and each one of us can conjure their power. Buy a pound of sea salt at the grocery store and place it in a bowl with ten drops each of jasmine and neroli or ylang ylang essential oil. Mix them together. Instead of a shower in the morning, take a bath with your Siren Salts. While submerged, visualize that you are turning heads with your mesmerizing mermaid beauty and silence. When ready, rise up and do not comb or towel dry yourself or your hair—drip dry naturally. As you go through the day, do more listening than talking. The compliments and attention will amaze you!

Calypso—Odyssean Nymph

One of the more illustrious water fairies, Calypso is prominent in Homer's *Odyssey* for rescuing the shipwrecked Odysseus and keeping him on her island for seven years. The Mediterranean nymph fell in love with the Greek hero of the Trojan War and beseeched him to forsake his wife and remain in her company. Odysseus's loyalty to his wife, Penelope, found favor with the great Zeus and the god commanded Calypso to guarantee Odysseus safe water passage to his home.

Cannered Noz—Washer Woman of the Night

Cannered Noz is actually a group of fairy water spirits local to the ancient area of Britannia (Brittany) in the corner of France closest to England. Local lore has it that the fairies manifest as old hags although they are even more frequently invisible to the human eye, so you really never know what they look like or where they are. Sounds of water splashing with no obvious reason is likely to be the handiwork of Cannered Noz. Why the splashing? Cannered Noz wash out the linens of sinners, people who die without the blessing of absolution for their sins. They are most often to be found near babbling brooks and streams. If you think you hear Cannered Noz, simply take the advice of the good people of Brittany and stay as far away as possible.

Ceasg—She Salmon of Scotland

If you happen by a loch and see a mesmerizingly beautiful woman bathing herself in the waters, don't let your eyes deceive you. She may well be something other than a woman—half salmon, perhaps. Ceasg is part woman, above water, and half salmon, below the water. The Highlanders also called her Maighdean na tuinne, "Maiden of the Wave." Ceasg's personality may not be entirely beautiful, either. She is a trickster spirit and very changeable in her nature. Beware if she comes in pursuit, as she prefers to swallow people. By the other token, if you can catch her, Ceasg must grant you three wishes. This Scottish mermaid may well be worth the risk of an encounter if you carefully choose your wishes.

Fin Folk—Shetland Sea Spirits

Off the shores of England and in the surrounding isles of Orkney and Shetland are a host of water spirits called Fin folk, who live under the water. They make their home on the sunken islands known as Eynhallow. They come in all shapes, sizes, and ages—there are the sensually appealing mermaids and selkies who appear as gorgeous women and there are "Fin wives," who are hideous hags and crumpled crones. According to Shetlander lore, the Fin wives grow to be so wretchedly ugly that the Fin men swim ashore, go on land, and hunt down human wives, which they kidnap and take under the sea. This myth is most famously told through the story of Evie, a Shetland fisherman whose wife was stolen by the Fin men. Evie found a way to outsmart the Fin folk by performing a secret ritual, during which he made an offering to Odin at the Odin Stone at the Stories of Stenness. He asked Odin to enable him to see through the deep waters of the Atlantic Ocean all the way to the sunken Eynhallow Islands so he could learn if his wife was being held captive there. Sure enough, she was there, and he, through mighty struggle and sacrifice, brought her back home to dry land.

Gwragedd Annwyn—The Ladies of the Lake

The Gwragedd Annwyn are gorgeous, golden-haired, and completely benevolent water fairies of Wales who live in sympathy with humans. They differ from mermaids in that they have a human shape and no fish's tail. They are renowned for their gentleness and peace-loving natures. They so appreciate the company of humans that they sometimes marry mortal men. Otherwise, they live underwater in family communities. In one popular tale, a young man falls in love with a Gwragedd Annwyn when he happens upon her in the act of combing out her beautiful blonde hair. To win her, he has to endure tests of his character. The final test is that he must correctly choose her from her sisterhood of ladies of the lake. He prevails and she becomes his bride, after he promises that he will forever treat her gently and lovingly. His fairy wife brings to him and his widowed mother a large dowry of valuable cattle. They live together happily for some years and then, one day, he forgets his pledge and hits her. Instantly, his wife and all her gifts to him vanish, never to be seen again.

Jenny Greenteeth—The Nursemaid's Nemesis

This is a nasty bogie first heard of in Lancashire, Great Britain. She is feared and dreaded because of her habit of kidnapping unsuspecting children who come too near the water where she lurks and pulls them underwater to drown. Jenny Greenteeth is so named because of her hideous green fangs and can be avoided by looking out for bodies of water that are filled with the bright green slime of algae.

Jer Kuba—Lake Jer Bodaz Protectors

In a remote part of the now-defunct Soviet Union, a pair of malevolent creatures harassed the people of the Mari region. They are denizens of the large lake of Jer Bodaz. The pair is known in Mari folktales as Jer Kuba and Jer Kugaza, which basically translate to "Lake Old Woman" and "Lake Old Man," and they are the guardians of this body of water. If by some chance you are wandering by this lake and see a cow mooing on the shore, you may well have encountered Jer Kuba. Make sure you please this water spirit; you will have great luck with your fishing. If the spirit is displeased, watch out! How do you offend this being? By soiling the waters of the lake with dirty laundry or bathing and washing dirty hair. How is vengeance exacted? The poor unfortunate will probably become very ill or all the fish will seemingly disappear. If the crime is severe, a great flood will strike the region or the water guardian will move the lake entirely.

Kelpy—Drowning Demon

Kelpies are to be avoided at all costs as they mean nothing but harm. They are difficult to recognize when they take the form of a very attractive young man or the opposite, a grizzled old man. Kelpies are easier to tell when they are in the form of a horse, usually coal black or dapple gray. You can tell them by their wild eyes and the telltale water reeds in their mane, revealing their watery origins. Sighting a kelpy is an augury of a coming drowning or some form of death by water. The kelpy's wickedness comes when he lures children into the water and eats them or craftily appears to a young woman as her husband or boyfriend

Liban—Sister of the Sacred Spring

Liban is an Irish girl whose effigy can be seen on many churches in Ireland. She became a part of lore and legend when she was swept away in a flood that came about as a result of the neglect of a sacred spring. The torrent of water took her and her beloved pet dog to an underwater cave where she remained for a year, unable to escape from the watery depths. In fact, she was very nearly the only survivor of her entire village. Finally, in utter desperation she prayed to become like a fish. Immediately, her prayer was answered and she was changed into a fish below the waist, just like a mermaid. Her canine companion was transformed into an otter. Liban lived in the waters, swimming and singing as happily as she could in her half-fish, half-human form for a long 300 years. Finally, a miracle happened. A priest by the name of Beoc happened to hear her lovely song and sought her out. Liban begged the cleric to help her. She wanted to get out of the water and go with him to St. Comgall. Beoc obliged and baptized the mermaid. According to the tale, she was offered the choice of 300 more years of life or to immediately ascend into heaven. She chose heaven.

Meremaiden—Water Deities

These water spirits are perhaps the most legendary of all, and for obvious reasons: mermaids usually appear as spectacularly beautiful women. From the waist up, they are lovely and lithe females and from the waist down they are fish. Meremaiden, more commonly known as mermaids, have been a part of the fabric of our myth and folklore for centuries. The most common image conjured is that of a lovely lady sitting on a rock by the sea or lake side, oftentimes with her fish tail hidden by water. The word *meremaid* means maiden of the sea. They make themselves known by their sultry singing, which can act as a lure to any men passing by within earshot of their songs, linking them with sirens. Sirens, however, seduce seafarers with their singing and usually lead them to their doom. From Homer to the fairy tales of Hans Christian Andersen, mermaids are supernatural beings who perform important roles from portending disaster to bestowing unforgettable gifts. Rescuing a mermaid is at your own risk.

Nasu—Demon of the Dead

Here is one of the most Goth of all spirits as Nasu is very concerned with the dead. This Zoroastrian being manifests as a fly and possesses the dead with the intention of making all humans so sick they, too, will die. Iranians believed that the watchful glare of a guard dog would frighten off the Nasu masquerading as a fly. Purification rituals are highly recommended!

Nidhogg—Envy Dragon

Beware this malicious being of Scandinavian lore; he is a lord of the underworld who threatens the very existence of the world by chewing on the deep underground roots of the Tree of Life—Yggdrasil—and the bodies of the dead. Nidhogg translates to "Envy Dragon," a hint at the dark heart of the nether-dwelling creature.

Pixies—Trooping Fairies

Southwestern England folklore is replete with stories of pixies, who are sometimes helpful, sometimes mischievous. They invariably wear green, pointy hats and are youthful in aspect with upturned noses and reddish hair. They are slight, as indicated by their name, seem to favor poor folks, and are even said to do domestic chores for penurious households. If you want to be rid of them, you simply have to lay out a set of new clothes for them. Other successful methods for sending them on their merry way is a bowl of cream or the tried and true "pixieworting" trick of setting out the last of the harvest apples for them under the tree.

Pixies are no friend of the lazy and torment anyone in the household with little bites, pokes, nips, and pinches. A trickster spirit, they sometimes scare people with unseen knocks and noise, similar to a poltergeist. The most severe crime they are accused of is stealing babies and leaving changelings in their place. Another of their tactics is to ride a horse all night in a fairy ring, leaving the horse in a lather of exhaustion and with a strangely knotted up mane and tail. If you have found yourself lost on a hike, dancing about, or going in circles because you always see a seemingly correct sign of your trail, then you have been "pixie led," in the way they love to devil travelers and wayfarers. Here is how you handle that: wear your jacket inside out. That stops the mischief. Pixies are believed to reside in small underground caves, mounds and barrows, or stone circles.

Pooka—Shapeshifter

Pookas or phookas are shapeshifters who most often manifest as wooly coated horses, sometimes with hanging chains on them. They can be found in remote and wild places, where their hauntings have the greatest effect. They like to lure young children onto their back and spirit them away. The rarest tales are of a pooka horse laboring for a poor farmer in the fields, pulling plows, and there is only one told by the great fairy expert Thomas Keightly of a pooka who, on the greatest of all witch's high holidays of Samhain, trod on a blackberry bramble and made prophecies.

Puck—Goat-Footed Nature Spirit

Even the name Puck conjures up the picture of mischief. Puck, who is known widely and in many countries, is called by the names Puckle, Poake, and Pug in Latvia; Pukis in Estonia; Puka in Iceland, Pouk in Germany; Pisca in Wales; and Pujk in Scandinavia. He is popular in English folklore and has been believed to take the forms of a brownie, goblin, elf, fairy, and hobgoblin. We can take this to indicate that Puck is a shapeshifter, but the vast majority of stories depict him as a very small and very hairy human-looking spirit with the feet of a goat. He is a colorful character in popular literature and can be found in the works of William Shakespeare and Rudyard Kipling. His main pursuits seem to be confusing and causing bits of trouble for unsuspecting people. Like a few other minor mischief makers, though, Puck's heart has a soft spot for impoverished country folk and helps them with gifts of food and money, even miraculously accomplishing difficult chores. He is a sometime patron of ill-fated lovers.

PUDDLEFOOT—BROWNIE OF THE BURN

It is my personal theory that no less than J.R.R. Tolkien himself was inspired by this spirit to create Gollum. Puddlefoot is a nature spirit who comes from one place only: a farm in Scotland. He was sort of a helper spirit; when not splashing around in his favorite pond or burn as they are called, he did housecleaning on the farm. Unfortunately, Puddlefoot never wiped his feet and usually made more of a mess. Once, a drunken Scot greeted him by name, causing Puddlefoot to disappear forever. Akin to the legends of Rumpelstiltskin and Tom Tit Tot, to name a spirit is to employ the power to send it away.

ROANE—SEAL SPIRIT

Roanes are placid beings said to be of a fairy form; the word *roane* is Scottish Gaelic for "seal." They can take human form as long as they have their seal skin with them to safely journey back to their underwater caves. They like to dance on the shores in warm weather, reveling in their human legs. In days of old, Scotsmen would spy out the most attractive of roane maids and steal their skin, trapping them in human form. Sometimes the roane females consented to being their wives, oftentimes departing the moment they retrieved their precious skin. One particular Scottish clan claims to be descended from a successful marriage between a roane and human, the MacOdums.

Gothic Arcana

For Egyptologists, there is the Rosetta Stone. For biblical and Gnostic scholars, there are the Dead Sea Scrolls. For students of the Gothic mystery school, there are two iconic objects of secrecy that bear consideration and study and perhaps contain some of the answers to the mysteries of the universe.

"The Magical Skull of Doom"

Skulls are one of the ultimate symbols of Gothdom, and this large, spectacular quartz crystal specimen is the definitive example. Very few objects have engendered as much controversy or imaginative conjecture as this crystal skull. First off, "The Magical Skull of Doom" is life size in its circumference and even in its likeness to the human head, and so far, it has defied all efforts to pinpoint the provenance and the origin of its making. To add to the fascination, there are a multitude of tales associated with the skull that tell of highly strange phenomena, leading some to believe it is haunted, others to believe it is cursed, and yet others to associate it with extraterrestrials.

As legend has it, the skull first turned up in the 1920s during an archaeological dig under an altar in the ruins of the great Mayan city of Lubaantun in British Honduras, now called Belize. Some of the greatest arguments are whether the Skull of Doom is actually pre-Columbian. While other crystal skulls have been discovered in Central American ruins, none can match the Skull of Doom for its perfection of craftsmanship and likeness to a real skull. Others suggest that the skull was never in Lubaantun at all. Perhaps the biggest mystery of all is that the crystal from which the skull was crafted is *not* even from Mayan territory. Evidently, it is the kind of crystal that is only derived from California.

One of the archaeologists at Lubaantun, Frederick Mitchell Hedges, who was present at the discovery, is rumored to have planted it on the site for his adopted daughter's birthday. Hedges named the large, mysterious hunk of crystal "The Magical Skull of Doom" and proclaimed that the skull was "used by the high priest of the Maya to concentrate on and will death," that it was "the embodiment of all evil," and that people who scoffed at the skull have died or "have been stricken and become seriously ill."

Frank Dortland, one of the later owners of the skull and a highly reputable art restorer, kept and studied the Skull of Doom. He swore that the skull gave off an "elusive perfume" and that it seemed to emanate sounds such as chiming bells, changed color at will, and was filled with ever changing, cloudy images. He also claimed that the skull from time to time showed crystal-clear images of temples, mountains, and myriad other striking scenes. Other folks who observed the skull when it was under Dortland's watch said a hazy aura would occasionally enshroud the skull. Still stranger are the reports of physiological phenomena affecting people who were near the skull—quickening of pulse, muscle spasms in legs and arms, and even eye twitching.

Maybe the fascination of "The Magical Skull of Doom" is simply in its inherent magnificence. It looks like it was formed and has few signs of tool marks. The artist who created this skull was a master of the highest order, whose handiwork is nothing less than spectacular. Simply polishing the skull would have been a labor of some years. For the final master stroke, the skull was crafted in such a way that light collects and refracts in the eye sockets, and so seems to be emitted eerily.

The Transylvanian Tablets

Archaeologists digging into a prehistoric mound in the mountainous Transylvanian village of Tartaria in the 1950s were actually only hoping to discover further information about the already well explored area and its unique history. Instead, they made a startling discovery: three small clay tablets with bizarre inscriptions. The inscriptions were believed by some to be sigils or magickal signs and others believed they were important documents left behind for the singular purpose of being found as time capsules. Scientists performed carbon 14 dating on the clay artifacts and dated them to circa 4000 B.C. and therein lies the biggest surprise of all. Up until then, it was believed that writing originated in Mesopotamia, specifically in Sumer in 3200 B.C.

It sent a shock through the civilized world to realize that writing may well have begun in the wild backwoods of woolly Transylvania—barbarians inventing writing? Interesting to say the least. The three tablets were found in a burial mound in the lowest layer of the dig, along with some human and animal remains, including some scattered bones from what appeared to be a sacrificial pit. They bore symbols quite similar to the inscriptions on tablets from Sumer and from the highly advanced Minoan civilization of Crete. But if the carbon dating was accurate, the Tartar tablets were made by a primitive Stone Age agricultural tribe known as the Vinca. The Vinca predated Sumerian writing by 1,000 years and the Minoan writing by 2,000 years. Most scholars believe that the inscriptions denote magickal cipher-spells and secret codes of this ancient farming tribe. The hash marks, swirls, x's, and shapes on the three tablets do cast a spell all their own, too.

The Sacred Art of Name-Giving

Native American tribes give tribal names to teenagers when they come of age. Tribes would welcome new people into their communities with naming ceremonies. These wonderful descriptive names are usually derived from an animal totem and a quality unique to the individual. For example, Thunder Horse may describe a very powerful and quick-moving person or Brother Sun Out of the Clouds might describe a very even-tempered and jolly sort. I had the distinct honor of getting to know the Native American teacher Jamie Sams when I worked at the publishing house that produced her divination decks. Sams, the creator of *The Medicine Cards* and *The Sacred Path Cards,* showed me the key to giving these tribal names: they should be earned, not given freely. The person needs to contribute to the tribe or community with service and to demonstrate he or she is a person of great honor. By observing the person over time, you will see into his or her heart and be able to describe his or her inner nature with a name, a true badge of honor.

If your circles are anything like mine, you know that Goths and pagans are tribal, too.

The following is the tribal naming ceremony I also learned to welcome new adults to the tribe. The elder Goth or tribal leader sets the date for the naming. In your case, it might be that you, as the parent, set the date for your circle and invite friends and family. Ideally, the ceremony should take place on the night of a new moon.

Goth Naming Ceremony

Your Goth name is an important signifier. It is a marker of your initiation and progress on your dark Wiccan path and lets the world know your intention and identity. When you are ready to take the step or induct a new Goth into your community or coven, this ritual is a beautiful way to ceremoniously mark the occasion.

Timing: This ritual is best performed on the new moon night.

Supplies:

Drums
Fire
Pipe with mild tobacco
Face paint
Feathers, leather, and beads for a headdress
"Gifts of wisdom" for the new Goth

1. Gather together the tribe and form a seated circle around the fire. Honor the new adult with "growing up stories." Any tales of courage, honesty, and generosity are encouraged for the telling as they show the best qualities of the new adult.

2. After story time, pass the pipe around for the blessing of smoke.

3. Present the new name with the explanation of the name. For example, "I name you 'Mistress Moonwater,' because you are wise and reflective, because you shine."

4. The tribe should welcome the newly christened Goth by going around the circle and speaking their hopes for the future. "Mistress Moon Water, may you see the world and find the place that speaks most deeply to your heart." Now is the time to present the newly named tribal member with the gifts of wisdom. Here, we are not referring to expensive new toys or watches but a book that changed your life and the reason why or an amber amulet for safekeeping.

5. Next, the tribe should decorate the celebrant with the paint and feathers, leather, and beads and cocreate a headdress, making it as magnificent as possible. This headdress is the insignia of newfound adulthood.

6. Drum and sing on this new moon night as an important new member of the tribe has just come into being!

Gothic Name Generator

If you are dressed like an eighteenth-century vampire, it's only fitting that your name be as ostentatious and extravagant as your appearance. Very few Goths use their given name, as it sounds boring. Instead, most Goths will create a moniker for themselves that corresponds with their Gothic persona. The objective is generally to create a title that is dark, mysterious, sexy, and romantic and extra points are given if it has an air of nobility. In renaming themselves, most Goths aren't shy about plucking a forename right out of a horror novel or other piece of Gothic mythology or literature. As Voltaire says, on a single visit to a Goth club you are likely to meet a couple of Ophelias or a handful of Vlads. Others may opt to take on the name of a notorious mythical figure, like Rasputina, Maleficent, or Lady Shelley, or that of a long dead writer, such as Emily Dickinson, Edgar Allen Poe, Dante, Lord Byron, or Verlaine.

Another commonly employed technique is to combine two words with dark connotations of their own to create a new, über-dark compound word; for instance, the ever popular Dark Angel (one of the most popular names in Gothdom), Raven Crow, Black Kat, or Eternal Mysterie. Others are content to simply choose a name from the pantheon of popular Goth names like Crow, Spider, Raven, Skull, Ankha, Damiana, or Lilith.

You can create a really ultra-Goth name for yourself using the unique Gothic Name Generator that follows. To use it, you can close your eyes and point or use two six-sided dice. Roll the dice to pick a title from column A, a name from column B, an occupation from column C, and subjects from column D. With any luck, you just might end up with a spiffy name like "Priestess Lilith, Defiler of the Clergymen" or "Empress Demona, Defenestrater of the Bats."

Mythic Name Generator—Embracing Our Mythology (Male)

Title	*Name*	*Occupation*	*Subjects*
1. Most	**1.** Dredd	**1.** Crawler	**1.** Trolls
2. Prince	**2.** Crow	**2.** Creator	**2.** Ravens
3. Lord	**3.** Dracul	**3.** Releaser	**3.** Seraphim
4. Count	**4.** Spider	**4.** Moonwatcher	**4.** Innocents
5. Baron	**5.** Nosferatu	**5.** Destroyer	**5.** Bats
6. Father	**6.** Sebastian	**6.** Nightbringer	**6.** Angels
7. Priest	**7.** Onyx	**7.** Liberator	**7.** Virgins
8. Sir	**8.** Byron	**8.** Flayer	**8.** Clergymen
9. Master	**9.** Diablo	**9.** Avenger	**9.** Dead
10. Duke	**10.** Darkness	**10.** Castigator	**10.** Crypt
11. Emperor	**11.** Barnabas	**11.** Necromancer	**11.** Succubae
12. Darth	**12.** Nocturnus	**12.** Defenestrater	**12.** Spiders

Gothic Name Generator (Female)

Title	*Name*	*Occupation*	*Subjects*
1. Heiness	**1.** Amber	**1.** Healer	**1.** Fairies
2. Princess	**2.** Acacia	**2.** Seductress	**2.** Night
3. Lady	**3.** Draculina	**3.** Keeper	**3.** Ravens
4. Madame	**4.** Lilith	**4.** Enchantress	**4.** Seraphim
5. Mother	**5.** Batty	**5.** Priestess	**5.** Innocents
6. Countess	**6.** Maleficent	**6.** Usurper	**6.** Bats
7. Mistress	**7.** Malora	**7.** Violator	**7.** Angels
8. Dame	**8.** Lucidia	**8.** Eradicator	**8.** Virgins
9. Czarina	**9.** Magdalena	**9.** Decimator	**9.** Nobles
10. Marquesa	**10.** Isis	**10.** Defenestrater	**10.** Black Veil
11. Queen	**11.** Vampira	**11.** Scourge	**11.** Succubae
12. Empress	**12.** Nocturna	**12.** Webmistress	**12.** Spiders

The Mythology of Magick— Gothic Gnostics

Gnosis is a form of knowledge concerning the cosmos to which the individual feels called. It is experiential and deeply personal, in the heart, body, and soul, and not intellectual or of the head. The Saturnian archetype from ancient teachings is a person who is independent, highly intelligent, original, inventive, strong willed, versatile, freedom seeking, self-disciplined, patient, and aloof. Many a Goth could be described in just these terms.

The Goth-Saturn connection goes back to Victorian times. A study of Victorian-era northern European magick and mysticism shows a lineage of magickal practitioners who were Fraternitas Saturni brethren. They were very concerned with achieving a high level of understanding of the cosmos and created an intricate doctrine for passing from a low level of knowledge to the very highest, a special path of initiation. In light of the fact that it is saturnine, it included a Luciferian aspect—Lucifer, the once most loved angel whose name meant "Morning Star." This Fraternitas Saturni's belief system was inclusive of a complete astral and planetary cosmosophy, one that contains a mythology and a chain of being with spirits and beings that guard doorways between worlds that open up to stars and planets beyond our own. This in no way means the group was Satanistic; its members were Gnostics for whom Lucifer was the highest angel who came to the earthly plane. It also seems that their religious lineage contained traces of the Ophite and the Barbelo Gnostics of thousands of years ago. The path of study of the Fraternitas Saturni was established to provide just such an occurrence of initiatory experience.

The rich lineage of Gnostic belief offers much to the modern Goth magician: it is a path where the highest mind and corridors of imagination meet the highest reaches of the spiritual. Through contemplation, Goth Gnosticism mines the riches of the inner world and calls forth a more disciplined, learned, and dedicated spirit worker. The Goth Gnosticism of antiquity consisted of quite a few sects, not entirely compatible in their beliefs but all with the same goal of experiential understanding. The commonality of all Gnostic beliefs is that godhead existed above all humanity and all of nature—a threefold deity in the fullness of being, "pleroma," or light. The dominion of divinity was outside of ordinary, or mundane, existence and was separated by a dividing area called "horos." Just how the realms of the universe came to be separate is a highly speculative subject.

Regardless, Gnostics agreed that our mundane world was not created by a divine entity but by an anomaly in the pleroma, that this anomalous flaw was a being who came about as result of the ever increasing distance from the fullness of being of the pleroma. Less powerful entities, called "Archons," grew in a hierarchical sphere called "aeions." Gnostics believed this episode was also possibly the result of the deliberate withdrawal of divine will, or "thelema."

The very powerful archon that created the world we know was a demiurge, and Gnostics believed this being to be the biblical Jehovah, YHVH, the god of the Old Testament. The last creation of this world was man, believed by Gnostics as originating in both the world of light, or divinity, and the world of darkness, the realm of the demiurge. And man, a being of both light and dark, can only be redeemed though gnosis. Redemption and being uplifted from the mundane and baser realm can only occur with direct experience, in which the soul is touched and enlightened. While Jehovah expects and demands simple, blind faith, or "pistis," the "Good God," an original divine will of Gnosticism, can only be reached through the personal process of illumination.

The secret Fraternal Order of Saturnius holds that Saturnus, the overlord and judge who ensures justice and who oversees all standards of measurement and numbers, will be brought to bear and bring about reason, logic, and intelligence—higher mind. This sect of Saturn-Gnosis believed the god Saturn to be the focal point for the expression of the demiurge, who is identified with Lucifer, the "bringer of light." Having been thrown out of the highest sphere because he shared this divine secret of gnosis with humanity, he is the "Guardian of the Threshold" and holds the key to gnosis and true initiation.

The secret society of the Saturnus order is one in which the initiate secludes in darkness and seeks the light of initiation. It can be a lonely path, one that has the light of gnosis shining at the end. Thus, the initiate must seek seclusion, to be liberated from base influences. Eventually, the seeker feels no need for connection to the masses and feels an inner sense of joy from self-containment and contentment born of solitude. Similarly, the Gothic path is a solitary one, removed from the mentality and aims of the masses, a growing light in the darkness.

The Great Secret—Sex Rites of the Fraternus Saturni

Goth magic takes place in a realm of secrecy, taking that which is taboo and reveling in it. Modern Goths desire to know all, to experience the deepest, darkest secrets. We have here one of the most well-guarded secrets of magick of all time. Every secret sect holds its private rituals dear. Even within the orders themselves, higher-level rites and practices are concealed from lower-ranking members, who must first pass through a series of testing before they can participate in the great mysteries of initiation. While some secret orders such as the Order Templar Orientalis, founded by Aleister Crowley, have at the highest degrees of initiation ceremonies of sexual magick, the Fraternus Saturni performs the highest level of sex magick at the eighteenth degree, or the Pentalphic stage. The most commonly practiced erotic ritual for the saturnine sect, however, is the "erita," which is derived from the philosophy of Hindu Tantra. A central concept of Tantra is to induce astral images, called "psychogenes," through the concentration of sexual energies. Psychogenes are talismanic entities created through magickal work of the magicians during the sacred rite. This being has a supernaturally created psyche, or soul, but abides by the will of its creators, controlled by their energy. The following is this great *secret ritual*, the Saturni Rite of Five M.

Saturni Rite of Five M

This deeply guarded secret ritual is a high and holy occasion to be undertaken with great reverence and preparation of your "inner temple." This is an intermingling of the divine.

1. Before entering the inner sanctum of the temple, the male and female magicians who are to perform the erotic ritual, or "maithuna," Sanskrit for Eros, will partake in a sacramental meal of "matsya," or fish, and "mudra," or grain, as well as "mansa," or meal, and "madya," or wine. These are the five Ms symbolized by the name of the ceremony.

It is essential to have a woman and a man from the ranks of the order who are drawn and bound to each other by intense erotic desire.

Building this craving necessitates abstinence and meditation before the Five M.

2. The first stage of the ritual is preparation of the temple. The sanctuary room should be hung with black satin banners that have silver pentagrams in the inverse. Aprons for this ritual are black with red pentagram reversed. If the initiates have ascended to holding the eighteenth degree, they will also be wearing the rings of that degree.

3. The second stage is the entry into the temple of the male and female magicians who step into the inner circle. Inside the circle is a low stool on which the man sits. The woman takes a crouching position between the man's outspread legs.

4. Next, a parchment, which is to be charged magickally, is laid out between the male magician, or "magus," and his medium, the female magician. On the paper are the sigils of the psychogene to be called on. A series of breathing techniques ensues to raise energy.

5. The working stage of the Five M ritual begins when the woman stands up and sexually mounts the man and brings him to a climax. She, in turn, is brought to climax, after which she rises and the magickally induced sexual fluids are gathered onto the parchment. Now, the paper becomes the central focus of the ritual for the purpose of invoking a psychogene.

CHAPTER EIGHT

Supernatural Sex: Romantic Rituals and Make-Out Magic

Goth culture has evolved to be very sexualized, stemming from the punk roots of the late 1970s with the playful approach to S&M. The magick of love and sex is an important aspect of Goth magick. At their heat, every dark Wiccan is also a Romantigoth.

Have you ever wondered why so many witches were burned at the stake? It's because they were too darned hot! If you look at records of the witch hunts from the extremely Goth Dark Ages and eighteenth-century Salem, witches were accused of consorting with everyone from the Devil to the preacher. Clearly, the sexual prowess of witches was intimidating, which stands to reason because we know how to unleash the most uncontrollable desires, even in times of extreme repression.

Witches are so in tune with their sexuality that they have dedicated an entire high holiday—Beltane or May Day—to sex. On that day, we celebrate seduction by dancing around the Maypole through the moonlit night and answering our wildest urges with complete abandon. As witches, we appreciate the transcendental nature of sex. After all, we worship the Goddess, who embodies the feminine mystique. With her guidance, we revel in the art of lovemaking and taste the full spectrum of erotic pleasure. For centuries, we have honed our craft and developed our mastery of the fiery arts to unleash the power of seduction within us.

Sex resides in a magickal realm where body, mind, and soul meet. It is a heightened state where raw emotions and primal passion reach their peak. To make love with another person is to give of yourself completely and to receive pleasure with just as much surrender. It is a chance to use every sense, including your intuition, as you blur the lines between your body and your spirit. By practicing Goth magick, you reach this pure state through the time-tested spells and potions listed in this chapter. As with all witchcraft, turning carnal knowledge into sublime spirituality requires clarity, intention, and authenticity. Conscious sex isn't a random act, but the result of focus and self-awareness.

Think of this collection of sex and love spells in this chapter as a sort of "pillow book." It is intended as encouragement for you and your lover to seek joy and intensity, to revel in the heights of ecstasy, and above all to have *meaningful* experiences.

But be forewarned that the sexual power of witchcraft can be scary and threatening to people, so discretion and caution are advised. I urge you to keep in mind your sense of ethics. These sex spells are for positive pleasure between consenting adults. No manipulation, no coercion. Harm to none.

Here, I have gathered together spells of my own design and those passed down from the sisterhood. I have also learned much about sex from the men in my life and this, too, I share so you can have a juicy and joy-filled sex life. I encourage you to share your secrets, as well. I believe we all have unique gifts and special talents. Pass them on.

And please remember, nothing is as sexy as an open mind.

Aphrodisiacal Altar

To prepare for new relationships and to deepen the expression of feeling and intensity of your lovemaking, you have to create a center from which to renew your erotic spirit—your altar. Here, you can concentrate your energy, clarify your intentions, and make wishes come true! If you already have an altar, incorporate some special elements to enhance your sex life. As always, the more you use your altar, the more powerful your spells will be.

Your altar can sit on a low table, a big box, or any flat surface you decorate and dedicate to magick. One friend of mine has her sex altar at the head of her bed. Another Goth Grrrl has hers in a cozy closet complete with a nestlike bed for magickal trysts.

Begin by purifying the space with a sage smudge stick—a bundle of sage that you burn as you pass it around the space. Then cover your altar with a large, red, silky-smooth fabric. Place two red candles at the center of your altar and then place a "soul-mate crystal" at the far right corner. Soul-mate, or Twinned, crystals are any crystals that formed fused together. They are available at metaphysical stores and through the resources listed in the Gothic Resources: Fashion, Clothing, and Culture at the back of this book.

Anoint your candles with jasmine and neroli oil. Keep the incense you think is the sexiest on your altar, too. For me, it is currently peach and amber musk, which I simply love smelling. Your sex altar is also a place you can keep sex toys you want to imbue with magick. Place fresh Casablanca lilies in a vase and change them the minute they begin to fade. Lilies are heralded as exotic *and* erotic flowers prized for their seductive scent.

Exotic Erotic Altar Dedication

Here, at your magical power source, you can "santify your love." Collect your tools, meaningful symbols, and erotic iconography and prepare for the sacred rituals of love.

Supplies:

Red and pink candles
Incense
Victorian violet and rose essential oils

1. Light the candles and incense and dab the essential oils between your breasts, near your heart. Speak aloud:

I light the flame of desire,
I fan the flame of passion,
Each candle I burn is a wish
And I come to you as a witch.
My lust will never wane.
I desire and I will be desired.
Harm to none, so mote it be.

Enticing New Love

This is the perfect spell of enchantment to use when you have met a "special someone" and you wish to enhance your personal charm and magnetism. With this invocation, you are sure to attract your heart's desire!

Supplies:

1 red and 1 pink candle
Essential oil (jasmine and rose have very powerful love vibrations to attract and charm a lover)

1. Stand before your altar with tokens representing love. Light the candles. Scent your wrists, throat, and your left breast over your heart with the same oil.

2. If you desire sexual results, look into the flame of the red candle; if your desire is affection or flirtation, look at the pink candle instead. Said aloud, this spell creates loving magick:

Venus, cast light on me,
A Goddess today I'll be.
A lover, strong, brave, and true,
I seek as a reflection of you.

Attracting That Attractive Stranger

This surefire attraction spell will bring that stranger to you. It is a "come-hither conjuration" with simple yet supernatural magnetic pull. Use wisely!

Timing: Begin this ritual on a Friday, Venus's Day.

Supplies:

Mandrake root, or any photograph or figure of a man or woman
Pink roses and candles
2 goblets of wine

1. Place on your altar a man-shaped mandrake root or whatever image you have chosen. Also place the goblets of wine on your altar.

2. Burn the candles every night for a week starting on a Friday. Sip from the goblets and recite:

Merry stranger, my heart,
Merry may we meet again.
Hail, fair fellow, well met,
With this wine I toast you,
As we merry meet again.

3. Make sure you look your best, and you will soon lock eyes again.

Oil of Love

Indulge in this sensually satisfying ritual bath that will make your skin glow and surround you with a seductive aura.

Supplies:

3 ounces apricot kernel oil
3 ounces sweet almond oil
1 ounce aloe vera gel
½ ounce rosewater
13 drops jasmine essential oil
6 drops rose essential oil
2 ounces dried chamomile flowers and yarrow
Rose or red candle

1. Shake this mixture together before pouring into a tub sprinkled with dried chamomile flowers and yarrow.

2. Light a rose or red candle (for passion) and say:

My heart is open, my spirit soars.
Goddess bring my love to me. Blessed be.

3. No towels, air dry afterward.

Goth Glamour Blessing

The word "glamour" comes from the meaning "enhanced beauty through artifice" and includes the magical arts. The truest beauty comes from within and you can enhance that greatly with this charm.

Timing: This ritual is best performed during the waxing moon.

Supplies:

Vervain, thistle, chamomile, and elder flower
Salt
Your favorite jewelry

1. To prepare for a night of true love, during the waxing moon take the rings, necklace, and earrings you are planning to wear during a special tryst and lay them on your altar.

2. Mix together the dried herbs of vervain, thistle, chamomile, and elder flower. Cover your jewelry with the herb mixture and then sprinkle salt on top. Hold the jewelry in your hands and say:

Bless these jewels and the hand and heart of the wearer with light and heaven above. May all who look on me see me through the eyes of love.

Lover's Tea

Here's a recipe to create exactly the right mood for romance. The verse at the end references the Garden of Eden before the fall.

Supplies:

1 ounce dried hibiscus flowers
1 ounce dried and pulverized rosehips
½ ounce dried lemon balm
½ ounce dried mint (ideally peppermint)
½ ounce meadowsweet

1. Stir ingredients together in a clockwise motion. Store in a dark, lidded jar.

2. To make tea, add two teaspoons of herbs for each cup of boiled water. Steep for five minutes while visualizing your heart's desire and saying aloud:

Herbal brew of love's emotion,
With my wish I fortify.
When two people share this potion
Their love shall intensify
As in the Olde Garden of Love.

Pillow Talk

To secure lasting, blissful love from a nascent romance, a love pillow can cast a powerful, binding spell. This spell works best if you use a soft, homemade pillow.

Timing: This spell is best performed on a Friday.

Supplies:

2 yards pink satin fabric
Goose down
Dried red rose petals (the rose should be one you've grown or that you have received from your lover)
Golden thread
Amber and rose oil

1. Take the satin fabric and stuff it with the goose down and the dried rose petals.

2. Sew it with the golden thread while you whisper:

Here rests the head of my true mate fair.
Nightly rapture is ours to share. So mote it be.

3. Anoint the thread with amber and rose oil, especially when you "entertain." You can "refresh" the threads from time to time.

Dreaming Destiny

This charm will help you see whether a newfound interest will become long term. Arrange a romantic evening and prepare this amulet for clairvoyance.

Supplies:

Small red velvet scarf or pouch
Lavender, thyme, cinnamon, and cloves
1 vanilla bean pod
Jasmine oil

1. Take the velvet scarf or pouch and stuff it with the herbs. Add the vanilla bean pod and a drop of jasmine oil.

2. Tie the ends together and hold the pouch in both hands until your warmth and energy fully infuse the potpourri. Recite:

Venus guide my dreams tonight—Is he [she] the one?

3. Tuck your amulet into a pillowcase before bedtime. On waking, record the night's dream. You will receive your answer immediately.

Binding Love Potion

This spell will ensure a faithful relationship.

Supplies:

Magnolia buds gathered under a waxing moon
Honey

1. Sweeten the magnolia buds with honey and brew in a tea, sprinkle in a salad, or stir into a soup. Chant this simple spell as you stir:

Lover be faithful, lover be true.
Give thy heart to nobody but me.
This is my will.

2. Before you both consume, whisper this wish:

Honey magnolia, Goddess's herb,
Perform this enchantment superb,
Let [name] and I be as one.
With this, the spell is done.

3. Seal with a kiss between you and your lover. Then feed your lover and his or her loyalty will never sway.

Belles Lettres That Bind

Love letters are an ancient art that always deepens intimacy.

Supplies:

Special paper and ink
Perfume
Wax

1. Take a sheet of paper and write with a magickal colored ink, which you can either make yourself with berry juice or can buy at the nearest metaphysical five and dime. Perfume the letter with your signature scent or one your lover appreciates, like amber, vanilla, or ylang-ylang. Seal it with a wax you have also scented with a drop of essential oil and, of course, a kiss.

2. Before your love letter is delivered, light a candle anointed with your preferred scent and say:

Eros, speed my message on your wings of desire.
Make my lover burn with desire.

3. Make sure you send your letter RSVP.

Enchantment Ink

In the days of yore, people often made their inks, thus imbuing them with personal energy. When it comes to matters of the heart, an artfully made ink can help you write unforgettable letters of love.

Timing: This spell is best performed during the waning moon.

Supplies:

Vial
Dark red ink
Crushed berry juice
Drops of burgundy wine from the bottom of your lover's glass
Fruity essential oil (apple blossom, apricot, or peach are excellent chioces)
Paper

1. Fill the vial with the ink, juice, and wine and add one drop of essential oil.

2. Incant aloud:

By my hand, this spell I have wrought.
With this sacred ink, I will author my own destiny,
And have the happy love I sought.
Blessed be.

3. Now write that fate you envision for yourself and your love with enchanted ink. You can keep it on your love altar or burn in the flame of a candle while visualizing the future.

Gypsy Love Herbs

The folklore of the gypsies is replete with love magick, charms, and enchantments. The way to a person's heart can truly be a dish of delight, spiced up with magickal herbs.

Supplies:

Rye
Pimento

1. Many a gypsy woman has enjoyed the fruits of long-lasting love by reciting this charm while mixing a pinch of rye and pimento into almost every dish. While stirring in these amorous herbs, recite:

Rye of earth, pimento of fire,
Eaten surely fuels desire.
Served to he [she] whose love I crave
And his [her] heart I will enslave!

Conjuring Pleasure

Make a vow to bring forth all your erotic powers. You will radiate passion and be intensely drawn to your lover.

Timing: Perform this ritual at the next full moon.

Supplies:

Essential oils
Candles
Drink of your choice

1. Begin with a blissful bath in oil-scented water. Sit in a darkened room.

2. Raise a cup of jasmine tea, a glass of wine, or whatever your drink is and speak this spell aloud:

Now I awaken the Goddess in me.
I surrender to love's power.
Tonight I will heat the night with my fire.
As I drink this cup, my juices flower.
I am alive! I am love! And so it is.

Lover's Oil Rub

This ritual permeates your handmade massage oil with passion. Your intention and intuition add a lovely and loving magick to your time together.

Supplies:

Cup of almond or sesame oil
Musk, sandalwood, or orange-blossom oil

1. In the cup of almond or sesame oil, stir 20 drops of your chosen oil. Heat in a double boiler slowly on the stove very carefully.

2. While you are warming it, look into the candle or gas flame and whisper:

My lover's eyes are like the sun,
His [her] body like the land,
His [her] skin is soft as rain.
Tonight we are one.

3. When the oil is the perfect temperature to your touch, pour it into a bowl beside the bed. Tenderly undress your lover and gently lay him or her down on towels. Each caress will deepen his or her desire and raise his or her temperature. Tonight, two lovers will slide into ecstasy.

Tantric Trysting

Transform your bedroom into a bower of love and sacred sexuality with a few flowers and this body blessing. With thoughtful preparation, your night of lovemaking will be spellbinding.

Supplies:

Gardenia flowers

1. Fill your room with the gardenia flowers. Undress and light a single gardenia-scented candle at the head of the bed. Rub gardenia petals into your skin and say this love spell:

> ***From your feet to the holy lingam* [or *yoni*] *to the hair crowning you, I will worship you tonight. Lover and God* [or *Goddess*]*—I share my entire being in ecstasy.***

2. Wearing nothing but one of the priceless blossoms behind your left ear, greet your lover at the door. Sit him or her in the bower bed and worshipfully wash, dry, and anoint his or her feet. Lovemaking afterward will reach new heights of passion and spiritual intensity.

Aphrodite's Oil

For men, this oil stimulates desire and prowess. For women, it . . .

Supplies:

5 drops rosemary oil
5 drops patchouli
10 drops yohimbe extract
A pinch of powdered ginseng root and yohimbe*
2 tablespoons sesame oil

*For women substitute pinches of saffron and ground dong quai (also known as angelica root) for the ginseng root and yohimbe.

1. Mix these ingredients in a favorite bottle or jar, ideally red or pink.

2. Use the oil on your fingers to anoint candles or to massage your lover's body. Speak lovingly to the object of your affections while you rub the magick massage oil into his or her skin.

The Wisdom of the Wind

Helping a jilted friend get over a bad relationship is good medicine for all.

Supplies:

2 long-stemmed white roses
Aromatic lavender

1. Take the petals from one rose and mix them with a cup of lavender. Bless the concoction by saying:

Eastern wind, wise and free,
Help [name] to see,
A better love will come from thee.

2. Scatter the petals along your friend's path so he or she will step on the flowers and release their curative powers. Place the other long-stemmed rose at his or her door with a friendly note and invitation to visit. Their spirits will soar and you will be blessed with wonderful company.

Spell for Letting Go

Most of us have had problems giving up on a relationship. This ritual will help you let go.

Timing: Perform this ritual during the waning moon, when things can be put to rest.

Supplies:

Black string
A symbol of your ex
Scissors

1. Tie the black string around your waist and attach it to the symbol of your ex—a photo, a memento, or a lock of hair.

2. Bless the pair of scissors by saying:

Bygones be and lovers part,
I'm asking you to leave my heart.
Go in peace, harm to none.
My new life is begun.

3. Cut the string and toss away the memento. You will feel freer and lighter immediately and will begin to attract many new potential paramours.

New Beginnings

This spell can be used to meet someone new or to bring on a new phase in an existing relationship.

Timing: This spell is best performed on a Monday morning before dawn.

Supplies:

1 pink and 1 blue candle
Lily or jasmine oil
Cinnamon tea and cinnamon sticks

1. Anoint both candles with the essential oils

2. Light both and say:

Healing starts with new beginnings.
My heart is open, I'm ready now.
Goddess, you will show me how.

3. Drink a cup of cinnamon tea that you stirred counterclockwise with a cinnamon stick. Sprinkle cinnamon at your front door. When the cinnamon is crushed underfoot, its regenerative energy will help you start a fresh chapter in your love life.

Bedroom Feng Shui for the Romantigoth in You

Surely one of the main reasons for clearing space in your home and bedroom is to make room for a happy love life. Before you attempt to enhance your prospects of love and sex, you need to create a relationship corner (described in the following pages) and follow these simple steps of "sex shui":

1. Remove all pictures of yourself in which you are alone

2. Remove all empty cups, jars, vases, and bottles

3. Remove all photos of past partners or your favorite dead icons (they can go in the hallway)

4. Ensure there are even numbers of decorative objects such as candles, frames, tables, and so on

5. Feature special feng shui love symbols such as an open red fan, a pair of dove figurines, or two red hearts; a Victorian or pre-Raphaelite print will work quite well here, too

On your bed use rich, luxurious fabrics and colors; I have a sumptuous burgundy tapestry quilt sewn from handmade Indian saris as my bedspread. It should feel wonderful on the skin and be very inviting with comfy pillows, soft silks, and plush velvets.

Good in Bed—A Bed Blessing

Anoint your bed with this special charm.

Supplies:

Red cup or Goth goblet
Jasmine and rose oil

1. In your goblet, mix a half-teaspoon of jasmine oil and a half-teaspoon of rose oil. Hold it with both hands and speak:

In this bed, I show my love.
In this bed, I share my body.

In this bed, I give my heart.
In this bed, we are as one.
Here, my happiness lies as I give and live in total joy.
Blessed be to me and thee.

As you say "Blessed be," flick drops of your bed blessing oil from your fingers all across the bed until the cup is empty.

2. Now, lie down and roll around in the bed. After all, that is what it is for!

Kindling Sex Energy—Your Relationship Corner

As you walk into your bedroom, the relationship corner will be at the far right in the back right corner. Your love and sex energy has to be nurtured there, and you might well consider placing your altar there to serve as your personal wellspring of Eros.

1. Look at this area with a fresh eye—what is cluttering your love corner with "dead energy"? Half-empty perfume bottles or near-empty cosmetic bottles could be impairing your relationship energy. You must cleanse your space of unhappiness and clear the area of clutter by getting rid of all unnecessary objects and tidying up.

2. To further cleanse the area, ring a hand bell anywhere clutter has accumulated, giving special attention to your bed and pillows.

Dispelling Old Energy

Here is pagan feng shui for the bedroom that will prevent problems before they even happen! Fill your home with the energy of love and happiness with some of the simplest and most effective magick of all by creating sacred and safe space for yourself and your loved ones.

Never bring old pillows into a new home! Old pillows can cause poor sleep and bad dreams, and they can kill a relationship. Old pillows can carry old sexual energy, too.

Never place your bed in the center of a room, as it will cause anxiety and get in the way of a healthy sex life.

Never have the foot of the bed facing the door, as it brings very bad luck.

Always make the bed and change the linens often to keep your lovemaking fresh.

Place these objects in your bedroom to attract loving energy:

Two crystals of rose quartz of equivalent size

Pink, orange, or red fabric

Two red candles

Images of two butterflies (but never two dead butterflies)

New Moon Candle

If you are "lookin' for love" and feel like you need the physical release of sex, perform this spell and you will find a lover quickly.

Timing: This ritual should be performed on the new moon night.

Supplies:

2 pieces of rose quartz
2 red candles

1. Take the pieces of rose quartz and place them on the floor in the center of your bedroom. Light both red candles and use this affirming chant twice:

Beautiful crystal I hold this night,
Flame with love for my delight,
Goddess of Love I ask of you
Guide me in the path that is true.
Harm to none as love comes to me.
This I ask and so it shall be.

2. Now, make yourself ready!

Lust Dust

Nowadays, you can buy body glitter almost anywhere. I've noticed that we witchy types were way ahead on the glitter curve. Whether it is baby powder, a body glitter, or the edible Honey Dust sold by the inimitable Kama Sutra body product company, start with a powder that feels comfortable on your body.

Supplies:

Your chosen powder
1 drop of amber oil
1 drop of vanilla oil
1 teaspoon lotus root powder
¼ teaspoon of cinnamon

1. Add the ingredients to your powder. Stir or shake and let it dry out before stirring again.

2. Stand naked and gently rub the powder all over your body while you whisper this charm:

I feel the warmth of your hands,
I feel the hardness of your body against mine,
I feel your tongue.
I am yours for your pleasure.
You are mine for my pleasure.
This dust, our lust,
Together, we must!

All day or night, your skin will feel tingly and ever so slightly warm. Notice the interested glances wherever you go. Soon, your body will be a map for exploration.

Breast Blessing

Celebrate the beauty of your body. Your breasts (and probably all the rest of you) will receive much attention during your lovemaking, so loving attention from you beforehand will consecrate the temple of your body.

Supplies:

1 cup natural beeswax
¼ cup sesame oil
Sandalwood, lemon, and rose oil

1. Take the cup of beeswax, chip it into a double boiler, and heat very slowly and gently. Add the sesame oil and stir with a wooden spoon until the wax has melted and blended with the oil.

2. Let it cool to skin temperature and add:

8 drops sandalwood oil
5 drops lemon oil
2 drops rose oil

3. Anoint yourself with the oil by dabbing a bit on your fingertip and then placing it on each nipple, circling clockwise outward until the entire breast is blessed. This should be done slowly, gently, and lovingly as you cup each breast and speak aloud:

We all come from the Goddess.
I am she and she is me.
My breasts are holy and wholly beautiful.
I love myself, I love my body, and I love my breasts.
I am consecrated.
Lover, come to me now.

Festive Friday Frolic

Venus rules this most popular day of the week. Small wonder this is the night for a tryst. To prepare yourself for a night of lovemaking, you should take a goddess bath with the following potion in a special cup or bowl. I call mine the Venus Vial.

Timing: Perform this rite on a Friday night.

Supplies:

1 cup sesame oil
6 drops orange blossom oil
4 drops gardenia oil
Bowl

1. Combine ingredients into the bowl and stir with your finger six times, silently repeating three times:

I am a daughter of Venus, I embody love.
My body is a temple of pleasure, and I am all that is beautiful.
Tonight, I will drink fully from the cup of love.

2. Pour the Venusian mixture into a steaming bath and meditate on your evening plans. As you rise from your bath, repeat the Venus prayer once more.

3. Allow your skin to dry naturally. Your lover will compliment the softness of your skin, and indeed, you will be at your sexiest. The rest is up to you.

Make-Out Magic

Ah—the big date you've been looking forward to all week. And you, clever one, planned it on a new moon night. If this new moon happens to be in the sign of Taurus, Scorpio, Libra, or Pisces, you are *really* in for a treat tonight! Here is a last-minute preparation that guarantees you will have the time of your life.

Timing: This ritual is best performed on the new moon night.
Supplies:

2 red candles
Your favorite essential oil (mine is vamber, an equal parts vanilla and amber concoction that makes me feel instantly erotic)
Thorn of a rose

1. Take the two red candles and anoint them with your essential oil. Take the thorn and scratch your name in one candle and your lover's name in the other.

2. Anoint yourself between your breasts and over your heart, and then speak aloud twice:

Tonight, under this moon's light,
We will fall under each other's spell.
Tonight, under these stars so bright,
We will ignite a fire and never quell.
With these lips, this mouth, and my art
I will explore the sacred mysteries
Of the human heart.

3. When your object of desire arrives, you should both get comfortable. At an opportune moment, ask your lover to light the two candles. Take his or her hand and place it over your heart, lean forward, and very gently kiss him or her. For this magick to blossom into full power, you should remain standing and only kiss, slowly and gently but with increasing intensity, for at least 30 minutes. The art of kissing begins with lips only, gently tickling, licking, and nibbling on your partner's lips before moving onto the fabulous French kiss.

Fanning the Flames

Have you exchanged meaningful eye contact with an appealing stranger at a coffee shop? Seen an artistic-looking individual at a gallery opening? Felt that tug in your tummy, the lingering heat of his or her gaze?

Here is what you can do about it—simple and powerful love magick to ensure you will "merry meet again!"

Supernatural Soul Mates

This conjuration utilizes the secret language of flowers to bring your ideal love into your life. With visualization and daily spell work, you can create the love of a lifetime, custom fit to your specifications.

Supplies:

Candles shaped like human figures, or two pink candles
Rosemary and rose oil
2 fresh roses

1. Any witchy five and dime will have candles shaped like human figures that are usually red in color. Get a man and a woman (or whatever configuration suits your need) and place them on your altar. If you can't find these waxen figures, take two pink candles and place them in a bowl of rosemary and rose oil. Also take the two fresh roses of your favorite color and place them in a vase on your altar.

2. Rub rosemary essential oil on each candle and do the same with rose oil. Rosemary is for remembrance, and rose is for sweetness and affection. Now light the candles and whisper:

Brother mine, brother fair **[substitute *sister* if that fits the scenario],**
New friend of my heart,
Merry may we meet and merry may we greet again.
I draw you with my art.
One rose for you, one rose for me.
And so it shall be.

3. Each night when you go to sleep, you should visualize your next meeting and what you will say. Each morning, you should wear one of the roses in the buttonhole of your jacket. Sooner than you think, the mysterious stranger will reappear. Mother Nature, one of the guises of the Goddess, will take her course.

Two Hearts Beat as One

To transform the object of your desire into your partner in passion, try this powerful attraction spell.

Supplies:

Plain muslin cloth
Dried sage
1 seven-day pink candle
Red thread and needle or stapler

1. Take the plain muslin and cut it into two heart shapes. Sew (or staple if you are in a hurry) the two hearts together and leave a hole so you can stuff it with dried sage. Then sew it shut and either write or, if you are really crafty, embroider the name of the object of your affections onto the muslin heart. Put it on your altar.

2. Each night at midnight, the witching hour, light the pink candle for thirty minutes beside the heart sachet and say aloud three times:

To ___ I offer affection.
To ___ I offer attention.
To ___ I offer joy.
And in return, I shall have the same.
So mote it be.

Now, your crush will return your attention and be ready to return your affection.

Tantric Tryst

To strengthen the closeness between you and your lover, plan a special evening on the next full moon. This Eastern wisdom mix may well have been used by Cleopatra when she and Mark Anthony made mad love on the banks of the Nile.

Timing: Perform this rite on the full moon.
Supplies:

1 part amber
1 part sandalwood
1 part frankincense
Gardenia oil

1. Mix the amber, sandalwood, and frankincense, and then add four generous drops of gardenia and grind the mixture together.

2. You should remove your lover's clothes and walk around him or her holding the smoking incense bowl to bless his or her physical body. Then, he or she should remove your clothes and circle you, in your full glory, with the incense.

3. Now, speak the following Full Moon Blessing together. Or you can do it before your lover arrives, if you prefer, but the spell is more powerful with both of your intentions intertwined.

With every word, I draw you closer to me.
With every breath, I do you embrace.
Tonight we bind our hearts.
Tonight we twine our bodies.
So mote it be.

4. Place the incense beside your bed and sit facing each other, eyes open. With the lightest possible touch, brush your finger on his or her skin, starting with the face and working your way down. Go *very slowly*. It should take at least a half-hour each for this Tantric Touch spell. Then, you should please each other manually while still looking in each other's eyes. At this point, anything can happen—and should!

Seduction Spell

For heightened and sustained erotic pleasure, try this sacred spell.

Supplies:

2 goblets
1 red and 1 white rose ("fire and ice")
Nutmeg
Fine red wine
1 yard of red thread
Red ink and a slip of paper
Rose oil
Bowl of strawberries

1. Sprinkle a dash of nutmeg in each goblet. Uncork a bottle of fine red wine for later, allowing it to breathe.

2. With red ink and a slip of paper, write your lover's name on the paper and what your hopes and intentions are for the night. For example, it could be: "Robert—my gift for you, a full massage and two orgasms." Let your imagination run wild here.

3. Take the red thread and tie five knots, reciting this as you tie each:

With a knot of one, this spell is begun.
Knot number two, for me and for you.
Knot number three, you come to me.
Knot number four, you knock on my door.
Knot number five, our passion comes alive.

4. Anoint the red thread with one drop of the red wine and one drop of rose oil. Tie the red thread around your waist and place the parchment under your bed.

5. Welcome your lover at the door with the roses, a glass of wine, and a bowl of strawberries wearing only the red thread. Wear the magick cord until it falls off, usually after 30 days. This is a very intense sexual spell, so be prepared to spend a *lot* of time in bed.

Yohimbe Root Tea

Centuries before there was Viagra, there was yohimbe root, now commonly sold in health food stores. Yohimbe is a very potent, natural way to maximize any man's vigor before a special night.

Supplies:

1 part sandalwood
1 part myrrh
1 part yohimbe root
3 drops tuberose oil
Yohimbe root tea

1. Make an incense by grinding together the ingredients.

2. Light the incense and burn it while brewing your yohimbe root tea. Speak the following aloud:

Lover of my heart,
My passion I impart.
Lover of my flesh,
My passion is fresh.
Lover of my mind,
Your passion to me binds.

Leaves of Lovemaking

After drinking your yohimbe root tea, let the leaves guide you to your lover's lair. The answer to *where* you should make love lies at the bottom of the cup.

1. As you study the leaves, keep in mind that the tea cup handle is south, and going clockwise around the circle, left is west, the top is north, and the east is right of the handle.

North, you should make love outside
West, you should go to your bedroom
South is in the kitchen or living room
East is at your lover's house.

Passion Plays

This section of spell work relates to the arts of love, starting with the first kiss. Make that kiss unforgettable! Tattoo your touch onto your lover's skin! Leave more than an impression and, most important, merge into a oneness that is truest enchantment.

Anointed Lips—The Vampire's Kiss

From time immemorial, witches have enchanted everyone with their magickal beauty. That's because we know how to supplement Mother Nature's gifts. Before a special evening, I usually employ a "glamour gloss" of my own design, so that each kiss is a passion spark.

Supplies:

Lip gloss
Oil of clove

1. Take your favorite pot of lip gloss and add one drop of oil of clove and stir counterclockwise, saying aloud three times:

The ripest fruit, the perfect petal,
My lips are the honey in the flower.
Each kiss a spell of utmost bliss.
So mote it be.

This will make your lips tingle and give your kisses "spice." The lucky recipient of your kisses will be spellbound.

Kama Sutra Kiss

"Whatever thing may be done by one of the lovers to the other, the same should be returned by the other." (Chapter 3, the Kama Sutra*).*

The kiss is the gateway to bliss and amorous experience. The kiss provokes erotic ardor, excites the heart, and is an incitation to the natural gift of yourself that you share with your beloved. After you have performed the Anointed Lips spell, think of your kiss as an offering of enchantment.

Goth Is in the Details

The following is a list of actual Kama Sutra kisses:

Bent kiss—the classic movie kiss where lovers lean into each other in this classic movie-style kiss

Throbbing kiss—the woman touches her lover's mouth with her lower lip

Touching kiss—the woman touches her lover's lips with her tongue and eyes and places her hands on her lover's hands

Turned kiss—one kisser turns up the face of the other by holding the head and chin and then kissing

Pressed kiss—the one lover from below or underneath presses the lower lip of the lover from above with both lips

Greatly pressed kiss—taking the lip between two fingers, touching the lip with the tongue, and then applying great pressure with the lips upon lips in the kiss.

Love Potion No. 69

This witch's brew is intended to enhance the act of its namesake. Upon imbibing the drink and indulging in erotic exploits, mutual orgasms are guaranteed.

Supplies:

1/3 cup dried vervain
9 dried apricots
Honey
Brandy
Glass decanter

1. Using a mortar and pestle, grind to a powder the dried vervain (hemp can also be substituted here if you are so inclined).

2. Dip 9 dried apricots in honey and then roll them in the powder you've just made. Steep the apricots in 1 cup of your best brandy and store in a tightly sealed glass decanter.

3. Store the liquor in a cool, dark place for one complete cycle of the moon. Whenever you have an erotic thought, go shake the potion, while fantasizing about mind-blowing sex. Consult your moon calendar and wait until the moon is in Cancer, Pisces, or Scorpio before straining and serving. Drink and total bliss is yours for the asking.

The Art of Mystical Massage

Set the stage for hands-on pleasure before you knead your lover's body into ecstasy. Start with your favorite music. I prefer Indian ragas because they seem to have a naturally sexual rhythm. Whether it is classic guitar, angelic harps, or an ambient electronic band from Iceland, it should relax and bring pleasure. Light pink, red, and brown candles to create a loving, sexual atmosphere that is strongly grounded. Light incense your lover has complimented before and lay out towels you have warmed and oils and lubricants you have also warmed. Turn up the heat a bit and turn down the lights, simply to create a "spa" feeling for utter unwinding. I have some goose feathers, honey, and edible raspberry-and-mint rub I like to share as well.

Serve an herbal tea. I recommend clary sage, eucalyptus, or lavender, but feel free to choose your personal favorite. Clean cotton sheets that have been warmed are a nice touch, and soft, fake fur is irresistible.

1. First undress your partner, very slowly and gently.

2. If your partner is open-minded to pagan ways, you should speak this incantation in his or her presence. If not, it is your silent prayer:

I call on you, Pan,
God of the woods, goat, man, and boy.
I ask your blessing on this day of joy.
I call on you, Venus, Goddess of this night,
May we find new seasons of delight.
What I want is here and now.
And so it shall be.

3. Start with the warmed oil and give a classic massage while your partner relaxes facedown on the bed or massage table. The basic principles of magickal massage are rhythmic yet sensitive gliding strokes, gradually going to deeper strokes. Use your body weight for firmer pressure.

4. After relaxing your partner's back, legs, and feet, have him or her turn over. Massage the chest, arms, and hands. Then glide down to the legs, occasionally brushing the genitals with a light touch. After you finish the legs and feet, slide back up the body and very delicately brush the genitals in a teasing way. Draw the tease out as long as you can so the energy builds and grows. Now is the time to start shifting the focus to more explicitly erotic activities.

5. One of the most important tips for an amazing connection: look your partner in the eye as you pleasure him or her. Locking the eyes and keeping them open during sex opens new dimensions of gratification.

Goth Is in the Details

Oral Fixation

Food can be foreplay! A wonderful prelude to a night of lovemaking can be feeding each other and, of course, a little whipped cream and chocolate placed strategically is a delicious lover's treat. The following is a list of amazing aphrodisiacs that will ensure pleasure, arousal, and help you explore the erotic possibilities of your witch's pantry fully:

Almonds or erotically shaped marzipan

Arugula is also called "rocket seed"—need I say more?

Avocado was referred to by the ancient Aztecs as the "testicle tree"

Both bananas and the banana flowers have phallic shapes

Chocolate is quite rightly called "the food of the gods"

Coffee is stimulating in more than one way

Garlic is the heat to light the flame of desire

Figs are another symbol of ultimate femininity—just eating one is a turn on

Honey—the term *honeymoon* came from a bee-sweetened drink served to newlyweds

Nutmeg is the traditional aphrodisiac for Chinese women; eat enough and you will hallucinate

Oysters were prized by Romans for their effect and their resemblance to a woman's genitals

Strawberries—well, why do you think erotic literature so often compares them to nipples?

Vanilla is captivating for both the scent and flavor

Wine, drunk from each other's mouths, is unspeakably erotic

A Price Above Rubies

If you are like me, you can't exactly afford to buy a ruby on impulse. But I have been gladdened lately by the appearance of $3 "rough rubies" at PlanetWeavers, a store at Haight and Ashbury in San Francisco.

If one isn't near you, you can shop online at Mystic Traders or Pacific Spirit, who have wonderful imported stones from all over the world.

Rubies are stones of great passion. Here is a simple way to light a fire by day that will catch flame with your lover by night.

1. Hold your ruby in your left hand over your heart and speak aloud three times:

I can feel the heat of your skin
And your mouth.
I can taste the kisses sweet.
Your hands on me,
My hands on you,
Oh, lover, hear my song.
Tonight, we will be as one,
All night long.

2. Now carry your heart-warmed, red ruby in your pocket all day long. Don't forget to give your lover a call and invite him or her over for a long and lovely night.

Elixirs are very simple potions made by placing a crystal or gemstone in a glass of water for at least seven hours. Remove the stone and drink the "crystallized water." The water will now carry the vibrational energy of the stone, the very essence of the crystal. This is one of the easiest ways to "take in" crystal healing, and it is immediate. The red stones always hold the "lust for life," so to push the envelope, put as many red stones into your elixir as you can get your hands on.

Supplies:

Red stones and crystals such as Carnelian, garnet, rough ruby, red coral, red jade, red jasper, red sardonyx, cuprite, aventurine, or red calcite
Jar or glass of water

Amber incense
Red candle

Mix and match the red stones and remember, if you only have access to a rough ruby and a tiny chunk of red jasper, so be it—that is still a lot of love in a jar!

1. Place the stones and/or crystals into the jar of water.

2. Place the Ecstatic Elixir in the love corner of your room or on your altar. Light the amber incense and red candle and speak aloud:

This jade is my joy, the garnet my grace.

3. Leave the water on your altar for seven hours or overnight and drink it upon awakening. Your life energy will quicken and you should feel very upbeat and "good to go."

Orgasmic Oil

I use this potion for a combination body care oil, massage oil, and lubricant. This is a tip I picked up from a "professional" who shared her confidential formula with me and added, "All my clients marvel at how soft and yummy my skin is." I have acquired several trade secrets from her that I have used to great effect. A total goddess, she also has her clients and lovers worship at her sex altar before they make love. I have to note that she has many repeat customers.

Supplies:

1 cup of sesame oil (you can cheat and get the sesame-scented oil from the pharmacy or grocery store, which works just as well in a pinch)
Clove, cinnamon, and ginger
Bergamot, amber, and jasmine oil
Amber-colored jar
Magnetite

1. Take the sesame oil and add a pinch each of all the spices. Then add a drop of citrusy bergamot and a teaspoon each of the amber and jasmine oil.

2. Stir gently and then place in an amber-colored jar with a stopper. Place the jar beside a piece of magnetite, or lodestone, which draws people to you. Let it sit for a full week, and then use it to bring yourself and your lover to orgasm—again and again.

Note: This is not for safe sex, if you are using a latex condom.

CHAPTER NINE

Modern Primitives and Hipster Heathens

In the late 1970s, people on the fringe of culture recognized each other by their markings—piercings, scarification, and a certain glint in the eye. They were the "modern primitives" who employed a strange juxtaposition of high technology and "low" tribalism, animism, and body modification. Goths, many of whom are Rivetheads, decorating themselves with metal in many places on their body, represent an aspect of modern primitivism. It is not just a personal aesthetic, either; it is a way of letting the world know your spiritual stance.

The modern primitives like Stelarc and Fakir Mustafar are perhaps best known for their use of body distortion, modification (elongation, coloration, and so on), and piercing. Many moderns were familiar (from visual anthropology) with the practices found in "less civilized" cultures such as foot binding, elongating the neck or skull, or ritual incision. Body manipulation is not anything alien to modernity, with its use of more antiseptic and clinical plastic surgery, but then neither is tattooing or piercing either. Moderns never gave up the urge to inscribe and mark the body or to alter and distort its features. Indeed, a preeminent feature of modernity was the pursuit of unattainable somatic norms, especially for women. Still, many people see body marking (tattooing) as transgressive, exotic, and "primitive," and this is one reason why modern primitives embrace it as a custom.

What does make the modern primitive movement unusual is its pursuit of sensation. Borrowing from the S&M sexual subculture, the modern primitives suggest that one of the effects of modernization and industrialization has been psychic numbing. People no longer know either authentic pleasure or pain and have forgotten the curious neurochemical ways in which they are interwoven. Piercing is more than just inscription; piercing is pain, especially during sexual intercourse, but it is a pain that becomes part of the ecstasy for modern primitives. There is this idea of a knowing *through* pain that modernity has forgotten.

When they pierce themselves with sharp painful implements, they are duplicating a practice found all over the world. It is a key ritual for many "primitive" and other societies for the person to go into trance and to demonstrate his or her "absorption" by the divine through the negation of pain and injury. The moden primitives claim that their performances are a pursuit of transcendence, proving the ability of the mind to go beyond the taxings and limitations of the body. Hipster heathens also embrace dance gatherings such as raves as a sign of the uniting of past and future. The rave is at once primitive and modern, with its gathering of "tribes." Besides raves and piercing, modern primitives are perhaps best known for their attempts at juxtaposing magick and science by combining Crowleyan occultism with chaos theory, neopaganism and Wicca with mimetics and information theory, and use of ancient hallucinogens with the latest findings in neuroscience. Shamanism is shown to have a basis in quantum mechanics, and Hermeticism in astrophysical cosmology. This new blend of the ancient and the modern is a sort of "roll your own religion," if you will. Now, a rave with thousands of people throbbing together on a beach can be a spirit-opening ritual, while a tattoo of your personal deity makes your body a temple.

Tattoos

One ancient practice that is very much alive today is the art of tattooing. Up until the early 1980s, only "freaky people" had tattoos. That, of course, included advanced Goths, rockers, Hell's Angels, hippies, sailors, and ex-cons. Outside of North America, tribal tattooing had never ceased. Nowadays, tattoo aficionados are aplenty. Tattoos have had spiritual significance since the first Stone Age man scarred himself with ink from Paleolithic plants. Maori warded off supernatural enemies with their singularly blue tattoos and certain Native American tribes of North America applied tattoos to guard against premature death.

What Is Tattooing?

In short, it is a process that originated in Paleolithic times of scarring or ingraining a permanent pigment onto the skin. The great historian Herodotus wrote that Greeks had their backs tattooed with Scythian symbology, floral patterns, and images of animals, with some chieftains going so far as to have their entire bodies covered with animal tattoos to connote courage and cunning. Similarly, Thracian nobility was fond of tattoos representing motifs important to their culture. The Egyptians, always at the vanguard of any art, used skin art as a way to designate the class and station of their architects, who bore triangles, and the priesthood, who were tattooed on their backs with special symbols. Throughout history, military personnel have worn tattoos as badges of honor. Only a few armies required ink, including the Moroccans and Adolf Hitler's SS, who sported tattoos for both soldiers and prisoners.

Henna

Henna is an herbaceous shrub that prefers dry and very warm climates and has been used over 7,000 years by people in various parts of the world as both a medicine and a decorative dye for body art. Used medicinally, Henna helps reduce fever and swelling and can help with skin and intestinal issues. In India, it is called "mehndi" and it specifically refers to the henna tattoos that last a few weeks. Even though it is perhaps most popular in India, the use of henna as body art was first recorded at Çatalhüyük (in modern-day Turkey) and was used in Africa long before it reached India. Once it arrived on the shores of the subcontinent, however, it reached record popularity and was applied in rituals and ceremonies, such as a preparation and a signifier of a special event—weddings, especially. The Berber peoples of North Africa have used it for centuries, and it has become favored by Europeans and Americans in the last ten years.

If you are interested in trying this kind of body art, go to a skilled mehndi artist, usually found near a college or university or the nearest "India Town" in your area. Mehndi is more that just a fashion, it is a spiritual endeavor. A true henna artist is a "negasseh" and he or she goes into a trance state before illustrating your skin with the henna paint. The purpose of the trance is to connect with the spirit world and also to see which spirit and gods and goddesses are right for you—they act as the guides for your ritual tattoo choice. Combining the heart symbol and hexagram would be a powerful love mandala.

Patterns of Personal Meaning

It takes a commitment to endure hours of intricate henna drawing or needles injecting ink into your skin. The wisest choice would clearly be a visual symbol that you not only like but truly *love*, such as your favorite deity, an imago of the sacred imbued with meaning. Even better, an imago or symbol expressing your spiritual belief. The word *sigil* means "a seal" or "device," but the word usually denotes a magickal sigil, a glyph used in ritual or sympathetic magick as a focus.

Signs and Sigils

The heart is a universal symbol of love. This sweet design would make an excellent blessing to a romantic relationship or as a gift to loved ones.

Triangles with the base at the top represent the Christian Holy Trinity and also Egyptian spirituality and wisdom. A pyramid power mandala could be created with the base at the bottom. The downward-pointing triangle represents the "yoni yantra" and signifies the female, water, and the ability to create. A mandala blessing for an expectant mother should include the downward-pointing triangle. Water signs Cancer, Scorpio, and Pisces would do well to honor themselves with this design. Double triangles in Tantrism mean all of creation, the conjunction of male and female energies, and infinity. A relationship mandala, especially in the sensual realm, will work well with double triangles. If you want to connect to the great universe, the symbol of infinity is essential. This symbol is the best for creativity mandalas.

A hexagram or Star of David (interestingly, the symbol of the nation of Israel), is a recent phenomena of the last hundred years. In India, it indicates Kali in union with Shiva and it is also the symbol for the heart chakra. If you want to create a mandala for blessing a relationship or to open your heart, the hexagram is an excellent choice. Combining the heart symbol and hexagram would be a powerful love mandala.

Earrings and Other Piercing Possibilities

Earrings were once worn to guard ears from potential disease and from hearing bad news. Earrings were also once believed to strengthen weak eyes, especially if set with emeralds. Earrings help to balance both hemispheres of the brain and also are a stabilizing factor to the throat chakra. The earlobes are a sensory center on the body and usually benefit from the stimulation of a gem or crystal. Jade and tiger's eye are great for reviving and refreshing. You generally will feel quite good with these two earring choices! Sapphires will bring you greater wisdom. However, lapis lazuli and opal can be overstimulating as earrings, so watch this carefully and see how your body reacts to them. Some people feel lightheaded with these two stones placed so high on the body. Malachite can be too spiritually stimulating as earrings, so don't wear them unless you want to be in a soulful or dreamy reverie. Garnet earrings will enhance your popularity. Rose quartz is wonderful for the skin and can even slow aging!

A Chakra Jewelry Placement Guide

The concept of chakras originated many thousands of years ago in Asia. The ancient philosophers and metaphysicians identified seven main energy centers in the body with each chakra seen as a color of the rainbow emanating energy that affects the mental, physical, and spiritual balance of every person. Chakra theory is at the basis of many Eastern healing practices. One of the simplest ways to achieve well-being is to place a crystal on the part of the body where certain chakras are centered. Many people I know credit their clarity and health to chakra therapy. One sure way to relieve stress and enhance the emotional body is the chakric application of crystals. A Goth princess pal of mine placed an amber stone in her navel when she was starting a business and her personal power and drive soared. These things do work! In your case, you might choose a ring for your left nipple with a lovely peridot bead to open your heart and bring both love and serenity. Now it does not get better than that, does it?

Chakra Chart

Chakra	*Color*	*Energies*	*Corresponding Crystals*
7th Chakra, Crown	Violet	Holy bliss; all is one	Diamond, amethyst
6th Chakra, Third eye	Indigo	Perception, intuitiveness	Lapis lazuli, fluorite
5th Chakra, Throat	Blue	Creativity, originality	Blue quartz, tiger's eye

4th Chakra, Heart	Green	Love, abundance, serenity	Peridot, rose quartz
3rd Chakra, Solar plexus	Yellow	Personal power, drive	Topaz, citrine, amber
2nd Chakra, Sacral	Orange	Pleasure center	Carnelian, amber
1st Chakra, Root	Red	Survival, security	Smoky quartz, garnet

Blotting—Modern Pagans and Animal Sacrifice

"Blot," which translates "to strengthen the gods," is the old Norse word meaning "sacrifice" and has become the term today for a ritual of offering to the gods, inferring that this also strengthens the worshipper and the community at large. These sacrifices are really a path of self-empowerment and a method of garnering great favor and intimacy with the gods. Quite simply, sacrificing the animals for blood is a way of offering a drink to the gods in the form of the animal's blood, often followed by a communal cooking and feasting on the flesh of the beast. While animal sacrifice sounds to many twenty-first century folk as outlandish as Old Testament or Bronze Age practices, it has remained a mainstay among the Scandinavian Asatru and vampire set, as well as among those who proudly call themselves "heathens." You may wish to substitute mead and red wine in making offerings to the God and Goddess. For others, providing cooked food is a favored offering.

Why make a sacrifice? The reasons have not changed at all through the centuries: we make sacrifices out of devotion to the gods and to show our gratitude for the beneficence of the gods. We also make sacrifice out of need. A modern way to "go to battle" is when you know you have a difficult or possibly contentiuns meeting ahead of you. If so, it would behoove you to make a sacrifice to the gods who can sway things to act in your favor. You can do "vegan sacrifice" with wine, beer, foodstuffs, and ritual implements and candles, or you can perform your show of respect in the traditional Viking style of veneration by killing an animal. It is worth noting, however, that many modern heathens and pagan farmers point out that beasts selected for sacrifice are treated in the best possible way, usually living lives where they are given the greatest care. In these cases, an animal's death in a sacred ritual is much more quick and humane than the typical treatment in a commercialized slaughter house. It is almost always part of the ritual to roast and eat the animal's flesh and share it in communal feast with great gratitude for the giving of the gift to the gods and the receiving of the animal's sacrifice to the greater good. It is important to remember to not offer the gods the sacrificed meat—the animal's sacrificing of life is the gift. While the number of modern Asatru who perform this ancient method of blot as real blood sacrifice is small, it has grown in just the last few years. Blotting today usually consists of pouring offerings of grog, beer, wine, and honeyed mead or a home-brewed pagan potion—a goodly amount of alcohol will turn anyone into a proper heathen!

Chapter Ten

Goth Astrology

Goth astrology is the same set of stars set in a much darker sky. Actually, the planets are all identical as are the birth dates and signs, but, as a practicing astrologer, I noticed in Gothdom that each placement in the zodiac has a slightly different permutation. It is the same astrological worldview through the slightly skewed lens of Goth magick. Do bear in mind that the exact days each sign begins and ends varies slightly. To be sure, I recommend www.astro.com. This astrological Web site features some of the best astrologers alive today: Liz Greene and Robert Hand, to name but a few. Best of all, you can check your planetary transits each day and get a two-year forecast free of charge.

Aries—March 21–April 19

The cardinal fire sign, and first of the twelve signs of the zodiac, the Gothic Aries's idea of a good time usually involves a bonfire. Characterized by strong will, the Aries Ram drives forward without looking from side to side. Flaming red streaks are the Gothic Aries's trademark hair color and bright red lips complete the look. Whether or not this is your sun sign, you can honor your inner Gothic fire with the color red and the driving force that can get you into wicked trouble!

Gothic Roles

Flamethrower
Fire dancer

Taurus—April 20–May 20

The fixed earth sign of Taurus, represented as the mighty Bull, will not tolerate lies, dishonor, or false pledges. Characterized as the wielding earth goddess of all dark forces, the healing Taurus will be seen gathering wild herbs to brew a wicked tea; so it is best to be on her good side. Lovely in dark greens and maroons, the Gothic Taurus can honor her earth sign with vibrant green hair and pointy-toed shoes.

Gothic Roles

Wiccan witch
Gothic gardener

Gemini—May 21–June 20

The Twins is an air sign to outwit all air signs. Gothic Gemini is the ever present ghost in the graveyard that you never actually see. Prone to outbursts of brilliant mania and stifling repression, the intuitive and poetic Gemini will out prose any one. With a mastery of the elusive haunting existence of a true Goth, the Gemini is capable of explaining the alternative to the most mainstream of mortals. Manifest your Gothic Gemini by wearing tons of silver jewelry and investing in a lot of electronic devices, almost like you have antennas!

Gothic Roles

Gothic educator/advocate
Troubled poet

Cancer—June 21–July 22

Moody Cancer, ruled by the beloved moon, is the Gothic type from birth. Morose to perfection, the Gothic Cancer will be spotted roaming among the granite angels and headstones throughout the day and weeping on her meticulously upholstered velveteen fainting couch at night. Flowing black robes look smashing, with a cobalt blue streak for accent in the hair. She wears her heart on her black lace–covered sleeve. Manifest your inner Cancer by dancing under the full moon light, in the safety of your benevolent rule.

Gothic Roles

Martyr
Gothic interior decorator

Leo—July 23–August 22

A fire sign known by the symbol of a Lion, the Gothic Leo will be seen sporting long black tresses and form-fitting pants, best for strutting in. Inspiring, and huge of heart, the Gothic Leo will make you want to paint, sing, and dance out your inner angst. The life of the darkest party, the Gothic Leo will express effortlessly what others have been writhing to know. Tap your inner Gothic Lion by dawning a necklace that looks like medieval armor and a bracelet that shines with metal studs.

Gothic Roles

Goth rock star
Actress

Virgo—August 23–September 22

Beloved Virgo, the Virginal Goth, is apt to stroll nonchalantly around in a multilock chastity belt, reading volumes of poetry by Sylvia Plath, all the while analyzing the other Goths in the room, just for fun. An earth sign, the ability to rationalize is the gift of the Virgo Goth; she will never question the need for the dark side to come shining through the cobwebs, though she may have to clean the cobwebs anyway. Although she is fond of earth tones, the Gothic Virgo looks smashing in the Catholic school girl motif. Bring out your Virgo Goth side with some knee-high socks and dangling crosses.

Gothic Role

Writer
Psychiatrist

Libra—September 23–October 22

Represented by the Scales, Libras are known for a desire to create harmony and balance. Gothic Libras love to find that balance between the macabre and the everyday, the dark and the light. The Gothic Libra calmly declares her love of the morbid with a giant winged skeleton sitting on her desk at the office, and a penchant for old horror movies. Ruled by Venus, goddess of love, Libras are also romantic souls, so they love to indulge in Victorian mourning wear and velvet drapery. Balance your own inner Gothic Libra with a sweeping hair style, baroque jewelry, and an old Bela Lugosi movie before performing a love spell or two.

Gothic Roles

Diplomat
Archivist

Scorpio—October 23–November 21

The quintessential Goth, Scorpios are fixed water signs that are represented by the vicious Scorpion, whose sting is defensive and deadly. The Gothic Scorpio will be seen wearing all black, all the time, with the deepest, darkest dyed-black hair and black nails. Her favorite outfit is usually made of vinyl and involves a corset. Secretive, mysterious, and alluring, the Scorpio Goth will be found at night, prowling the streets for Gothic companions. Engage your innermost Scorpio self with a solo spiritual journey to a place that scares you. Face your demons, return to society, and then give yourself over to love as only you can.

Gothic Roles

Sultry temptress
Vampire

Sagittarius—November 22–December 21

Brazen, forward thinking, and fiery, Sagittarius is characterized by a half-man/half-beast character, shooting its arrow into the sky. Never one to look back and linger for too long, Sagittarius moves forward with a definitive swiftness that can sometimes go unnoticed. This is the person who is granted permission to come to the front of the line, yet never brags about his or her privilege. Quick witted and self-assured, the Gothic Sagittarius likes the simpler Goth outfits, preferring multiple zippers to straps and hooks. Sagittarius wants clothes to come on and off with ease, and looks best in all shades of black. A little orange or red to the outfit and your sweetest inner Sagittarius can be expressed.

GOTHIC ROLES

Club owner
Executive

Capricorn—December 22–January 20

Characterized by the Goat, the Capricorn is naturally Gothic, with a sharp disposition ready to cause mischief backed up with a fantastically artistic side. Morose when her way is not rolled out red-velvet style, this Goth Diva is one of the few Goth signs that can pull off the color gold. Earthy and full of drive, your inner Goth Capricorn can be tapped by donning a flowing, gold lame scarf over your vinyl ball gown and giving orders to everyone in your entourage.

GOTH ROLES

Diva
Dominatrix

Aquarius—January 21–February 19

Ah, sweet Aquarius, death's personal dreamer and musical genius. The Gothic Aquarian not only has your number, she accurately dreamed it three days before you ever met her. A musical goddess and esoteric junky, the Aquarian Goth girl dresses like a witch and acts like an angel. Scatterbrained when it comes to details, the Goth Aquarian is best left alone to dream as often as possible. Pick up the latest edition of Crowley's *The Book of the Law* and snuggle into a bed of finely spun silken sheets, preferably the color of night.

Gothic Roles

Composer
Guru

Pisces—February 20–March 20

These silver Fish are the Gothic girl's best friend; they are psychic, sensitive, and love twirling parasols to keep their Gothic beauty preserved. Simple in their elegance, yet complex in their tastes, these mellow Fish will transform into vampires and circus performers at night, only to melt into silver shimmering mermaids when the light of day hits their fins. Almost any Gothic outfit is suited to Pisces Goths—they are mutable, very chameleon-like, and excel at whatever they need be for the moment; however gorgeously scented candles and a few CDs of haunting and spiritual music that really move you are essential to set the mood for meditation and contemplation of the meaning of it all.

Gothic Roles

Creative director
Tightrope walker

Sex by the Stars, the Sun, and the Moon

The specialized astrology relating to relationships is called "synastry" and is endlessly fascinating and well worth anyone's study. Liz Greene's brilliant book *Astrology for Loves* is the best on the subject and you will turn to it again and again. By learning the sun and moon sign of your love interest and comparing it to your own, you can determine your compatibility in every regard. With Goths, who are even more romantic and sensitive than mundanes, it is even more important to keep track of the moon. A basic knowledge of synastry, the sexy side of the stars, can take you far!

The best relationships happen when one person's moon sign is the same as the other's moon. Opposites also attract as many a lusty Leo and quirky Aquarian can attest, so you should also check out the person right across from you in the zodiac. Some of the most delightful and exciting sex can happen when people are very different and compliment each other with refreshing new sex techniques. This section will provide you with the basics.

Fire Lovers

Fire signs are intense, usually positive, and often impetuous. Fire signs get things moving. They are passionate and need a match of enthusiasm in the bedroom. Fire signs belong together. Sparks can also fly if your moon or Venus is in a fire sign.

Warrior Aries angers easily, but the "kiss and make up" part can be fun. Tell a Leo he or she is wonderful and sexy (and he or she really is), and you will be amply rewarded with dramatic fireworks between the sheets. Adventurous Sagittarians like to make love outdoors. Try a hike followed by skinny-dipping and an erotic workout.

Air Lovers

Air signs are the great communicators and philosopher/techies of the zodiac. They are always thinking. These fun and social creatures really get along with everyone, although earth signs may try to keep them too grounded. They live in the world of ideas and can sometimes intellectualize sex. You can turn this trio on with sex toys, porn, and books of erotica. Geminis are very verbal during sex, so a little erotic talk can drive them crazy with desire! Libras are the most partnership-oriented of all signs, so a very romantic approach will bode extremely well here. Libras are ruled by Venus and have refined lovemaking to an art form. Aquarians are wildly experimental. Together, you'll go through all the Kama Sutra positions and beyond.

Earth Lovers

Earth signs are at once solid, practical, and extremely sensual. Grounded and security-oriented, they are the most involved with the physical body of anyone in the zodiac.

Tauruses are ruled by Venus, so they are very amorous. Bring a fine wine and some food into the bedroom for an after-sex snack. Soft fabric, good music, perfumed oils—all senses are explored with Taurus Bulls in bed. Virgos are not fussy neatniks. They are highly skilled and service-oriented lovers—two wonderful attributes, erotically speaking. Capricorns work just as hard in the bedroom as they do in the boardroom. Support them as they strive for success and you will be amply rewarded by an attentive lover who will sweep you off for weekend trysts.

Water Lovers

Water is the most emotional and sensitive of the signs. Water signs feel things intensely, and their empathy and sensitivity can make for exquisite sex. A passionate group, to say the least. Cancers are very nurturing; this is a lover who will take care of you and meet your every need, sexual and otherwise. They are home-oriented, so the bedroom should be a palace with every comfort and erotic toy. Scorpios are reputedly the most passionate of *any* sign—they are walking sex and they know it! They love mystery and want to make love for hours. In bed and out, they want to dominate and own you. Whisper that you want that, too, at the exact right moment for ultimate pleasure. Pisceans are dream lovers, so intuitive they can anticipate your every need and give you unceasing sensuous attention. These trysting Fish would *never* get out of bed if they didn't have to!

Once you are grounded in a good understanding of your own sign, your own astrological chart, and those of your friends and significant others, you can begin to use this new knowledge to enhance your life and well-being and to bring joy to the lives of others. Astrology is an excellent tool to help you understand yourself and others. It is also a science, handed down through the centuries. Each sign and planet has many associations and magickal correspondences. By learning about these correspondences, you can begin to wisely wield the art of astrology.

Goth Astrology: Talisman and Totems

The ancient art and science of astrology comes down to us from 6,000 years ago when the Sumerians, denizens of the "cradle of civilization" in Mesopotamia, began marking the metaphysical meanings of the map of the stars. Their neighbors in Ur, the Chaldeans, took notice and took this a step further when they observed certain affinities between precious gems and "star seasons." At the time, their interests were primarily bounteous crops, bounteous babies, and less plentiful enemies. But the canny Chaldeans were great record keepers and they noticed that these recurring patterns tracked with the sky chart and that constellations helped them predict what would happen at certain times of the years. Their greatest minds, scholar-scientists and mathematician-philosophers, cocreated what would become the very dense and deeply meaningful pursuit of astrology. Once they got going, they could predict the future, as evidenced by the great biblical story of Jesus's birth and the three kings—astrologers all.

Six thousand years ago, learned men were often also the priest, doctor, and seer, along with being the astronomer and the teacher. These special groups of men were also the gemologists, who cut, polished, and studied the gems, rocks, and crystals of their earthly domain. They knew which gems should accompany the dead to the underworld, which rocks portended good fortune over the doorways, and which crystals offered benefits to the body.

The ancient Sumerians had enormous knowledge, for example, about the Dog Star, properly referred to as Sirius A, and its mate, Sirius B; they knew the densities of the stars and the length of the orbit (fifty years), and since Sirius A was the brightest star in the night sky, they connected it to the beautiful blue stone they considered to be both powerful and precious: lapis lazuli. They devised a color coding as the basis for their system:

Rose and red for planet Mars
Green for Venus
Blue for Mercury
Yellow for the sun
Purple for Saturn
Light blue for Jupiter
White for the moon

This was just the most basic beginning point for a study that would grow and continue for thousands of years, but this was the basis for today's chemistry and astronomy as well as the human study of astrology. Without knowing about the big bang theory, the Chaldeans and Sumerians still knew we are all made of the same "stuff" and come from the same place. We are all interconnected; the minerals from the meteorites that literally fall from the heavens are of the same minerals and elements as our terrestrial rocks. The spectacular process of creations, stemming from the original biggest of bangs, is still happening. Diamonds are the result of millions of years and millions of pounds of pressure on coal, a rather unlovely hunk of earth. The diamonds on our ring fingers started out as coal under our feet.

The universe revolves around us in regular cycles and change is happening at every moment. So, like the clever Chaldeans and the scholarly Sumerians, let us see what we can learn from the stars in the sky and the rocks beneath our feet. Let us learn from patterns, cycles, and connections between the earth and sky.

We started out as sun worshippers on this planet and it is the center of our planetary system as my birthday mate (February 19) Nicolaus Copernicus pointed out long ago. Composed mostly of hydrogen and helium, our fantastic and fiery sun is actually a midsized and rather ordinary star in the whole scheme of things. An impressive 870,331 miles in diameter, the sun is 300,000 times the size of the earth, and it affects all bodies within a range of nearly a billion miles, which is why earth and all the other planets circle it so loyally. The temperature at the sun's core has been estimated at 17 million degrees Centigrade and with a surface heart of 5,500 degrees. Astrologically, the sun is linked with the planet Leo, the Lion. Naturally, fire is the element of our sun. Around "Old Sol" all the planets rotate, pulled by the gravitational force of the star. Each of the stones and astrological signs has a planetary influence.

Each sign also has a precious gem, a talismanic power stone. Talismans are lucky omens and I highly recommend them as altar crystals. Use these rocks and gems to augment your magickal workings as well as wearing them for healing and protection.

Aries, First Half—March 20–April 3

Sunstone, ruled by Mars, is the talismanic stone for early Aries folks. Appropriately red with an iridescent glow, sunstone is a gold-flecked good luck charm. Jasper and heliotrope, commonly called bloodstone, are the other talismans for this part of the year. Jasper is an opaque and fine-grained variety of chalcedony. It is found in all colors including red, brown, pink, yellow, green, gray/white, and shades of blue and purple. Bloodstone is a green stone with red spots. It also occurs in shades of dark green with red, brown, and multicolored spots. The iron minerals cause the deep red and brown colors.

Aries, Second Half—April 4–April 18

The talisman for this half of Aries is bowenite, a mossy green-colored stone of great strength and power. While many of the crystals designated to late Aries are red or pink, the green bowenite signifies the other side of the planet Mars. Bowenite is especially precious and sacred to the Maoris of New Zealand, where some of the finest specimens come from, and to the ancient Indians and Persians. Another strong talisman for the second half of Aries is the umber-colored chalcedony known as carnelian. It was ceremoniously carved by the Egyptians, Greeks, and Phoenicians in the pre-Christian era.

Taurus, First Half—April 19–May 2

The talisman for the first half of Taurus is another gorgeous green stone: malachite, corresponding again to the planet Venus. An earthy rock, it is befitting to this earth sign of the zodiac and has many magickal tales to its credit. Malachite is said to aid in the regeneration of body cells, creates calm and peace, and aids one's sleep.

A stunningly gorgeous stone, malachite is worn by many to detect impending danger by using it to scry. This beautiful green stone offers bands of varying hues and is believed by many to lend extra energy. It is believed that gazing at malachite or holding it relaxes the nervous system and calms stormy emotions. Malachite is said to bring harmony into one's life. It is also believed that malachite gives knowledge and patience.

Taurus, Second Half—May 3–May 19

Jadeite, the lucky stone for late Tauruses, comes in many colors. Jadeite also rings with a lovely tone when struck and this is the most natural musical sign. This stone calms the soul and heals the bones. Jadeite also abets the easy expression of love, enabling you to say what is in your heart honestly and easily.

Gemini, First Half—May 20–June 4

Moss agate, which is a form of quartz with a plantlike pattern caused by metallic crystalline grains, perfectly represents the dualism of the twin-signed Geminis. The ancients actually believed it was fossilized moss inside the stone with the dark green markings inside and often used it for water divining. Moss agate is associated with the metal-rich planet Mercury, ruler of the sign of the twins. This stone makes a great grounding stone for this airy air sign and Geminis need to keep their feet on the ground, making this member of the quartz family the perfect talisman stone for this sign.

Gemini, Second Half—June 5–June 20

Late Geminis can count on the garnet known as Transvaal jade or "grossularia" for their talisman. People most often think of garnets as red stones of great clarity, but this garnet is opaque and a beautiful, bright green. Under certain light, it appears as a blazing yellow color, symbolizing the dual nature of the June born. This stone, originating so many millions of years ago in the deep core of the earth, contains many metals in its makeup, also corresponding to the Gemini nature, with so many different qualities and talents. Wearing this garnet can awaken hidden talents and bring them to the fore for Geminis.

Geodes, usually coming in two split halves are the ideal soul stone for late Geminis. Geminis must have *both* halves! This will help integrate the two parts of their nature and make for a complete, whole person. Geodes are formed from old volcanic bubbles and are usually solid agate outside with a center of gorgeous amethyst, opal, or rock crystal. I recommend keeping one of the geode halves at home on your altar or in a special spot where you can see it every day. Keep the other half at your place of work, reflecting and connecting the two parts of the Gemini nature.

Cancer, First Half—June 21–July 4

Pearl is the talisman of early Cancers. Pearls have a long and rich history, first written about in China 4,000 years ago and celebrated in all the ancient cultures of the world since humankind first opened a shell and found the prize inside. As Cancers are the great historians of the zodiac with their incredible memories, pearls are connected to Cancers through the ocean and the tides, since their ruler, the moon, influences the flow of the waters of the earth. Cancers should wear pearls on occasion, not constantly, and decorate their homes and workspaces with shells to honor their native element, water, and to stay secure, refreshed, and relaxed. This will enable Cancerians to avoid their great nemesis: worry.

Cancer, Second Half—July 5–July 21

Red coral is the talisman for the second half of Cancer. Coral is composed of the stone formed by lime secreted by sea creatures. One memorable old story associated with oceanic coral is the ancient Greek belief that sea sprites stole Medusa's severed head and took it to the ocean bottom and that each drop of her blood formed a red coral. It was (and still is) believed to have healing and protective qualities. For Cancers, red coral is good for vitality, a symbol of life, love, and health.

Leo, First Half—July 22–August 5

Early Leos can count zircon for their talisman, beloved by the early cultures. They resemble diamonds in many ways, except for their chemical compounds and the simple fact that they are not nearly as rare and hard. There is much lore throughout history regarding the brilliant zircon; it was believed to be a safeguard against poison and was thought to be a holy healer in ancient India. In the early Roman Catholic Church, it was held to be the sign of humility. For Leos, whose downfall can be pride, zircon can guard against this and keep astrological lions on an even keel.

Leo, Second Half—August 6–August 21

Heliodor, named for the sun, is the ultimate talismanic stone for late Leos. Heliodor is a member of the beryl family, the sunny yellow specimen and sister stone to the emerald (green beryl) and aquamarine (blue beryl). Heliodor is formed under high temperature and pressure. Heliodor can help Leos call on their greatest qualities and talents and provide the impetus to go out and try to make their dreams come true!

Virgo, First Half—August 22–September 5

The early Virgo's talisman is labradorite, the lovely iridescent stone originally discovered in Labrador. Virgos are also ruled by Mercury, as are Geminis, and this quicksilver, peacock-hued crystal is good for mental swiftness. Virgos constantly feel the need to accomplish all their goals for this life. This type of feldspar can reflect every color of the spectrum and helps Virgos from becoming too task-oriented, too focused on one thing. No one can work harder than Virgos and labradorite can prevent exhaustion from overwork and can also ensure that these early Virgos can activate other talents.

Virgo, Second Half—September 6–September 22

Tiger's eye is the late Virgo talisman, another iridescent stone; this one denoting strength, courage, and great perception. Virgos are the great critics, missing no flaw and tiger's eye can help them also have great vision and be able to see wonderful possibilities. Tiger's eye typically has lustrous alternating brown and yellow bands and to some, this resembles the eye of a tiger, thus the name. Tiger's eye is used for focusing the mind. It is said that tiger's eye offers protection during travel and strengthens convictions and confidence. This very warm stone is beneficial for the weak and sick as a protective talisman.

Libra, First Half—September 23–October 6

Dioptase is the talisman for early Libras. A deeper green than any emerald, dioptase has an extensive copper content. Venus is associated with the color green and the intensity of this gorgeous green stone makes it a love crystal for Librans, both in relationships and in the higher love for humankind. Dioptase can awaken the spiritual side of Libras, making this usually attractive sign beautiful both inside and out. Dioptase is difficult to cut for jewelry because of its brittleness, but it can be placed in settings in its crystal form and is also a lovely object to place in uncut crystal clusters all around the home, in shrines, and in the bedroom.

Libra, Second Half—October 7–October 22

Like Taurus, the late Libran's own talisman is green jadeite, sometimes called "Imperial Green Jade." The Chinese, who highly prized this stone in their lengthy history and culture, "Yu Shih," believed that this jade contains all that you need for a long, happy life: courage, modesty, charity, wisdom, and, most important for the Libra scale to be in balance, justice.

Scorpio, First Half—October 23–November 6

Early Scorpios have a most unusual talisman stone: Blue John, which is found in only one place in the world, in the underground caverns beneath a hill in the county of Derbyshire, England. Blue John is the rarest of fluorites and has dark blue and reddish-purple bands on a white background, relating to Pluto, the second ruling planet of Scorpio. Scorpios are the sign of the underworld and of secrets and the origin of the name of their talisman is a mystery no one has yet solved. While Blue John is going to be difficult to come by, other fluorites are more common and a blue fluorite will substitute nicely for Blue John. Fluorite is a stone that heals bones and wounds that lie beneath the surface, such as broken blood vessels or infections. Secretive Scorpios carry many hurts beneath their strong exterior and over time fluorite can gently resolve them.

SCORPIO, SECOND HALF—NOVEMBER 7–NOVEMBER 21

Everybody thinks of amethyst as the February crystal for Aquarians and Pisceans, but it is also the talisman for late Scorpios. The purple color relates to the purple planet Pluto and it is also a stone corresponding to the element of water. Scorpios are the third water sign and amethyst can open the love vibration for Scorpios. Wearing amethyst jewelry and keeping chunks of amethyst crystal in the home and workplace can reveal the sweet, funny, smart, approachable, and loveable side of Scorpios, thereby offering a much greater chance for happiness for this most misunderstood and enormously powerful sign.

SAGITTARIUS, FIRST HALF—NOVEMBER 22–DECEMBER 5

Amber is the talisman for early Sagittarians; this rock formed from fossilized tree sap and resin, is an organic crystal. Amber was thought by the ancients to have trapped the sun and was called "electron" by the Greeks, who observed its negative electrical change. Amber keeps your energy surging, which is good for wildly active Sagittarians, but it can be weakening if worn all the time, as even Sagittarians can become exhausted. Amber helps performers—actors and musicians swear by it.

SAGITTARIUS, SECOND HALF—DECEMBER 6–DECEMBER 20

Late Sagittarians have a turquoise talisman. This rock has a rich and colorful history and it was valued in the extreme by Persians, Egyptians, Mexicans, Bedouins, Chinese, Tibetans, Native Americans, and Turks. Sagittarians are the centaurs of the zodiac, half-man, half-horse, and turquoise is a strong fit, as it is associated with horses and riders. Turquoise, once revered as the "Eye of Ra," lends great sight and aids travel. Wearing this stone will help people born in this part of the year to find their purpose, harness their passion, and keep the vision to see it through.

CAPRICORN, FIRST HALF—DECEMBER 21–JANUARY 6

As a talisman, early Capricorns have both jet and lazulite, stones having a dark and shadowy appearance representative of the Capricorn planet of Saturn. Jet, named for its intense black color and hardness, is one of the oldest stones known to man, a match that is perfect for slow and steady Capricorns, who are reputed to grow more youthful as they get older. Capricorns also have great longevity; they live long and prosper! Lazulite, opaque and often the dark and cloudy blue of the planet Saturn, is good for mental processes and stimulates the frontal lobe. Dogged and hardworking Capricorns will do well to keep this concentration-enhancing talisman nearby at all times.

CAPRICORN, SECOND HALF—JANUARY 7–JANUARY 19

Late Capricorns get to have lapis lazuli as their talismanic crystal. This crystal was absolutely revered by the Egyptians and other Mesopotamian cultures. A brighter saturnine blue, this stone connotes wisdom, accomplishment, and value as befits the latter half of Capricorn. Capricorns sometimes seem slow and plodding to others, but they are really anything but. Capricorns are surefooted and careful and will get to the top of the mountain while others fall behind.

AQUARIUS, FIRST HALF—JANUARY 20–FEBRUARY 3

Onyx is the deep, dark talisman for early Aquarians—a stone beloved by the people of prehistory and of the craftsman of the classical era. It was one of the first stones to be used as a tool and for decoration by the ancients. Another option for early Aquarians is moldavite. With its otherworldly origins as a meteorite, it is perfect for the Uranian "bolt from the blue" these scientist-philosophers represent. Moldavite is a mysterious and powerful crystal with many mist-shrouded legends and theories. No doubt, an Aquarius will get to the bottom of it all one day. Visionary Aquarians are some of the great thinkers and scientific researchers of the entire zodiac and frequently awe us with their discoveries.

AQUARIUS, SECOND HALF—FEBRUARY 4–FEBRUARY 18

Diopside is the beautiful blue talismanic gemstone for the late Aquarians. This stone has correspondence to both Uranus, the official ruling planet of Aquarians, and Saturn, the former ruler before Uranus was discovered. In the same way, the gem-grade diopside was discovered comparatively recently. In 1964, star diopside, an included type, was found; it is a magickal and stunningly gorgeous stone that has a star-struck quality of electric enlightenment, just like these February-born inventor, artist, and creative types. Diopside is believed to improve intellectual, mathematical, and analytical abilities and brings practicality to these applications. As such, this is the perfect talismanic stone to bring airy Aquarians back to earth. The late Aquarians also have jade for their talisman, a universal healer and love stone to keep these very intellectual people in touch with their hearts.

Pisces, First Half—February 19–March 4

Interestingly, the sign of the Fish is affected by three different moons by three different planets: Triton, Io, and our moon. The gem for this sector of the astrological wheel is the oceanic blue-green diamond, regarded as Neptunian, the ruling planet of Pisces. Aquamarine relates to all three of the aforementioned moons and is a second talisman for the Fishes, a dual sign needing dual crystals. Aquamarine was once believed to be the dried tears of sea nymphs.

Pisces, Second Half—March 5–March 19

The talismanic stone for the late Pisces people is the apple-green type of chalcedony known as chrysophrase. This is a stone revered through the ages. Chrysophrase was assigned sovereignty and utilized by high priests of nearly every era. This crystal is perfect for the sign that can attain the highest level of spiritual evolution. Crystal lore says that chrysophrase bridges the awareness of spiritual self and physical self. This brings healing, joy, and laughter. It is said that chrysophrase teaches how to love life and yourself—as well as your shortcomings.

Astrological Herbology

You can choose the herbs for your altar based on your sun or moon sign. You should explore using celestial correspondences when making tinctures, incense, oils, potpourri, and other magickal potions for your rituals. For example, if the new moon is in Aries when you are performing an attraction ritual, try using peppermint or fennel, two herbs sacred to the sign of the Ram. Or, if you are creating a special altar for the time during which the sun is in the sign of Cancer the Crab, use incense, oils, teas, and herbs corresponding to that astrological energy, such as jasmine and lemon. These correspondences create a synthesis of energies, adding to the effectiveness of your ceremonial work.

Sanctuary and Serenity Magickal Potpourri

Potpourri, now a popular household item, was a medieval custom revived by the Victorians who utilized the meaning and power of flowers. Collect and dry these flowers either by growing them in your kitchen garden or by buying and drying cut flowers. Choose flowers that connect with your astrological sign and personal energy from the following:

Aries, ruled by Mars: carnation, cedar, clove, cumin, fennel, juniper, peppermint, pine

Taurus, ruled by Venus: apple, daisy, lilac, magnolia, oak moss, orchid, plumeria, rose, thyme, tonka bean, vanilla, violet

Gemini, ruled by Mercury: almond, bergamot mint, clover, dill, lavender, lemongrass, lily, parsley

Cancer, ruled by the moon: eucalyptus, gardenia, jasmine, lemon, lotus, rose, myrrh, sandalwood

Leo, ruled by the sun: acacia, cinnamon, heliotrope, nutmeg, orange, rosemary

Virgo, ruled by Mercury: almond, bergamot mint, cypress, mace, moss, patchouli

Libra, ruled by Venus: catnip, marjoram, mugwort, spearmint, sweet pea, thyme, vanilla

Scorpio, ruled by Pluto: allspice, basil, cumin, galangal, ginger

Sagittarius, ruled by Jupiter: anise, cedar wood, sassafras, star anise, honeysuckle

Aquarius, ruled by Uranus: gum, acacia, almond, citron, cypress, lavender, mimosa, peppermint, pine

Pisces, ruled by Neptune: anise, catnip, clove, gardenia, lemon, orris, sarsaparilla, sweet pea

Capricorn, ruled by Saturn: mimosa, vervain, vetiver

CHAPTER ELEVEN

Dark Divination

Divination takes many forms: scrying, tarot, palmistry, throwing bones or stones, tea leaves, even reading the livers of sheep, to name but a few. Goth divination is all of these and also some intriguing post-modern variations such as the swinging of a pendulum, the TV remote oracle, and a very "in-your-face" style of tarot involving a set of dice and the Major Arcana from your favorite tarot deck. Learn about your future, your past, and, best of all, the here and now with these delicious Gothic forms of divination and "pomo" tarot.

TV Remote Oracle—Roulette-o-Mancy

The TV remote oracle is the most punk rock form of divination possible. You can think of your remote control as a wand, and "White Wizard" Lon DuQuette says, "TV is a medieval magician's dream come true—a magick mirror that informs, entertains, and (if we're not careful) enchants." So, whether you spend all of your time watching the Sci-Fi Channel or *Charmed*, even if you only watch the Sci-Fi Channel constantly since we know those cable witches of *Charmed* are way too vanilla for you, you can still wield your magickal powers with your remote control.

The next time you sit down to watch your favorite show, try this:

With the remote, hit "mute" so the volume is completely down on the television.

Close your eyes, ask your question aloud. Begin flipping through channels as many or as few as you want.

When it "feels right" or when the spirit moves you, press mute to bring back the volume.

Listen to and write down the first few seconds of sound. Hit the mute button again so all is silent and ponder the wisdom you have been given.

Goth Is in the Details

On the Road and On the Bus

Neal Cassady and Jack Kerouac utilized a form of divination they called "Radio I Ching" on the road, later echoed and carried on by the Grateful Dead, who were famously driven across America by the same Neal Cassady in the psychedelically painted bus Further. Their trip was a continuation of the shamanic journey undertaken by medicine men and tribal leaders to heal society. Today's cyber-Goth and techno pagan can V Jam and also do an I Pod I Ching for the latest take on this great beatnik hippie tradition of transcendental divination.

Shamanic Visioning

The psychedelic "trip" into inner space replicated the shaman's magick journey, from which he returned with secret knowledge for his tribe. This myth of a spiritual journey was a motif of tribal societies from Central Asia to the Amazon River basin. It is possible that hallucinatory shamanism was widespread in Native American cultures because it was brought from Siberia by the Indians' North Asian ancestors when they immigrated across the Bering Strait. (*Shaman* is a Ural-Altaic word.) Furthermore, North America, in contrast to Africa, is especially fertile in hallucinogenic plants. Even the species of strong tobacco (*nicotiana rustica*) used in Native American rituals had hallucinogenic properties.

Divination Facilitation

Many ritual practices, such as fasting and marathon drumming, have been used throughout history to induce trance and facilitate divination. In some cases, techniques of flagellation or mutilation resemble those of the modern S&M scene, whose devotees claim to attain a beatific state. Mushrooms eaten by Siberian shamans caused convulsions. Hallucinogens, perhaps mushrooms, were used by worshippers in the Eleusinian mysteries. Possessed by Apollo, the Delphic oracle went into paroxysms after intoxication by fumes from a cleft in the earth. Fault lines have recently been identified in the bedrock at Delphi by an archaeologist and geologist, who speculate that the priestess was maddened by oozing petrochemical vapors such as ethylene (prized by modern glue-sniffers). Drugs were also used in medieval European witchcraft. The iconic Halloween image of the witch flying on a broomstick is another version of the shaman's visionary journey: ritual staffs were smeared with a greenish hallucinogenic ointment and "ridden," to autoerotic effect.

The massive drug taking in the 1960s, promoted by arts leaders and pop stars, redefined the culture and set the stage for the decade's religious vision. But shamanistic drug taking in tribal societies took place within small communities unified by a coherent belief system. Hippies and college students casually sampling hallucinogens were relative strangers and brought with them a mélange of private problems, identity issues, and family psychodramas. What they shared was a yearning humanitarianism—and rock music, which urged the liberation of sexual desire. Sex was portrayed as a revolutionary agent: the establishment, like the walls of Jericho, would fall before sensuality unbound. This overestimation of sex—the faith that sexual energy freed of social controls is inherently benign—was one reason for the dissipation of the authentic spiritual discoveries made by the 1960s generation. A philosophy of random contacts and "good vibrations" built little that could be passed on to the next generation.

Pendulum

The pendulum is regarded as the most mysterious form of divination of all. It is also the simplest and the most unique of all oracular tools in that you, the diviner, become part of the pendulum, your electromagnetic energy, your body, and your own psychism. Similar to dowsing, or radiostheseia, you become a vehicle for "the force." Experts in the field say that if you use a pendulum regularly, you hone that psychic ability and become a more reliable instrument. All the more reason to obtain a pendulum *now*! You can also make one easily enough. Clear spheres on a black cord held by a silver claw or skull make a terrific Goth pendulum. A crafty option is to choose the crystal you are most drawn to and tie it to a black silken cord. Simply ask it to "show me 'yes' and show me 'no,'" and you'll soon be divining all the answers to the questions in your mind.

The Tarot of Brutal Honesty

Divination by the throw of the dice can provide brutally honest insight, making it more Goth than not. Goths are willing to looking into the deepest, darkest parts of their soul and this is exactly what you will see with this method of tarot and dice. Many people divine for greater understanding of the self, which is an excellent way to use these magickal tools. Similarly, this take on tarot is for self-discernment. In other words, this is a tarot of awakening or, at least, wake up, dammit! Concentrate, focus, ask your questions, then take a deep breath and prepare to learn a lot about your past, your present, your future, and, most important, yourself! So, pull out all the Major Arcana or "trumps" in the deck you are using and stack them after a good shuffle. Roll the dice and look at the number they add up to. Pick the card that matches. You should roll the dice only thrice. That is definitely enough brutal honestly and self-knowledge for one day!

0. The Fool

If your throw results in the Fool, it is obvious that, whatever the question may be, you are being an idiot about the situation. This draw is a warning to stop with the stupidity and take a long, hard look at yourself to see why you are appearing foolish to your friends and why they know this but you don't.

1. The Magician

You are guilty of sleight of hand here and, in truth, you are really slighting yourself and all you are undertaking. You are behaving like a cheap magician of the rabbit-out-of-the-hat variety, and your shtick is wearing thin. You are just about to drop all the plates you are spinning and, while you think you are being very clever, really you are tricking yourself with your own bullshit. Enough!

2. The High Priestess

You're late, you're late for a very important date! And, to further complicate things, you can't even remember what it is about. The High Priestess card is about to deal up a very painful truth and you are blanking out trying to avoid facing this uncomfortable aspect of yourself. Allow the memories to flood back and, in so doing, you will change yourself for the better. Face the music!

3. The Empress

If you were asking about love, whether man or woman, the Empress card represents a diva second to none—a total pain in the ass. If your question was about you, well, it is fairly evident that you yourself are a bit of a prima donna. Yes, you are Goth, you are fabulous, but the universe does not revolve around you and you need to get real about it. Humility is a rare and wonderful thing indeed. Try it!

4. The Emperor

This card represents a present situation in which you are the dominating force. Power is a funny thing and rare is the person who handles it with grace. Having power can corrupt, confuse, and raise petty and pitiful ego issues. Beware and carefully consider whatever it is that can invoke your ugly side. Does the phrase "control freak" sound at all familiar?

5. The Hierophant

This is a question about a question and it is doubtless a very important and pivotal one in your life right now. If it is a spiritual question, you need to consult your god, your goddess, your guru. If not, try the man or boss lady upstairs or even your lover, a bartender, or a best friend. Ask the question honestly and listen, even if it is hard to hear. You can grow toward heirophancy yourself if you handle this right. Don't revolve, evolve.

6. The Lovers

I can almost see your smile on getting this card. Surely, it is all good, brimming with peace, love, happiness, and maybe even some great sex, right? Guess again. It is really about your ability to make decisions, particularly about partnership. In the very near future, you are about to receive an invitation—maybe to join a band or a new coven, maybe a new business venture, or a new relationship. The cards are trying to tell you something—do this thing! Whether a new friendship or a new job, make up your mind and commit. The Universe will commit right back.

7. The Chariot

A wonderful card, glory be at long last. You are finally on your way, the going is good, and you're traveling in high style, too. A Rolls Royce hearse, maybe? Well, as long as you know where you are going. Oh, wait a minute, ummmm. Just where are you hurtling to in your hearse or Goth glamour mobile? Calm down, mediate, let go of that fraudulence complex, own your authentic self, and go for it. Keep your head about you and all will be well.

8. Strength

Wow, even without Red Bull, Jolt, depth-charge espressos, or absinthe you are a ball of fire. You have so much energy brewing inside you, you're like a bottle rocket. And, would you like to hear the really great news? It is love energy! Here is one of the rare cases wherein you should let your heart take the lead and just turn that big, beautiful brain off. Don't overthink anything, just let your own light shine and don't even worry about being corny. Since Goths are the most romantic of folks, that should be lovely, indeed. Remember, you have unbelievable strength and the highest level of energy of your life, so get wild!

9. The Hermit

Go Goth and spend some serious time by yourself. You need to look deep inside and take a temporary vow of silence. You have gotten away from the truth and need to take up the lantern of enlightenment—no one else can help you. This isolation will help you see things as they really are, starting with yourself.

10. The Wheel of Fortune

Here is the true meaning of the phrase "down on your luck." You can think of this wheel as "the rack" if you like, similar to that of the Spanish Inquisition. Your luck is about to change and not necessarily for the better! Take a moment to assess your life; now how bad can it be? You have a place to sleep (even if it is a coffin in a dark dungeon) and an interesting Goth lifestyle. You are spiritual and have a group of fascinating friends, right? Well, this card is letting you know your luck is about to change. If you are in a good phase, get ready for a run of really back luck. If your luck has been down in the gutter, then look on the bright side—there is no way but up from here. In any case, enjoy the spinning sensation!

11. Justice

Here is the brutal truth: Lady Justice has decided you are going to get exactly what you deserve. In much the same way that the Wheel of Fortune spins up or down depending on your position at the time you get the card, the scales of justice will swing out exactly according to your current karmic bank balance. Have you been good? Then you deserve better. Have you been bad? You better get ready!

12. The Hanged Man

Uh oh—is all the blood rushing to your head? You are in a trap of your own making and only *you* can untie your hands and climb down from the noose. Get busy freeing yourself and stop throwing so many obstacles in your own path. Obstacles may include bad attitude, egoism, negativity, pride, sloth, envy, jealousy, or any number of traits you should face squarely and overcome in your path to higher consciousness. I say unto you: go forth and be excellent.

13. Death

As a Goth, you probably interpret this card as something other than the end of a life. And rightly so. This is an ending of a journey, a relationship, a phase of your life. We can grow from endings and let go of old patterns that no longer serve us in our spiritual evolution. This card is drawing your attention to something you maybe have not yet realized is over. Take a look around and, if you are in denial about something that is broken in your life, fix it by moving on. Celebrate this death as only a Goth pagan can—memorialize, sentimentalize, honor, and begin a brand-new dance.

14. Temperance

Slow down, you have been going too fast, too hard, too much. Maybe you are partying and overindulging in absinthe or your poison of choice, be it lust, power, work, you name it. Everything in moderation, even magick. You need to recalibrate and get your balance back and the bounce in your step that has been missing.

15. THE DEVIL

Are you looking in a mirror? No doubt you are. Face it, you have an evil twin residing among your many personalities and this is the least charming one. Feeling pangs of guilt? Some aspects of the Devil card turning up in your life can be lust (we know you are dead sexy, but really!), greed (how many ankhs and crosses do you need?), or ambition (are your coworkers calling you Rasputin behind your back?), so don't be afraid to look at how you function in the world and treat other people. It is good to get ahead and look good while doing it but not at the very high price of your soul. My advice: get over your "bad self."

16. THE TOWER

Well, get ready. Bad things are going to happen and you probably even know what they are. Breakups, getting fired, being kicked out of your house—major transformation, period. The good thing is that you start over again with a clean slate after this master disaster!

17. THE STAR

This star is a ray of light of true inspiration, directly from the gods and goddesses and sent right to you. You are special and you need to cultivate the light within *you*! What is your real art you are to create? Meditate on this out under the stars when you get this card and you will "receive" your message. And, remember, you are a star!

18. THE MOON

This card represents deception—someone is lying to you and it might be yourself. The moon can be a silvery orb of delusion and can represent being out of touch with reality. Stop moon-gazing and take a strong hard look at your life and make sure you are not living in a fantasy world.

19. THE SUN

For the most part, this is a positive card; the sun *is* shining after all. This card might also indicate that you are a bit of an egotist and an attention hog. You think too well of yourself. Try on a little humility for size and everyone will love you even more.

20. Judgment

Yes, it is you everyone is talking about. And with good reason. You have done something either very good or kind of bad. The sad thing is that you don't even know yourself. Instead of trying to hear what they are whispering, why don't you ask someone to be brutally honest with you? You need some truth serum and once you have swallowed the bitter pill, you can begin again and get on the right track.

21. The World

Hit the road, Jack. You need to get out more. You have been stuck in your own little world of your own invention and it is getting stale in there. You need to see, to experience, to become more of the world you really live in. It will be a wonderful thing if you do some traveling; think of it as a pilgrimage to your self. You will grow enormously if you do this. Bon voyage! Send postcards.

How to Determine a Tarot Trump Card by a Toss of Two Dice

0	Fool	0	(If the dice "escape" and roll away, you've accomplished the Fool's toss!)
1	Magician	1-1	
2	High Priestess	1-2	
3	Empress	1-2	
4	Emperor	1-4	
5	Hierophant	1-5	
6	Lovers	1-6	
7	Chariot	2-2	
8	Strength	2-3	
9	Hermit	2-4	
10	Fortune	2-5	
11	Justice	2-6	

12	Hanged Man	3-3
13	Death	3-4
14	Temperance	3-5
15	Devil	3-6
16	Tower	4-4
17	Star	4-5
18	Moon	4-6
19	Sun	5-5
20	Judgment	5-6
21	World	6-6

Casting Stones

Give your tarot cards a rest and create a one-of-a-kind divination tool: a bag of crystals you can do readings with. It is very easy to do. Collect stones you have picked up on travels, and keep your eye out as you go about your daily business for crystals. You can gather up relatively inexpensive stones such as garnets, agates, amethysts, and tiny citrines at your favorite metaphysical five and dime. Select a favorite velvet bag and when the need arises, turn to crystal visions for your enlightenment. Most of us cannot afford diamonds in our bag of crystals, so substitute clear quartz here, for emeralds, switch to peridot, and garnets can substitute nicely for rubies. A wonderful New Age Web site, www.Mystic Trader.com, has "rough rubies" and "rough emerald" pieces at $3 each, so the real deal is more available all the time.

Casting the stones is as easy as one, two, three:

1. Shake the bag well.
2. Ask a question.
3. Remove the first three stones you touch and then interpret from the following guide.

How to read the stones:

Agate: business success and notoriety
Amethyst: change is coming
Black agate: monetary gain

Red agate: long life and health
Aventurine: new horizons and positive growth
Blue lace agate: the need for spiritual and physical healing
Citrine: the universe offers enlightenment
Diamond: stability
Emerald: lushness
Hematite: new prospects
Jade: everlasting life
Red jasper: the need for grounding
Lapis Lazuli: heavenly fortune
Quartz: clarity where there was none
Rose quartz: love is in your life
Ruby: deep passion and personal power
Sapphire: truth
Snowflake obsidian: your troubles are at an end
Tiger's eye: the situation is not as it appears
Snow quartz: major changes

Looking into the Days of Future Past: Crystal Balls

While the crystal ball is a little understood mode of divination, it is one method, if not the most enticing, of augury. There are probably as many definitions of crystal balls as there are opinionated people. However, it is usual to group these individuals into three categories: the ancients, the geologists; and the seers or scryers. The ancients supposed crystals to be congealed water or ice petrified by some long-continued natural process. These long-ago people invoked the power of the crystal to change the fate of individuals, and often to modify the course of a country's events. It is reported that the Roman historian Pliny the Elder subscribed to this belief and that the Roman statesman and philosopher Seneca the younger supported his opinion. This belief extended well into the Middle Ages. John Dee, the great alchemist and master of magick and a forefather of modern Goth magick, used a crystal ball and a black obsidian scrying mirror to "break on through to the other side" and call down angelic beings, as well as to see deeply into the future. Not only is a crystal ball the ultimate vessel for seers, it is a marvelous way in which a Goth magician can train the psychic muscles on the way to becoming an adept.

Highly polished, glasslike spheres of beryl and quartz crystal have been used in divination for thousands of years. Biblical priests used shewstones, as crystal balls were known in those times to communicate with higher beings and divine the future. Abbot Tritheim, who taught the fifteenth-century German mystic and alchemist Cornelius Agrippa von Nettesheim, had very specific guidelines for the size and color of crystal balls. He recommended they be "the bigness of a small orange" and also have complete and absolute clarity. Furthermore, he urged diviners to mount their stone on a pedestal engraved with the "tetragrammaton," or the holy four-lettered name of the Jehovah, YHVH, along with the names of Michael, Gabriel, Uriel, and Raphael, the four archangelic rulers of the sun, moon, Venus, and Mercury, respectively.

Great figures throughout the ages have recommended crystal balls to help look into the future or to gain clarity on present situations. The great philosopher and physician Paracelsus declared during the height of the Renaissance that what he called "conjuring crystals" should be used in "observing everything rightly, earning and understanding what was." The scepter used by Scottish royalty contains a crystal ball, the usage of which was thought to have come down from the Druids. Another Scottish association is that of the "cairngorm," a large sphere of smoky quartz now housed in the British Museum, believed to be John Dee's own crystal ball. Sir Walter Scott referred to crystal balls as "stones of power." In Asia, some of the finest crystal balls are the result of many years of patient hand polishing. For the Japanese, the "tama" is a crystal ball held to be the symbol of eternity.

The value of crystal balls shows up in our culture and collective mindset. They can be found in mythic history: Merlin, the fabled wizard of Arthurian legend, was believed to have kept his crystal ball with him at all times. They can also be found in fairy tales, Disney stories, and even today's movies—the "palantirs" favored by the wizards in *The Lord of the Rings* were superpowered crystal balls

Scrying

It seems that everyone wants to see into the future, and scrying is an ancient method of doing exactly that. Scrying is the art of divining by gazing at or into an appropriate surface and receiving information about the future in the form of visions. The reflective surface can be water, a mirror, a crystal ball, or a slab of stone. Some people are quite talented at seeing visions in the flames of fire or in the bottom of a teacup. However, smooth, neutral surfaces are much less distracting.

We don't know how the art of scrying first began. Perhaps a chunk of shiny black obsidian was the first scrying mirror. We do know that ancient civilizations had special prophets and priestesses who engaged in foretelling the future. They made the tools of their trade from various crystals they found in their locale. No doubt these ancient future-seers would be delighted to know we are still using crystal balls made from translucent quartz and mysterious volcanic obsidian, the same materials they used!

Scrying is even mentioned in Genesis 44:4–5. Queen Elizabeth I entrusted all matters of the heavens and the future to John Dee. Dee used a mirror of polished black obsidian and employed scrying to great effect in calling on certain angels. He reported hearing knocking and even voices that sounded like an owl screeching during sessions. His skill and legacy led succeeding magicians and psychics to prefer black mirrors.

Scrying can be also be used to divine the past, present, and future. You can contact spirit guides, improve your skills of creative visualization, and even use it as a gateway to the astral plane. Any time you feel the need for insight and answers, scrying can lend illumination. Are you stymied at work? Are you restless and don't know why? Do you suspect someone isn't being honest with you? Try scrying!

The Search for the Secret of Crystal Gazing

Crystal gazing has been recognized in some form since the ancients used ice for divination. As time passed and ice gave way to quartz, there was even more interest in the crystal ball. In the Middle Ages, elaborate rituals were invoked before the seer took up the crystal ball and prayerfully read the symbols that appeared, believing they had heavenly origin. While many dismiss crystal gazing with a shrug, there are rare individuals with a thoroughly scientific attitude who endeavor to search for the truth and refuse to give credence to their own doubts. Such individuals are now looking at the crystal ball with renewed interest.

Lewis Spence, one of the world's foremost scholars of occult science, has this to say in his *An Encyclopedia of Occultism*, "The object of crystal gazing . . . is the induction of an hypnotic state giving rise to visionary hallucinations, the reflection of light in the crystal forming points de repére for such hallucinations. . . . There are many well-attested cases wherein the crystal has been successfully used for the purpose of tracing criminals, or recovering lost or stolen property."

Caring for Your Visionary Tool

A crystal ball is not a toy, and it should be treated with great respect and deference. If the owner is seriously considering seership, it is important to house the crystal ball in a room of its own. A small room is preferable, and it should be kept impeccably clean. This applies to the entire room—floors, walls, and windows, as well as the furnishings. Anything that might distract the attention should be eliminated. The furnishings should be kept simple and down to a minimum. A small, sturdy table to hold the crystal ball and two unpretentious but comfortable chairs should be sufficient. However, if the seer finds it necessary to record what the crystal ball has revealed, a small chest of drawers to accommodate stationery may be added. If you live in a studio apartment, as have I, keep your crystal ball in a special box or chest lined with soft cloth.

Keep the crystal ball clean! This is not a rule, it is a command. When its surface becomes soiled, make a mild solution of luke-warm water and the purest soap you can find in a small basin. Rest the crystal ball on a square of white flannel that has been placed on the bottom of the basin. Gently wash the crystal ball to remove all trace of soil. Then rinse in a solution of alcohol and water or of vinegar and water. Dry with a soft linen cloth, and polish with a piece of chamois kept for that purpose.

As has been said already, the crystal ball is not a toy to be handled indiscriminately by anyone out of curiosity. Ideally, only the seer's hands should touch it. The dedicated scryer magnetizes the crystal ball by passing the right hand over it to impart strength and might. Then the action should be repeated with the left hand to transmit more sensitiveness. Generally, when the seer is alone this exercise is carried out for five minutes at several periods during the day. Then, too, magnetism from the transcendental ethers collects on the surface of the crystal ball as the seer gazes fixedly on it. To put it simply in the words of the modern idiom, this is comparable to "recharging the battery."

It can be readily understood that handling by the curious actually destroys the sensitiveness of the crystal ball. However, it is conceded that the crystal ball is an inanimate object. It is powerless to say, "I shall allow only the seer's magnetism to collect on my surface." It is unable to move away from an alien intruder. Its power is to reveal to a sensitive that which lies quietly in its heart.

It is acknowledged that handling leaves magnetic vibrations that, mingled with the seer's, cause much confusion that is not only worthless but also detrimental to all concerned. If a person is equipped to become a consulting scryer, then that person must be strong enough to firmly but kindly refuse to allow the crystal ball to be held by unfamiliar hands. When William Shakespeare admonished Laertes in *Hamlet,* he spoke indirectly to all scryers:

This above all: to thine own self be true,
And it must follow, as the night the day,
Thou canst not then be false to any man.

When the crystal ball is not in use, it should be placed on its pedestal in the center of the table. A black silk handkerchief is the perfect cover for it. The cover not only protects the globe from dust, but its more subtle purpose is to refute random reflections, which would disturb the rest periods of the crystal ball. When leaving the room, the scryer should further protect the crystal ball by locking the door.

How to Use the Crystal Ball

From the beginning of time, the one persistent question has been, "How does one make direct contact with the crystal ball?" Immediately, three words present themselves: belief, concentration, and patience. All three are equally important; seership depends on them. If an individual has an inborn ability to fix the mind or to concentrate, that person is well on the way to becoming a scryer. However, none of the three will be as effective if the seer is not at ease physically. A posture chair will free the scryer from being distracted by seeking a more comfortable position.

Nothing is more vital than the breath, which is the source of all energy. It behooves every seer to learn to control the breath. All professional seers, like all professional clairvoyants, cultivate deep breathing, for they are aware that their psychic powers are enhanced by their lung capacity. Deep breathing is a great aid to concentration, just as physical ease helps erase irritability, and ensures a patient attitude.

The time factor enters strongly into gazing. There are three periods during the day that are ideal to consult the crystal ball: sunrise, midday, and sunset. It is generally accepted that sunrise is the most propitious, for it symbolizes a new beginning. This does not preclude other hours between dawn and dark. Times to avoid using the crystal ball are the dark hours from nine o'clock in the evening until dawn. During that period the scryer is renewing vital powers, either through sleep or meditation.

Parting the Clouds

As a novice scryer, you will notice the clouding of your crystal ball. This clouding may appear in various forms:

1. As a milky obscurity
2. As a smoky, impenetrable mist
3. As minuscule white clouds drifting through the crystal ball

White clouds are an affirmative indication of coming favors. If brilliance breaks through the clouds, it is indicative of the sun, which will light the way to better financial circumstances and to improved physical health. However, if a soft light lacking brilliance appears through the clouds, it is indicative of the moon, which foretells a period of inaction that may be likened to recuperating the vital forces. When the cloud is black, that is the time to be concerned, for a black cloud is unfavorable, even ill omened. The seriousness of the prediction is measured by the degree of blackness. Does the blackness appear in a small portion of the crystal ball, or does it fill the entire globe? Occasionally, the clouds take on a show of color. If green, blue, or violet suffuse the crystal ball, this is an excellent indication. When green clouds appear, the individual will be called on to assist as a neighborhood mediator in an educational, political, or religious capacity. If a blue cloud appears, an occasion will arise that requires shrewd discernment, which brings both honor and praise to the individual. When a violet cloud floats through the crystal ball, a latent talent may be recognized, or a worthy philosophical expression will be presented and well received. When clouds of red, orange, or yellow appear, the portents are ominous.

Red clouds foretell dangerous situations—accidents, serious illness, and grief. Orange clouds predict loss of material goods and friendships. Yellow clouds bring deception and ultimate betrayal by supposed friends.

Directions the Clouds Are Moving

Your questions may regard anything that is uppermost in your mind, such as business, health, housing, matrimony, social activities, or any of a myriad subjects. Clouds that move upward in the crystal ball are positive signs. Clouds that move downward in the crystal ball are negative. Every question you have asked earns a "no" or the indications are negative. However, it must be realized that it is the question itself that causes the cloud to appear and descend.

Clouds that move to the right of the seer announce the presence of spiritual beings. They are benign and ensure their willingness to assist both the seer and the individual seeking assistance. Clouds that move to the left of the seer indicate a refusal to continue the "sitting" at that time. Do not be discouraged! Dark divination is an excellent tool with which a Goth magician can hone psychic skills. Like a muscle, your intuition needs exercise. With this in your arsenal and bag of magick goodies, you will be a force to reckon with. With tarot, scrying, the pendulum, runes, and your trusty crystal ball by your side, your power grows and flourishes.

CHAPTER TWELVE

Living the Craft: Goth House Magick

Gothic house magick is a way of life. It is taking what is inside of you and reflecting it out into the world. Your home becomes a mirror of your sense and sensibility. More important, it reflects your inner spirit to the world. You have chosen to be Goth and to pursue the path of magick, so your home is a sanctuary and an incubator for the intense creativity you bring to everything: your clothing, personal style, body art, jewelry, music, art, work, and special sorcery. In this way, you create a positive, magickal, and harmonious energy flow through your home and world.

The old adage "know thyself" is mind magick. Through soul searching and spiritual seeking, you can achieve great self-understanding and you know what you want. With magick, you also know how to get it. Goth house magick is a magnificent way to exercise your personal power and help it to grow. It is also the best way to manifest the life you want because you are literally creating it! In this wild and wildly creative chapter, you will learn some highly unusual Goth crafting ideas, fantastic recipes, and some superb spells that will help you live an inspired life.

Making Gothic Candelabra for Your Altar

Nothing says Goth quite like a candelabrum. If you are a crafty Goth, you can make and customize your own. As you doubtless know, horror films are replete with many candelabra glittering and casting shadows in the background. Both elegant and romantic, with many layers of molten wax flowing down the side, these holders of candles can be nothing less than splendid. While you can always buy them, it is much better to make them and place your imprimatur and your own special kind of magick in them.

The following are the steps I learned from the one and only Voltaire, who was a writer, musician, animator, graphic novelist, comic, and all-around Renaissance man.

Supplies:

Empty wine bottles
Black spray paint
Spray adhesive
Paper images or stickers
Candles

1. Have fun by emptying some bottles of wine, preferably by drinking their contents! If you do not imbibe, you can get bottles from friends or from a recycling center.

2. Give the bottles a good spraying with flat black paint and let them dry.

3. You *can* stop here, but it is even better to refine your design with your own art, or stickers you particularly love, or even decoupaged (or spray-glued) photos evocative of your mood and magick. Voltaire recommends the "Bandelabra," featuring photos, stickers, lyrics, or an image representing your favorite band, such as Dead Can Dance's beautiful hands and serpent coils from their album covers, or a particularly spooky-looking shot of Siouxie Sioux, of Le Cure's Robert, or maybe of even the beautiful and very talented Voltaire! Another suggestion from the master of Goth décor is "The Fliker," with stills, shots, and poster images from favorite Goth movies. The Goth cinematic "A" list is inclusive of any and all Dracula movies, *The Rocky Horror Picture Show, The Crow,* and *The Nightmare Before Christmas.* As long as these are for your own enjoyment and edification, you do not have to be concerned about copyrights, but if you suddenly decide to start eBaying your handcrafted candelabra, you must get clearance!

My personal favorite Gothesque flick is Francis Ford Coppola's *Bram Stoker's Dracula* and, above all, my favorite moment in this gorgeous visual feast is the absinthe-inspired section with verdant greens, light and shadow play, and yearning past-life romance. So, I suggest leaving the wine bottle in its native green state and going for green candles and a touch of green glitter and emerald stick-on stones to evoke the green fairy.

I also highly recommend you obtain some imported absinthe from the greatly Gothic Eastern bloc. I prefer Czech absinthe. The highly creative people of the former Eastern bloc also bottle a wine called Vampire Wine. It comes to us from Transylvania and the vintners use a charming black bottle with a menacing label. So, this is the easiest Gothelabra of all—just place a candle inside, light it, and you have a very vampiric-looking light source.

Ritual Use of Absinthe

Absinthe originated in Switzerland, and its basic ingredient is wormwood, an extract of Artemisia Absinthium. In medieval times, wormwood was used to treat intestinal worms. Dr. Pierre Ordinaire created absinthe as a general medicinal drink. Later, Major Henri Dubied obtained the recipe from a group of nuns and began making batches of the liqueur from wormwood, juniper, Melissa, angelica, anise, fennel, hyssop, and nutmeg. Major Dubied, a patriot, gave this drink to soldiers to aid their libido, mental clarity, and sprits. Henri-Louis Pernod was the major's son-in-law and he set up the now famous absinthe factory in France in 1905. Drinking absinthe then and now requires a ritual approach: place a sugar cube on a special perforated spoon and hold it over the liquor and sprinkle water on the sugar. The absinthe instantly turns a milky, magickal green. In Prague, the additional ritual step of setting the sugar on fire adds to a nice finishing touch. Absinthe casts its own singular spell.

I had the fortune of going to Prague for a literary festival a few years ago for Women of the Beat Generation. As if that weren't wonderful enough, I was accompanied by Laurence Ferlingetti and ruth weiss, two legendary poets who were also going to Prague for the first time. We were enthralled with the city and its undisturbed medieval beauty, despite some unfortunate communist-era architectural monstrosities in the suburbs. Also, we got to stay near the city gate on Templova Street in an apartment building that had been a Knights Templar stronghold a mere 800 years ago.

Walking along the banks of the Charles River, it was like a dream. Get thee to Prague as soon as you can, it is a place of deep Goth magick and will doubtless inspire you.

From what I could tell, there seemed to be two Pragues. One is the day-to-day Prague with citizens going about their business as they always have, intermixing with tourists and the many ex-pats who (like I very nearly did) came to Prague to visit and simply never left. Then, there is the Prague by night, which has many discos and a glittery blend of Europeans and North American clubbers. Lit by candlelight and neon, this Prague takes on an otherworldly glow where pretty much anything is possible. For me, the most memorable public house of all is a bar whose name translates to "The Man with the Shot-Out Eye," a reference to Jan Hus. Our beatnik contingent decided to visit this bar on our last night in Prague, and when we arrived the pivo (Czech for "beer") and absinthe were flowing. I was an "absinthe virgin" and everybody was guessing I would not be able to handle it. Perhaps it was the romance of this trip but I *was* able to handle the absinthe. I think.

The bar was filled with mostly men that night, odds I was definitely appreciative of—Russians, Moravians, Slovenians, Slovakians, Czechs, Germans, Hungarians, Poles, and Estonians. And—I'm sure it was *not* the absinthe—they were the most interesting looking men, mostly with long hair and dark clothes, in short, pretty darn Goth. At one point, after my third glass of absinthe, all the colors in the room got just a little bit brighter and suffused with a sort of electric glow. I was talking to a particularly amiable young man with long blond hair. While he was explaining the wonders of the Eastern bloc to me, I had a perceptual shift. It was right after that that I had what I call my absinthe epiphany, in which I realized that J.R.R. Tolkien's Riders of Rohan were the Slovakians and that all the peoples of his Middle Earth (minus the Hobbits) were right here in the bar with me. I was thunderstruck and so overcome with excitement at my sudden understanding of Tolkien's *Lord of the Rings* that I tried to explain it to all of my new friends. They heartily agreed; my new Slovakian friend insisted I was correct, that he was a *Rohirrin* warrior. Shortly thereafter, we swept out into the streets to take Prague by storm. The next day, a bit headachy and sad to be leaving my new second home, I realized that I had a minor absinthe-induced hallucination. When the first of the *Lord of the Rings* movies came out in 2002, I was pleased to see that the casting director apparently saw Middle Earth the way I did.

Recipe Ritual: Making Absinthe Wine

Unless you are the kind of charming scofflaw who has the time and inclination to make actual absinthe, here is an easier and more law-abiding way to still create a supernatural drink.

Supplies:

2 pints of port
2 teaspoons dried wormwood
2 drops clove essence
2 teaspoons each of lavender, marjoram, peppermint, sage, and thyme

Mix and enjoy!

Eternal Flames—The Craft of Candlemaking

Burning candles has now grown into a full-blown obsession in today's culture. To Goth up and insert your intention into candles, you can adorn them with big sequins, curio crosses, symbols such as the Egyptian ankh, faux pearls, or anything lovely and suitably glittery into the sides of candles and have "stained glass" candles. Another technique is to mix your "objet," mixing them into the wax inside the mold. An even easier way to do this is to take a soft beeswax pillar candle and "stud" the sides and candle top with the crystal pieces that cost just pennies per pound. You can save yours from the melted candles and reuse them again and again. Nowadays, candlemaking classes abound and you can get leftover or "recycled" wax to use, melt, and pour into glass votives for your own uniquely magickal candle creations.

Candle Conjuration for a Happy Home

Select an item from your collection that you feel most reflects your inner Goth—perhaps it is a statue of a kneeling, winged fallen angel.

Maybe it is a fossil with an insect from the Paleolithic age embedded inside. It could be a rusted iron cross you found in an abandoned church cemetery or a tiny dried bat. Whatever it is, choose wisely and make sure it is an item that makes you feel inside, "Ah, now I am at home."

Supplies:

Your chosen object
Brown candle
Rose oil
Cinnamon incense
Sage

1. The brown candle will improve and secure positive, grounding energy in your home. Place it beside your sacred object. Anoint the candle with rose oil and light the cinnamon incense. Meditate to clear your mind of any distractions; a clear mind is essential to opening the mental and spiritual space necessary to create.

2. Once you feel focused, light the candle and then light the sage with the candle and speak aloud:

By my hand
And by the blessing of the spirit,
The fire of home and heart burns bright,
Burns long,
Burns eternal.
I offer my home to
New friends
And new love.
Welcome!

Gothic Gardening

Bringing together the dark and divine with the beauty of the plant kingdom can bring great pleasure to the surliest of Goths. Since many of these plants are black in nature, a green thumb is hardly necessary to create your own Gothic garden. Gargoyle statues, wrought-iron fencing, and black pots can add to the effect, but you do not need to have a large yard to create your own somber sanctuary. A small corner plot will do, as will a windowsill or balcony—in some cases, even indoor Gothic gardening is possible. As it is a Gothic garden, it is no coincidence that many of these plants love shade, or look best in the moonlight. The rare art of Gothic gardening serves to put you in closer touch with nature, which is essential to Goth Wiccans. Gardening is an amazingly peaceful pursuit, and working directly with the earth and her plants and flowers will teach you the secrets of our Great Gaia. Tending and growing these rare and wonderful Goth plants will usher you into a very specialized world. From this vantage point, you can dry herbs to make special teas, potions, tinctures, and flower essences that are uniquely Goth and magickal.

Black Calla

The black calla lily, *Arum palaestinum,* is arguably the mother of all Gothic plants. Even though it is not considered a true calla lily (*Zantedeschia aethiopica*), it is still a member of the same greater family, *Araceae.* The black calla's flowers bear a resemblance to the more familiar white calla, so often used in funeral arrangements, but with a dramatic difference. Where the common calla is white with a yellow spike in its center, the black calla is a deep blackish purple, with an intensely black spike. The spathe, or outer part of the flower, has a greenish exterior that uncurls to reveal the deep black velvet of the inside. Cradled inside this rich velvet is a thick solid black spadix. As the plant unfurls, the black velvet of the spathe fades to a deep purple, or in some cases, a blood red, with a tapered tip that dangles behind it like a tail. Truly one of the most fantastic Gothic plants in existence, it is bizarre, magnificent, and completely Gothic! It can be grown outdoors (in the shade of course) in milder climates, and in colder climates it can be grown as a marvelously macabre houseplant.

Vampire Lily

No Gothic garden is complete without the beloved vampire lily, *Dracunculus vulgaris*. Also called the dragon arum, it is in the *Araceae* family, along with the black calla. Sporting an incredible, deep red flower with a ruffled edge and a long black or deep purple spadix, the vampire lily brings to mind the gown you wished you had for last Halloween's Gothic Ball. Even the stems are Gothic; they are a mottled green and red, as if they have been splattered with blood. One of the creepiest aspects of this plant, and no doubt how it brought on the fantastically vampiric associations, is the fact that it emits a smell like that of rotting flesh. This attracts the flies and carrion beetles that pollinate it. Its deceptive beauty brings the garden visitor into its realm, luring him or her to inhale deeply into the blood-red curls of the blossom, only to horrify and repel the mortal with the smell of death, sweet and sickening. Truly Goth. Similar care to the black calla.

VOODOO LILY

What could be more bewitching than a plant with such a ghoulish name? The voodoo lily, *Sauromatum guttatum,* sometimes identified as *S. venosum,* derives its name from the wicked enchantment of a speckled, blood-red flower, coupled with the foul smell of a corpse. Another plant adapted to attracting flies and beetles as its pollinators, the voodoo lily's flower forms similarly to the black calla and vampire lily, with a tall central spike, or spadix, surrounded by the spathe. For the voodoo lily, the spadix is the richest of reds, and the spathe is a vibrant red spotted with deep burgundy. Especially enchanting even when not in bloom, the voodoo lily's speckled leaf spikes appear after the single flower has come and gone, shooting up and branching out to look like miniature Gothic tropical trees, green and smattered with blood-red spots at the base. Bizarre, enchanting, and gorgeously ghastly.

CORPSE FLOWER

No Gothic gardening list could be compiled without including the one and only corpse flower *Amorphophallus titanum.* So named for its extremely potent corpse-like smell, the corpse flower is also one of the largest flower structures in the world. Growing up to twelve feet tall and five feet wide in the wild, with leaves that can exceed twenty feet in length, this is like a giant version of the voodoo lily. Also known as the titan arum, the corpse flower is both ghastly and breathtaking (you will want to hold your breath when near it during its fullest bloom). As with the voodoo lily, the flower comes before the leaves, although the plant needs to be at least six years old before it can bloom. When it does, a large mottled spike pushes up from the ground, slowly unfurling to reveal a beautiful, deep red velvet outer spathe, and a three-foot spike that is dirty green in the center. When fully opened, the corpse flower begins to live up to its rotten reputation, for it emits the strongest and most foul of decomposing flesh-like odors, caused by the most Gothic of essential oils: putrescine and cadavarine! A foul beauty, it looks like something from *A Little Shop of Horrors*, and no Goth will be a true malcontent until he or she has witnessed the cadaverous horrors of the corpse flower in the flesh.

BLACK MONDO GRASS

Unlike many "black" plants in the Gothic kingdom, black mondo grass, *Ophiopogon planiscapus, "Nigrescens,"* is truly unique in color. A member of the turflily family, with a spidery growth habit, a blade of this black grass held up to the light reveals the depth of its utter blackness. Small occasional flower spikes of white or pale purple stars fade into purple berries that gradually turn to a shiny black. Keep your black mondo grass in a pot with chartreuse groundcover, such as saliganella or golden baby's tears, and the black only looks blacker. True to its Gothic nature, it can tolerate only partial sun, and likes it cool, although it does not like to freeze. It can be grown as a houseplant with some difficulty, but outdoors it is dark and divine!

ANDEAN SILVER SAGE

The Andean silver sage, *Salvia discolor*, lives up to its Gothic reputation. A silver-leafed sage that produces spikes of black flowers from soft silver sheaths, the deep indigo of the blooms counts as black in the Gothic garden book. Unbelievably pleasant in fragrance, it has a smell like the more common purifying white sage, but with flowers that prove it to be quite the opposite of white. Perhaps this sage should be burned to purify only the Gothiest of rooms. Unlike many of its sun-loving relatives, Andean silver sage prefers partial sun. If grown outdoors and protected from heavy frosts, it will provide you with hours of eerie entertainment.

GENTIA'S GREEN

The new Goth nickname for this plant should be *The Nightmare Before Christmas Tree*. Gentia's green, *Corokia cotoneaster,* is one of the most unique plants in the Gothic garden. Gray leaves on black stems make the untrained eye think this plant has already died, when it is in fact thriving in all its Gothic glory. Up close, one can see the black stems grow in an unusual zigzag pattern, that when pruned, can create a dramatic effect, especially if lit from underneath at night, casting the spookiest of silhouettes. This plant is hardy in most climates, and takes frost rather well. Look for the variety known as "little prince." It would look great with little Jack and Sally heads hanging from it at Christmastime. Nightmarish!

Psychic Protection Potpourri

This will safeguard you and your loved ones from psychic vampires and from outside influences that could be negative or disruptive.

Timing: Simmer this mixture whenever you feel the need to infuse your home and heart with the energies of protection.

Supplies:

$1/4$ cup rosemary
4 bay laurel leaves
1 tablespoon basil
$1/8$ cup sage
1 teaspoon dill weed
$1/8$ cup cedar
1 drop garlic oil
1 teaspoon juniper berries

1. Mix the herbs, oil, and berries together by hand. While you are doing this, close your eyes and visualize yourself and your space protected by a boundary of glowing white light. Imagine that the light runs through you to the herbs in your hand and charges them with the energy of safety, sanctity, and protection.

2. Add the mixture to a pan filled with simmering water. When the aromatic mist and steam rises, intone aloud:

By my own hand, I have made this balm;
This divine essence contains my calm.
By my own will, I make this charm;
This precious potpourri potion protects all from harm.
With harm to none and health to all, blessed be!

GOTHIC RESOURCES: FASHION, CLOTHING, AND CULTURE

Magazines

Gothic Beauty
4110 SE Hawthorne Blvd., #501
Portland, OR 97214
www.GothicBeauty.com
The premiere Gothic magazine, with everything from fashion to music reviews.

Morbid Curiosity
www.charnel.com/automatism/morbid.html
A fantastic Gothic online magazine with a literary bent, full of stories of the most morbid kind, as well as current topics among the macabre. Published by Automatism Press.

Shopping: Online, Catalog, and Retail

Arsenicfashions.com
PO Box 521411
Salt Lake City, UT 84152
Online fashion boutique extraordinaire! Gloves, jewelry, clothing, and more!

Black Phoenix Trading Post/Black Phoenix Alchemy Lab
www.blackphoenixtradingpost.com

By far one of the most exquisitely designed Web sites with detailed art that makes any Goth go wild. Go to "The Lab," where you will find themed blends of perfume, including voodoo blends and funereal oils.

Cheap Thrills
1324 Haight St.
San Francisco, CA 94117
415-252-8395
A bastion of punk rock and Goth girl (and guy) supplies, this shop is crammed full of cool clothing, toys, and accessories. Recently, this place proved invaluable to me when I found myself throwing a spontaneous Pirate Party—think skull and cross bone coasters and shot glasses.

Design Toscano, Inc.
1400 Morse Avenue
Elk Grove Village, IL 60007-5722
1-800-525-0733
DesignToscano.com
A catalog of statuary and accessories in the historical reproduction vein. It has a section of angels as well as a Gothic gallery, with plenty of gargoyle fun!

Goodgoth.com
"A Curious Coming Together of Objects Both Wonderful and Strange"
PO Box 1814
Westfield, MA 01086
413-568-1120
Primarily an online catalog, the site says the store will have a paper catalog available in the future, but the Web site is fantastic. It features lots of hair dye, great clothes, books, and jewelry.

Gothgiftbaskets.com
"Arrangements for the Subversively Inclined"
Goth Gift Baskets
PO Box 353
Northampton, MA 01060
This site provides gift baskets for the Goth in your life. It has several pre-made baskets, but the funnest part is the custom gift baskets, where you

get to choose from containers such as spider web baskets and cauldrons and fill them with any number of fun and morbid treats! Check it out.

Gravestone Art Wear
PO Box 141
York Harbor, ME 03911-0141
Studio
250 York Street
York Village, ME 03909
1-800-564-4310
Fax: 207-363-3268
www.gravestoneartwear.com
Super cool t-shirts and tanks with images made from gravestone rubbings Ol' New England style, handmade soaps, velvet treasure bags, cloaks, aprons, and even supplies to do your own headstone rubbings. You can order through links on the online site, but I recommend requesting the great catalog!

Hotgoth.net
An online resource for Goths, primarily personals, with some links for merchandise. An interesting way to meet some cyber-Goths out there.

Hot Topic
www.hottopic.com
Web site that allows for ordering most of the things that can be found in its line of retail stores. Great, affordable fashion for Goths! Shoes, accessories, and large chains.

Lip Service
www.lip-service.com
Producers of hot fetish and Gothic attire, available at many alternative clothing stores, including Hot Topic, as well as online.

MexicanSugarSkull.com
Loads of Dia de Los Muertos accessories, decorative items, and, best of all, sugar skull molds and recipes. A list of retail vendors is provided on the site. Many ways to celebrate and honor the dead year round!

Obscura Clothing
2030 S. 900 E
Sugarhouse, UT
Retail vendor of Arsenic Fashions and other Goth goods.

Siren
463 Queen Street West
Toronto, Ontario M5V 2A9
416-504-9288
Fax 416-504-5145
www.sirenweb.com
A beautiful retail store in Toronto, Canada, that now offers online ordering for many items.

INDEX